ADDISON CARTER

Copyright © 2022
J A Publishing All rights reserved

The characters and events portrayed in this book are fictitious. Any similarity to real persons, living or dead, is coincidental and not intended by the author.

No part of this book may be reproduced, or stored in a retrieval system, or transmitted in any form or by any means, electronic, mechanical, photocopying, recording, or otherwise, without express written permission of the publisher.

ISBN: 9798357980915

Cover design by: AF Designs
Library of Congress Control Number: 2018675309
Printed in the United States of America

Content Warning

This book contains some material that some readers might find difficult to read.
This includes strong language, graphic sexual content, grief, substance abuse, mentions of S.A, witnessed death, parental death, mild violence, heavy mental health topics including s/h, mild degradation.
If you have any concerns regarding anything, listed or not, please do not hesitate to reach out via direct message or email.
Email: Addisoncarterauthor@gmail.com
Instagram: @Addisoncarterauthor

For the ones who wanted to give up, but didn't.
I'm so happy you're here.
;

1

"You can spend the rest of your day dwelling on the bad, or you can forget it all and look for some good." Dad's words echoed in my head. He never let anything get him down for too long, and neither would I. My morning may have been a complete shitshow, but that didn't mean the rest of my day had to follow suit.

  I pushed the door open, making sure it locked into place, then made my way along the length of the bar, running my hand along the dented surface before ducking into the corridor and throwing open my office door. I cracked all of the windows, then shoved a fire extinguisher in front of the door to jam it open, hoping to create a breeze running through.

  It was one of the quickest ways I knew to boost my mood. Allowing the fresh, salty sea air to wash through and eliminate the lingering smell of bleach from last night's deep clean.

  I paused in the middle of the room, then laughed to myself. I hadn't opened the bar myself in weeks, and for a brief moment I forgot what I needed to do next. My bar manager, Clem, had completed her final shift yesterday and today was starting her maternity leave, so *all* responsibility would be falling back on to me until I trained someone to step up. Something I really should have considered doing way before Clem's leave began.

'Turn it into a bar,' they all said. Every single one of my friends had told me to do this. *'You've always wanted to run your own place.'* That was true. But they neglected to mention that it would be really hard work, *and* that when you inherited a complete dump of a restaurant from your parents when they died, and decided to turn it into a live music venue, that it would be really bloody expensive. And exhausting.

But despite it all, I love my bar, and I had big plans for it. The place was all me, all my hard work, and I was proud of that. I wouldn't want to put my money anywhere else, or my time and energy. My bar makes me happy, most of the time. And when it didn't, I found happiness elsewhere.

The bad mood that I was attempting to banish was all down to my sister. She may be the best friend I've ever had, but the girl was hard work. She was constantly getting herself into sticky situations, and I was the one who usually bailed her out.

This morning she had called me from Venice. She had been hysterical, screaming down the line because private photos had been leaked all over some site I had never heard of before. Photos that she had sent to one of her bandmates. The guys were going insane, the press were all over it – another thing to add to the ever growing list of gossip about my sister – and no one knew who was responsible *or* how to fix it. I had presumed this was something their manager would do, but apparently, he had disappeared. Not a single person had any idea where he was. So it was down to me to one, calm my dramatic big sister down, and two, work out how to get the pictures buried as quickly as possible.

Luckily for her, I have always been a quick thinker. So I had managed to find a solution before Bea had stopped sobbing. Maverick was on the case – being the most level-headed one of them all – and I had been making calls to all of the right people. Throwing her money in all the right places.

It had been dealt with. Done.

So my mood had calmed, I was no longer worried about my sister, until I received a call on my way down to the bar from a reporter who decided it would be a fantastic idea to attempt to drag *me* through the mud with Bea. It had happened before, so I knew how to handle it. But when you're not the rich, famous sibling, it's a lot harder to make stories go away for good. I had accepted that this wouldn't be the last time, finding out my secret wasn't as hard as uncovering any of hers.

I couldn't let the whole world know what had happened five years ago, and I definitely wouldn't let my sisters name get ruined by my past. So I bargained with him. Of course, he wanted money – they always do. I sent it, every last penny that I had saved up for the bar, to make the place perfect. And the arsehole had the audacity to fucking laugh as he thanked me for my 'cooperation'.

I had been left with a sour taste in my mouth, and an irritated shift in my mood. I didn't like feeling irritated. I needed a long swim, or…

Thank god I owned a bar. A bar that was stocked full of high-quality liquor. 11am might not be the most conventional time to start, or while I was working, but fuck it. One little drink wouldn't hurt.

Reaching up and pushing onto my tiptoes I

grabbed the tall crystal bottle from the very top shelf and snatched up a glass before heading to my office to begin the process of setting the bar up.

"Juney?" a gruff male voice called through the bar just as I finished counting my final till.

Leaning back in my chair, sipping the neat vodka, I peered down to the front door, wondering who on earth was here so early. I knew it would be one of the regulars, they were the only ones who would call me that. Important people – scary people – usually called me Juniper, and I insisted that everyone else call me Juno. Then there was Bea, who was the only person alive who could get away with calling me June-bug. I might be all sunshine and rainbows most of the time, but I would tear into anyone else who tried to call me that.

Hadley came strolling towards me, a wide grin on his weathered face as his heavy boots stomped along the permanently sticky – no matter how much I tried to clean it – floor.

"Hadley, you're here early," I declared, throwing back the last dribble of burning liquid and rising to my feet.

"I'm not here to drink. I'm just checking in on you, my love." He leaned against the doorframe and ran his fingers through a tangle of long, grey hair.

I gave him a wide grin, and grabbed the till, jerking my head towards the front of the bar. Hadley took the heavy tray from me, and I followed him, shaking my head and rolling my eyes as he walked ahead of me. I nudged the fire extinguisher and let my office door close behind me as I followed the huge man. He finished my set up for me as I continued to shake my head and scolded him for treating me like a weak little mouse.

"Stop complaining," he laughed. "Just let us take

care of you."

"You boys are too good to me." I winked, leaning against the bar and flipping open my laptop to find a playlist to suit my mood this morning. The Vodka had done a great job of perking me up, but I just needed a little something more, something to really turn my day around.

"You're too good to us," Hadley argued, moving around to the other side of the bar and pulling up a stool. He sat down and pulled out his phone, as usual, scrolling aimlessly and thinking that I didn't know what he was doing.

Every day this happened, if it wasn't him, it was one of the other two. My protective little gang of old dudes. They were pretty scary guys, all friends of my parents, and they had always treated us girls like family. So when I took over this place, they made a deal between themselves that one of them would always be looking out for me. It was cute, but what was even cuter was that they thought I didn't know.

"How's your sister?" he asked, glancing up at me as I put on a playlist of bouncy pop punk cover songs and hooked it up to the speakers, keeping the volume low enough to chat over.

"Drama follows that girl everywhere, I swear," I sighed, trying not to think too much about how my morning had gone. "I think they need a break, but they're determined to finish touring."

"She's so much like your mum."

I nodded in agreement. She was, and I was just like Dad. Dads life motto had been something like 'Every cloud has a silver lining', and I wholeheartedly agreed with that. Mums was more along the lines of 'What is life without a little risk?' Maybe that was why they worked so well together, she took crazy leaps and often messed up, and he found a solution while living life on the bright side.

Before I could dwell for too long on thoughts about my parents, another head popped through the door and in walked Jeremy – Hadley's twin brother.

"Must be my lucky day," I teased as the men scowled at each other, having clearly messed up their scheduling. But they quickly fell into comfortable chit-chat and managed to entertain me to no end with their bickering and fun – repetitive – tales of their youth.

Five hours later, happier and full of chips which Hadley had popped out to grab for me when I started to nibble on pork scratchings, they left me under the watchful eye of the third old dude. Carl. He had turned up to help me set up the stage for the evening. Fridays were always my favourite day of the week. Open mic night. We had all sorts come in on those nights, some talented, some not so much. But each and every one of them would be met with a raucous cheer at the end and a pint on the house.

Carl took up his spot for the night, sitting in the small booth he had made himself, and I took over a couple of glasses of lemonade to keep him going. Carl didn't drink alcohol anymore, which was great for me, since he also never paid for a single drink. Not that I minded as he was doing me a huge favour by running these nights.

Once the crowd had thickened out a bit, I jumped up onto the small stage at the very back and welcomed everyone. Then – as expected – Hadley's son got up on the stage and kicked off the night with a half decent cover of a City and Colour song. When he was done, he bounded off of the stage and straight up to the bar where I was waiting with a fresh pint of Otter ale, just like every week.

As I was wiping down the bar during the seventh performance of the evening, the man at the very end snorted a laugh, grabbing my full attention, and earning himself a raised brow.

"What's amused you?" I asked curiously, cocking my head and leaning against the bar so that he could whisper his response.

"I find it funny when people sing *their* songs." He rolled his dark eyes, and I glanced up at the stage where a woman was belting out a Hand That Feeds song quite impressively.

"She's good, so why is it funny? It's not like she's ruining a great song."

He slammed his whiskey glass down on a beermat with a grunt and narrowed his eyes. "Nothing to do with her. She's fine. It's the band that I hate."

"Well, let's hope the next person sings somethin' that you approve of, or better yet, get up there yourself?" I bit my tongue with a wide smile as I watched his jaw tense, and his lips pressed tightly together.

"Why the fuck would I do that?" he finally asked, his voice a low rumble that had my insides sparking with something warm and electric. There was no denying that the gorgeous grump was hot. I had noticed him the moment he had stepped foot in the door, talk, dark and mysteriously handsome. But now that he was speaking, I was realising that it wasn't just my eyes that appreciated his presence.

"Because it's fun," I said, earning myself another eye roll that I laughed off as I leaned even closer, slowly ran my tongue over my lower lip, blatantly flirting. "And because it means you can take control of what's being sung. No more *Hand that feeds*."

His gaze dropped to mine, cold and hard as he searched my face for a moment, then shook his head and raised his glass. "Nope, but I'll take another."

I sighed and straightened up, grabbing the bottle I had poured his first drink from and topping him up before locating the card machine.

A couple of songs later he piped up again. "How can you tolerate this shit?"

The man up on the stage was putting on a dramatically choreographed performance of an original song. His voice was awful, but he was entertaining my customers, and that was what this place was all about. Giving people a place to enjoy themselves, even if it wasn't everyone's cup of tea.

"That's my brother," I deadpanned, "don't be rude."

Something a little like embarrassment flashed across his face, but it was gone in a flash as he blew air loudly from his nose. "He looks old enough to be your dad. I'm calling bullshit."

I looked back at the man on the stage, realising that he was right as I tried to stop myself from laughing. He looked even older than my dad would have. "Fine," I chuckled, "You got me. But I *tolerate* it because it's fun."

"It hurts." He rubbed his finger and thumb hard against the bridge of his nose, then met my gaze, holding it as he pushed back his black hair before unhooking the pair of glasses tucked into the open collar of his linen shirt and sliding them up his nose, drawing my attention to the dark curls sitting just visible beneath the white fabric, the top two buttons hanging open in a relaxed way that didn't at all fit with the stern expression fixed on his face. "Pass me the sign-up sheet."

I did as he commanded, curiosity spiking and drowning out the fact that he was coming across as *a bit* of a rude arsehole. "You're gonna perform?"

He raised the pen, his jaw tightening. "No, I just wanted to draw a massive cock on it. Of course I'm going to perform, anything to show these poor people what real talent is."

Once again, I ignored his rudeness – and the way he said cock – and smiled as I took the sheet back and read his name aloud. "Nate, is that short for Natha-."

"And you are?" he cut me off abruptly.

"Juno." I said, holding out my hand for him to shake. He stared at my brightly painted nails, then jerked his head in greeting instead.

"Short for Juniper I'm guessing?"

"Good guess, but please, just call me Juno, pretty much everyone else does. So, what will you be playing for us?"

"Something impressive. Something that will put every other performer to shame." He boasted, and I had to clench my legs to stop myself from squirming. Apparently cocky confidence was my kryptonite.

What do they say? Opposites attract? Well that was a bloody understatement, on my part anyway. I definitely have a type – older, grouchy arseholes who rock the 'I hate everyone' look. I've always been a sucker for a guy who would more than likely treat me like rubbish. But I've also always bounced back straight after. Perks of that inherited optimism.

"I'm looking forward to it." I grinned, pouring him another whiskey and gesturing to it. "For the nerves, it can be quite scary when it's your first time up there."

He laughed coldly, ironically sending a rush of heat through me. "This isn't my first time, not that *you'd* know that, Juniper."

I bit my lip and nodded, "Well, in that case, get that down you, and get your ass up on my stage, baby. It's your time to shine."

2

Nate

It was barely a stage. Just a small platform really. Not big enough for my old band to fit comfortably on, even all those years ago, when we were still messing around and working out our dynamic, before they moved on and became one of the biggest bands in the world. Leaving me behind, to what? Play shitty open mic nights while working a dull as hell 9-5 and not knowing how to flirt with adorably cute girls who look like the last place they belong is behind the bar of a dark, dirty 'music venue'.

Not that it really mattered. A sweet young thing like her would never find what she wanted in someone like me. No one ever did.

And there was that blatant age gap. I probably had about fifteen years on her. Although sometimes it felt as though I had a hundred years on everyone I met. Living too many lifetimes already, yet not enough to be a better man.

I stood up and rolled my shoulders, threw down the large measure of whiskey she had just poured me, and walked away, winding through the half empty tables and approaching a guy standing at the side of the room.

"Can I borrow that?" I asked, nodding at the acoustic guitar propped up against the wall beside him. I wasn't prepared for this in any way, so I hoped that the guy was in an agreeable mood, and that the instrument was tuned correctly. There was nothing worse than sitting on a stage piss-arsing around with your instrument while the people watching lost interest.

"Sure thing man," he said, his smile wide as he pushed the guitar into my hands and slapped me on the back, wishing me luck as I stepped up the single step and sat down on the barstool that had been placed before a microphone in the middle of the platform.

"Up next, we have…" An old guy sitting in a makeshift sound booth spoke up loudly over the crowd, taking the sheet of paper from Juniper, who had left her place behind the bar and was standing beside him with an excited grin splitting her face. She tightened her ponytail and flicked the coiled curls back before smoothing down her strappy, short black dress.

"I'm sorry love, I can't read his handwriting," the old guy said, and I groaned irritably. What did it matter what my name was? No one in here really cared.

"Nate," Juniper announced in her upbeat west country accent, and I groaned once again, but this time it wasn't out of irritation.

"Nate, Great," he said, then laughed to himself. "That rhymed. Anywho, take it away, Nate."

I expected Juniper to go back behind the bar, but

she remained where she was, her head cocked as she – and every other person in the place – waited patiently for me to blow them away.

And blow them away I would.

I may not have been enough back in London. I would probably never make it big. But I was sure as shit a lot more talented than any of the other people I had heard in here tonight, even the woman who was singing that fucking Hand That Feeds song.

The chords were easy to recall, and the lyrics were practically branded on my soul. This was the one song I had refused to let them keep. It was mine, entirely fucking mine.

The words fell from my lips as my fingers positioned themselves expertly and I played with ease. Hand That Feeds would never have made this work for them anyway, so I would never feel an ounce of guilt for taking this away from them. Not that I should anyway, not after what they did.

I closed my eyes as the lyrics ripped through me, and each word that echoed around the room filled itself with its own special brand of pain. When I finally reached the closing line, I opened my eyes and allowed them to focus on the closest face. A face that I hadn't expected to be there, so close.

Juniper was standing right in front of me, the toes of her well-worn vans pressed up against the base of the 'stage' as she stared at me with wide blue eyes that shone and sparkled like the sea. She pulled her bottom lip between her teeth and smiled like what she had just heard might be the best sound to have ever filled this bar.

I held the final note, and her hands came colliding

together. She bounced up and down like an excited puppy. "Holy shit," she squealed, "you weren't joking about impressing me, you were *amazing.*"

Heat spread through my entire body like wildfire at her enthusiastic compliment, and I grunted, clearing my throat to avoid anyone seeing that her compliments were having a strange effect on me.

"I know," I said, cringing inwardly at how cocky I sounded. But she didn't seem bothered, so I pushed down the part of me that wanted to disappear into the night and stepped off of the stage, shoved the guitar back into its owners' hands, and made my way back to the empty barstool I had been sitting at since I'd arrived in this dump.

"So, what's your story then?" Juniper asked as she rounded the bar and went to work pouring pints for the young guys sitting at the far end. They waited patiently, seeming to be completely unphased by the fact she was sloshing their beer over the matts in front of them as they grinned and thanked her.

"What do you mean?" I asked. What did she want? My life story? That was a depressing tale to say the least, and one I absolutely would not be sharing with some random girl who would probably end up either staring at me with pity in her big ocean-blues, or sneering in disgust, not wanting to even be in the same room as someone like me.

Maybe she just wanted to simply know how I ended up walking into this place. That would be a far easier question to answer.

"I mean," she stretched out the second word as she turned her back on me and reached up on tiptoes to grab a bottle from the top shelf. I couldn't help but notice how her dress rose up almost a little too high, and that every guy sitting at the bar had noticed too, and they were shamelessly ogling her.

I glared daggers at the closest guy to me, and he jolted, averting his gaze with a sharp intake of breath. I guess that was one perk of being so unapproachable, I could scare people off, and sometimes use that power for good.

Except, *I* was clearly not *that* good, since my gaze shot back to the tops of her tanned thighs a split second later and my thoughts filled with ideas about what I might be gifted a view of if she just pushed herself a little further.

"Well?" She asked, glancing over her shoulder at me, and I realised that I hadn't listened to a word she had said.

"Well what?"

"Fuck me, Nate. Are those things on each side of your head just there for decoration or what?" She followed her question with a melodic laugh, but I was distracted again, because hearing those first three words leave her full pink lips was enough to make *any* hot-blooded male forget how to function.

Did she even realise what she had going on?

That cute, flirty girl next door vibe, mixed with a healthy dose of sunshine. I usually wasted nights with women who were dark and twisty, just like me, but shit, she could convince me to take a brief trip to the light side with just one flutter of those long lashes.

That realisation made my jaw clench so tight I felt it in my temple. It shouldn't be that easy. It *wouldn't* be that easy. Because I would never give up control like that, not for anyone.

A wall instantly shot up around me, and I breathed a sigh of relief that I was still able to do that. I knew I was in dangerous water right now, the high of my performance was lingering, and I had no idea where I was going to throw my emotions. I was feeling good, confident, better than I had in the six months I'd been living here. But I was not going to drag some cute little barmaid into my bed. That would just be reckless.

It was clear to me from watching her tonight that we were in completely different places, she was young and radiated optimism, and I was aged and cynical. A terrible match that wouldn't even work for a single night. Girls like her didn't do one night stands anyway.

She leaned against her side of the bar and slowly repeated what she had apparently said, "You're new in here, and I like to get to know my customers. You sing like you've got a story to tell, but I'll settle for somethin' random."

I considered what she was asking for a moment, wondering what was safe to share, then settled on something that I considered to be quite simple. "I moved here from London."

Simple, factual, and probably pretty obvious. I didn't fit in, but neither did this place. Situated between a string of ice cream parlours and souvenir shops, it was the last place you'd expect to find a dark bar filled with people who appreciate a live performance over a sweaty club playing the same songs every night. I stumbled across this place on my way home from work. I had taken a different route, opting for a seaside stroll for the first time ever. The sound of the music had caught my attention as I passed, and I knew the second I got home that I would be coming back to check the place out. If it was shit, I'd go home. And I almost did, except I was curious, and thirsty. I wanted to know what this place was all about. So I stayed.

"Why?" Juniper asked, sipping what I hoped was lemonade.

"Because I needed to."

"Sounds dramatic."

"Not really."

"I bet it is."

"Nope."

She wasn't wrong. My reason for hiding away down here wasn't a pleasant one. It wasn't that I was sick of the big city and wanted to slow down. It wasn't that I just loved the sea. No. It was all to do with that fucking band, those so-called friends, and that bitch who decided that I wasn't the right fit. There may have also been an outburst of sorts, but that's neither here nor there. The bottom line was that I left, and I was bitter as hell about it. *And* I wouldn't be opening up to anyone.

"So, you're really going to milk this whole dark, broody, mysterious thing then?" she asked.

"I'm not milking anything. Don't you have customers to serve?"

She looked thoughtful, then turned her attention to the room. "Anyone need a drink?" she hollered.

Amused faces turned to her, shaking their heads, and laughing as she met my gaze with a cheeky smirk. "Apparently not. But I'll leave you be, Mr Grumpypants. Shout if you need anything."

With that she glided to the other end of the bar and fell into an animated conversation with a couple of younger guys, laughing and smiling as she swayed to the music that was now coming through the speakers. I finished the drink that I hadn't even realised she had poured, slipped some cash under the glass, and slunk out of the bar without saying goodbye.

Twenty minutes later I slid down the back of my front door, falling to the floor as the switch hit. The high was over, and I had nowhere to go but down. Down down down into the depths of bleak emptiness. Down where I belong. Where I should have stayed.

3

I left a long trail of water from the front door to my office as I hurried past the bar, covering my face with my hand and hoping that no one noticed me. I had gotten a little too carried away with my late afternoon swim and was an hour late.

    I had opened the bar earlier, then ducked out for a while to enjoy a little 'me time' while Hannah handled things during the quietest part of the day. Poor thing was probably fuming about my disappearance.

    I yanked a towel out of the cupboard behind the door and roughly dried my hair then glanced down at my body. Thank god I was wearing black. I hadn't bothered to dry myself after my swim, instead I had thrown my dress on over my bikini and ran up here. By the time I'd poured my third pint I'd no doubt be dry, so I tossed the towel on my desk, shoved my bag underneath, and twisted my hair into a messy plait.

"I'm *so* sorry, Han," I whispered as I ducked under the hatch of the bar and gave my newest barmaid an apologetic smile.

"It's fine, boss. Nice swim?" The dark haired, heavily made-up girl asked.

"It's not. Just because it's my bar doesn't mean I can leave you and do whatever I want," I huffed, but she simply rolled her eyes at me. "It was great out there though."

"Good, you deserve a break. You should get them more often. I'm happy to take on some extra responsibility here, if you wanted me to. I love this place." She grabbed a bottle of vodka and spun it in her palm before messily filling two shot glasses, then launched them surprisingly smoothly down the bar towards the twins.

"Old dudes," I called out and saluted my friends. They returned the gesture then went back to their conversation.

"I definitely need some help, can you come in on Thursday at around 11am? I can give you a quick rundown of the opening routine then. Thursdays are usually easy."

Hannah's face lit up and she nodded eagerly. That was why I had hired her in the first place. Her past experience was great, but it was her passion for my dream that had convinced me to take her on. "Of course. Want me to stick around for a bit now?"

I glanced around the bar, it was no busier than any other night I had handled alone before, so I declined her offer and sent her home. It was the weekends that I'd struggle with. She could save her energy for then.

As I watched her leave, a set of dark eyes, shadowed by a deep frown, caught my attention, spiking my curiosity. They were focused on the beermat that he was mindlessly spinning between his fingers. Long fingers with silver rings that caught the neon lights, sending flashes of red and purple my way when he moved them in a certain way. The hot, moody singer from the other night. He had been so cold. It should have been off-putting. A man who snuck out when my back was turned. But there was something about him, something I reckoned could set my entire body on fire.

I itched to find out how that would feel.

"Juney, don't be silly," Hadley chastised gently, and I tore my gaze away from the man sitting alone in the corner.

"Hmm?" I gave him a puzzled look.

"You're making eyes at him, that moody looking arsehole. He looks like bad news, love. And he's far too old for you. So, maybe, just this once, don't be silly?" His kind eyes creased around the edges as concern furrowed his brow. Hadley knew me well; the old man had seen me chase after far too many inappropriate men over the last five years. But only one had ever ended in tears, for a bloody good reason.

"I'll be fine," I smiled. "But thanks for the concern, you're the best." I learned over the bar and placed a quick kiss on his stubbly cheek.

"I'd rather not be concerned in the first place," he grumbled. But when I pulled back, he smiled softly. "Can I rough him up a bit if you manage to charm him?"

"Of course you can." I patted his arm, causing him to grumble something under his breath, but I was no longer paying attention.

My gaze had slid back to the table where Nate was sitting, sipping whiskey, and avoiding making eye contact with anyone. Including me.

It was all well and good that my friend was concerned, but if the mysterious man was really as closed off as he seemed, I wasn't sure there was much need for it. I did have a talent for breaking down people's walls, but this man, he seemed far more stubborn than anyone I had ever met in my twenty-four years on this earth.

He drained the last drops of his whiskey, then glanced up, meeting my gaze and jolting backwards. 'Another?' I mouthed as he regained his composure and nodded sharply, his brows still tight and his posture far more rigid than before he had noticed me staring.

I placed two perfectly poured pints down in front of the twins, then rounded the bar with Nate's drink. Hadley made a frustrated noise under his breath, which I chose to ignore, carrying on over to the table.

"You came back," I announced brightly as I slid the glass across the table, using just enough force for it to stop before him without his need to catch it.

"I did," he said, his voice a low, rough rumble. He placed his hands around the glass and peered into it in what seemed to be an attempt to avoid talking to me.

"You gonna stick around for a bit? Or will you leave without saying goodbye, again?" I teased, taking a step closer and bumping my hip against the table, hoping to grab his full attention. I had never been one to give up too quickly.

"Who knows." He shrugged, keeping his eyes down as he swirled the liquid and hunched forward.

I pulled my lower lip between my teeth as I wondered how I was going to manage to crack this grumpy egg, when his voice filled the space between us. "Don't you have work to do?"

"This is work. I'm making sure that my customers are happy." I flashed my best smile down at him, not that he bothered to look up and notice.

"I'm fine. I'm sure your boss wouldn't be pleased with you giving me all of your attention," he said bitterly.

I looked around in bewilderment, wondering where exactly he thought my mythical boss was. The laugh that bubbled up from my throat was louder than I expected, and I clamped my hand over my mouth as his eyes shot up to mine.

"I'm sorry," I spluttered, as an intense, dangerous look filled his eyes. "Who do you think runs this place?"

"Fuck knows. I'm guessing your boss is one of those arseholes who never turns up and expects you to do everything, from the way you've just reacted." His gaze softened slightly.

"Oh yeah, she makes me do *everything*. It's almost like she has some crazy mind control thing going on," I joked, raising my brows and grinning. "Like she's constantly in my head telling me what to do."

"She sounds like a bitch," he snapped.

"Ouch." I feigned outrage. "I'm not a bitch."

My smile grew wider as two deep lines marred the smooth, pale skin between his brows, then another laugh fell from my lips as his mouth popped open in realisation.

"*You're* the boss." He couldn't have sounded more shocked if he had tried.

"This is my bar, so yes, I think it's safe to say that I'm the boss. And I *think* standing around talking to you is fine. No disciplinary action needed."

His eyes darted to my lips, and he cleared his throat as something dark flashed in his eyes. He opened his mouth as if to speak, then blinked hard and pursed his lips, dropping his focus back to his glass.

"Well." I filled the awkward silence between us. "I'll get on then. But the crowd here on a Monday usually dies down around 9pm, if you wanted to join me up at the bar later, that might be nice."

"Maybe," he mumbled, and I walked away, swaying my hips, hoping that he was watching. When I rounded the bar again and looked his way I groaned inwardly, finding his head bowed even lower than before. He had definitely not noticed.

I wondered for a moment if I was wasting my time? Or was this guy about to become my new challenge? I so enjoyed challenges.

Give it a week, I thought to myself. One week, and if I had made no progress, I'd give up.

Oh, who was I kidding, I was already way too intrigued by him to do that.

But still, I could lie to myself for now.

4

Friday night rolled around quickly, and once again I found myself sitting at the bar in Kim's. I had sat there every night since Monday. I hadn't come in over the weekend after reading the chalked board out the front when I had passed by on Saturday morning. Saturdays were for live music, local bands and occasionally slightly better-known faces, and on Sunday's she closed early to the public to allow for 'The old dudes poker night' to be held. I didn't really understand that, did they really need the whole bar to be shut down for a silly poker night? And was that even legal?

    I didn't know what it was that had kept drawing me back in, but each day when I arrived home from work, I made myself my pathetic single serving dinner, took a long, hot shower, and then strolled on down to Kim's. I never spoke to anyone, except for *her*, and even those conversations were minimal. I didn't see much point in getting to know anyone. But being in this place made me feel a little less… alone. Because that's what I was, every day that I had sat in my small flat since moving there six months ago I had felt so heavy with loneliness that I wondered if I would ever feel anything else ever again. And when I arrived home last Friday night, and hit another spiral, the first feeling that had consumed my body was that one. Closely followed by my old friend: unrelenting rage.

The emotions passed though, and I woke the next morning with a brighter outlook, until I read that chalked board. I had turned around straight away, and then spent the weekend in my dark room, cycling through the stages of grief over what I had lost. It had taken a lot to dispel the anger that stung deep in my chest on Monday morning, but I had forced myself to use the small set of coping skills that I had. The skills I forgot about most of the time.

It wasn't that I didn't *want* to get better. I did. Fuck, if I could see a way out of this shitty illness, I would run that way at full fucking speed without ever looking back.

But knowing my luck, I'd reach the exit, and have a sudden burst of euphoric joy, and I'd question why I would ever want to feel like other people do when I could feel happiness so intensely. I would forget about what comes later, and I'd walk away from that exit with a temporary ecstatic spring in my step.

I huffed quietly at the thoughts, feeling a spell of self-loathing coming on as I glanced across the bar at the stunning little brunette who had been trying so bloody hard to befriend me all week.

With a little more time, and with a different man, she might have succeeded; she was a persistent little thing. But the thing was, I didn't want to be her friend. She wouldn't win me over with her playfulness, kind words and upbeat personality. No. She would have no chance. Because the more time I spent around her, the more I realised that I wanted to be something entirely different to her. Something that I shouldn't be. And if I acted on that desire, well, that would give a sweet girl like her the complete wrong impression. And that put friendship firmly off the table.

I craved her flesh, I wanted to possess her in the rawest way I could. And that was all. I wouldn't even allow myself to want anything deeper from her. It wasn't who I was. I could never have, *give,* anything more. That was off the table too.

Unlovable.

That's what I've always been. It's a fact, and it hurts. It will never change. If I was going to be anything else, it would have happened by now. So instead of letting anyone realise the painful fact, the disappointing truth, I keep them at a distance. Holding them in a place where I can use them for what I need, and never truly take what I want.

Looking at her, I can see that she's not the type of girl who had a one-night-stand. She's the type of girl you take home to meet your parents. She bakes gingerbread with your mum at Christmas, and laughs at your dads' awful jokes, and every time she looks your way, she's gazing at you with utter adoration in her eyes. Because you are the most wonderful man in the world, according to her.

I can't give her that. Even if I wanted to, I don't have it. And I'm not the most wonderful man, I'm so fucking far from it. So I would have to continue keeping up a cold front towards her.

"I'm starting to think you enjoy my company, Nate," she said as she reached my corner of the bar to fill a tall glass with ice.

"I enjoy your bar," I corrected her and pointed down at my empty glass. "When you're ready."

She laughed lightly and glided back to the customer she had been serving, her curly, long ponytail swaying from side to side as she busied herself pouring drinks. I forced my attention away from her as filthy thoughts filled my mind. If she was anything like my usual type, I would have already taken what I wanted from her, and she'd know exactly what I fantasised about doing with her hair.

But she was too nice, too…sunny.

Sunny girls don't want their hair wrapped around a man's fist as they get their backs cracked like fucking glowsticks while screaming for more.

Do they?

"You gonna sing tonight?" Her voice pulled me out of my inappropriately curious musings, and I shrugged noncommittally. I shouldn't have been thinking about her in that way anyway.

"I might." I had enjoyed myself a lot when I had stepped up to sing the previous week, but arriving home and hitting that sudden spiral was not something I was excited about repeating. Then again, I knew now that I had little to no control over *when* that shit happened, I could fall into a pit of darkness the second I stepped out of the limelight, or it could happen in three days' time. So feeling the high that I only got from performing was something I'd probably risk any time it was offered. No matter how badly it hurt after.

Maybe I'm a masochist?

"I'd love to hear you again, and everyone has been talking about your performance last week," she gushed, and I rolled my eyes.

"Fine."

The smile that bit into her cheeks was so infectious that no matter how badly I wanted to push her away I couldn't help but be drawn in. I mirrored her for a moment, then managed to get a hold of myself. It was too late though; she had already noticed.

"Holy crap," she murmured, then drew her bottom lip between her teeth. "You should do that more often."

"Do what?"

"Smile." I swear to fucking god I saw little hearts appear in her sparkling ocean eyes.

Shit.

It wasn't that I thought I was irresistible or something. Well, not often. Occasionally I did, but that god-like feeling never lasted for long. But I was certain that she felt some kind of attraction towards me. She had been pushing for friendship, but her eyes were saying something entirely different. Something more. And that was bad. I could practically see a flashing neon warning above her head - *Do not ruin this girl. She cannot handle it.*

I shook my head at her, then dropped my gaze down to my freshly poured whiskey. "When am I on then?"

She squealed and my eyes darted up at the sudden movement of her jumping up and down, looking like a puppy about to get a treat. She wriggled, momentarily lost in the cutest little dance I've ever seen, and I had to use every last drop of self-control to stop myself from smiling. Which was more of a challenge than it should have been.

"You can go on next if you want?"

"Sure." I swallowed down half of my drink, then turned and headed to the stage, swapping places with a leggy blonde who was covered in dark ink and had just been completely destroying Blondie's 'Call Me'.

Juniper rushed around the end of the bar, ducked under a hatch, and grabbed a guitar from another patron with a polite, excited ramble of words before she stood in front of me. "Do you want this?"

"Yeah. Thanks." I made a mental note that if I decided to keep this up, I should probably start bringing one of my own guitars. I hated using strangers' instruments. And no one felt quite as perfect in my hands as Lola, my Ibanez with her stunning starburst body. Aly may have been a close second though, she was cleaner, newer, but didn't hold as much history.

She handed over the guitar and I quickly checked its tuning, it wasn't perfect, so I irritably fiddled around for a minute as the same old guy from last week introduced me and Juniper headed back behind the bar. I let my fingers and ear focus on the tuning as I watched her. She quickly poured a line of shots, then leaned her elbows against the sticky bar top, resting her chin on her dainty fists. Her gaze locked onto mine, and there wasn't a single damn thing I could do about it. I couldn't blink, or look away, or fucking *anything*.

All I could force myself to do was play. Deciding to do a cover this time, knowing full well that if I sang the song that was sitting on the tip of my tongue I'd be in deep, deep trouble. Those lyrics were best kept locked away. They were too honest, too painful.

Juniper's lips parted as I sang a particularly difficult part, and I finally managed to blink away from her, closing my eyes and losing myself to the rest of the words.

*"And I'm, I'm out making rounds
On every side of town
That I've been through, that I know
To find my reason to come back home."*

A loud applause erupted around the bar, and I finally let go, smiling as a tidal wave of pride and confidence flooded over me. As I made my way back to the bar I was greeted with compliment after compliment, and my heart soared. It felt amazing, everything felt so fucking good, and I prayed I could cling to the feeling forever.

I finished my drink and smirked at Juniper.

"You're quite impressive, aren't you, Mr," she stated, and placed the bottle of whiskey down beside my empty glass. "Will you stay a while tonight?"

"You know what, I think I will," I said, nodding as my smirk turned into a genuine smile.

"Great, help yourself." She gestured to the bottle, and I frowned slightly. "Promise to keep coming back and I'll forget how much that shit costs." She answered my silent question and I frowned deeper. "You're good for business." She answered another question that never passed my lips and my head tilted. Another question sitting on the tip of my tongue. "I'm really good at reading people." There it was again.

I swallowed hard and mulled over that statement as she was called to the other end of the bar. If she was that good at reading people, then perhaps she already knew what kind of man I was, the content of the thoughts that filled my head, and exactly how little I could give to her. My tongue pressed into my cheek as I continued on that train of thought. If she saw that, then maybe I was wrong about her. Maybe I had seen her in the wrong light entirely. And maybe she *could* handle a single night. There was an unexpected chance that she was capable of taking all that I could give, and that she wouldn't need anything more. Maybe I was wrong about sunny girls.

"If you're so good at reading people, what am I thinking right now?" I asked, testing her as she passed me to grab ice.

She paused, squinted, and cocked her head before answering. "You're thinking that I'm never going to guess right, and I've not given you long enough to think of somethin' hard." She smiled, filled the glass, then locked her gaze on mine. "Now you're having inappropriate thoughts because I said hard."

Her tongue darted out and slid across her bottom lip, "And now..." she trailed off and leaned closer. "Nate," she gasped, "I cannot say *that* out loud."

She wasn't wrong. Not at all. And from the way she giggled as she leaned back and drifted away from me was enough to confirm my suspicion. I was seeing her in a completely different light than I had not ten minutes ago, and she was shocking. A single, short conversation, and everything in my head had changed. And I knew, without a doubt, that I was going to give in, and I was going to end up finding out exactly what was hidden beneath that bright, lovely exterior.

I raised the bottle and poured a large measure, feeling a tiny stab of guilt as I watched the liquid flow. If I caved to my desires, I wouldn't be coming back. I may not have voiced anything, but the action of filling my glass was acting as a silent promise. And it was one that I would never keep.

Once the night was over that would be it. No more visits to Kim's. Juniper would never see me again. I would go back to my lonely pit of despair, until I found something else to bring a smile to my face. The same old cycle.

I sipped my whiskey and watched her work. The smile on my lips never budging. Come morning it would be gone. I'd realise what I had done. But for now, I was happy to sit at her bar, growing hard beneath my jeans at the thought of trying something new.

I was going to destroy little miss sunshine.

"How about you stay and help me clean up then?" Juniper suggested when I told her that it wasn't right that she would be all alone once I had left. She had called last orders twenty minutes ago and was attempting to kick everyone out. Luckily the Friday night crowd seemed to be quite cooperative, minus the group of guys who I had found out were those infamous 'Old Dude's' who hosted their poker games here. They were hovering, looking like a cross between a gang of scary old bikers, and overprotective grandads.

"We can help. He can get going, can't you lad?" One of the twins said, folding his huge, tattooed arms, and glaring at me with a clear threat written across his face.

Lad? What am I? Fucking 12?

"Don't be silly Jer. Anyway, this one owes me, he's been drinking on the house most of the night," Juniper said, clamping a hand down on my shoulder with a far tighter grip than I imagined her to have.

"Juney, remember what I said," the other twin said, giving her a pointed look.

"Yep. And remember what *I* said." She smiled at the man, and he cracked his knuckles. She laughed lightly, "Not now you big brute. We'll be fine, won't we, Nate?"

"Of course." I forced a smile.

"I'd feel better if *we* helped instead." *Jer* said, stepping forward and picking up a cloth from the bar.

"Well, I s'pose you can all help then," Juniper said, still smiling as she released me and moved behind the bar, stacking glasses into a dishwasher and humming happily to herself.

"It won't take all five of us to shut down the bar," I spoke up, not liking the way she had just caved to their protests. I got it, they cared. But as I had told myself all evening – every time that I had wondered if I should walk away from Juniper – *she* was a grown fucking woman. And *I* understood the word no. So what was the problem?

"It'll get done quicker," the third man said. I

recognised him as the guy who handled the sound system, and when I met his gaze, I found a slightly softer expression in his eyes. He was still fiercely protective, but apparently a little more trusting than the other two.

Although gaining their trust wasn't exactly something I needed to do. Still, I gave him a half assed shrug, not bothering to argue with a man who was clearly just trying to keep the peace.

"Well, it will if you lot stop hovering around and actually *do* somethin'," Juniper said and playfully whipped each of us with her damp cloth. "Now get to it."

Annoyed by our lack of alone time, but too curious to walk away, I headed to the furthest corner and began to collect glasses, wiping each table down as I moved along to the next. It was about as much fun as licking envelopes, but I had come this far, and I was determined now to see this night through. So I silently cleaned up while the 'old dudes' chatted away, pausing from time to time to glare at me, their gazes all so cold, so full of hatred. By the time we were done, and Juniper had gone to cash up, I was feeling pretty close to sober, and just a little uncomfortable.

"You'll stay away from our Juney if ya know what's good for ya," one of the twins said. I had noticed that Hadley was the more aggressive one, so I presumed that was who had just lightly threatened me.

I pushed my tongue into my cheek and tilted my head. "What the hell is your problem?" I hissed through my teeth, low enough that 'Juney' wouldn't hear from her office.

"You. You're my problem. That girl is an angel, and you come in here with your dark, mysterious act, wooing her with pretty songs, corrupting her and *taking advantage* of her. It's disgusting. I can see it in your eyes, you're bad news, and I don't want our girl getting hurt." He stepped close to me, the stale scent of the beer on his breath filling the small space between us.

"I'm sure your girl can handle herself, so maybe wait until she asks for your help before you attack me," I whispered, glaring at him.

"I fucking knew it; you *are* going to hurt he-" He raised his voice, but hers cut over, stopping him in his tracks just before his clenched fist could collide with my stomach.

"All done," she sang, completely oblivious to what had almost just gone down. "Nate, will you walk me home?"

Her eyes widened and her bottom lip popped out as though her request was more of a plea, and I felt my cock unexpectedly twitch excitedly in my jeans. *That* was not what usually got me going.

"Sure," I agreed, and as she turned her back on us all to lock the office door I smirked darkly at the men. They all looked as though they might strangle me if they were given a chance. It was a look I was used to receiving though. I wasn't exactly likable.

That thought suddenly made me second guess my intentions with Juniper, again. Maybe I shouldn't...

She grabbed my arm and bounced out of the bar before I could debate the thought, dragging me along with the three men stomping behind us.

"See you tomorrow boys," she called out as she let them out first, quickly locked the doors, and pulled me in the opposite direction that they had started heading in.

"We can wal-" one of them began but she shot them a shockingly fierce glare before pulling me more quickly away from Kim's.

"Juniper," I began, not sure exactly what I was going to say to her. I had never second guessed going home with anyone. I had regrets, sure, but they had always come the morning after.

"Oooh, ominous," she said with a laugh, "you say my name like you're about to tell me you're a serial killer with a taste for twenty-somethin' brunettes."

"I am," I said, completely dead pan as I stopped us from taking another step forward.

"Awesome. I knew tonight would be the night, I could feel it in my bones," she laughed again and tugged on my arm where she was still gripping me, but her hand slipped away as I refused to move.

"Juniper," I said, firmer this time, and she turned to face me, her ponytail swishing with the rapid movement and the skirt of her black dress fanning out before settling against her thighs again. "This, do you know what you're doing?"

"Walking home, and probably inviting you in." She smiled and reached for my arm again, her warm fingers so small compared to my wide, toned bicep.

"And is that what you want? A night with me?" I asked, my voice low as I narrowed my eyes and held her sparkling gaze.

She bit her lip and tightened her grip on me. "I know I'm not great at saying no, but I'm not an idiot. I wouldn't be making moves like this if I didn't know what I was doing."

"Moves like what?" I tilted my head, confused.

Sure, she was literally dragging me to her place, but I'd hardly call that a 'move'.

"This." Her gaze suddenly darkened, the bright ocean morphing into a swirling, stormy sea as she stepped forward, wrapped her free arm around my neck, pushed herself up, and dragged my lips to hers.

I forgot how to breathe. In that moment she had stolen every last breath from my lungs, and I began to drown in her. The taste of her cherry lips sprinkled with a hint of vodka had my head spinning. And when she released me all too soon, I refused to suck down the heavy gasps of air that my body was begging for. Instead I snared the back of her head with one hand and crushed my lips back to hers. My fingers roaming through her hair until I found the tie securing her ponytail and wrapped the length once around my palm. I tugged hard and swallowed down her yelp of pain, thrusting my tongue between her parted lips as she twisted both arms around my neck and ground her body into mine.

Unexpected.

That's what she was. And I was certain I didn't have enough control to allow her to take me home before I enjoyed her.

"Come with me," I commanded against her perfect lips. My voice rough with need.

Before I could lead the way, she took my hand and dragged me in the exact direction that I had been about to take her. We barrelled down the stony beach until we hit damp sand. A moment later she was ripping my white shirt, buttons flying, and landing god knew where as she stepped back, raked her gaze down my torso, and groaned happily.

"You're like every crush I've ever had rolled into one."

I bit back a grin at her interesting compliment and closed the space between us. Her fingers grazed the skin just above my jeans, and before I could take control, she had my belt unhooked and was fumbling with the button.

"Patience," I scolded as I warred with myself. I loved how forward and confident she was, but I hated that she was taking the control away from me. I wanted her beneath me, begging to come. Not on top of me forcing me to submit.

It turned out that all I had to do to take back what I needed was to push her down onto the sand, drop between her thighs, and rip off her bikini bottoms. I tossed the damp fabric across the ground, not giving a single fuck about where it landed. We were close to the water's edge, and there was a high chance that the tide would come in before we were done, but I was already drowning in carnal need, I could handle the sea.

She squirmed excitedly against the sand, and hoisted her dress up, exposing her bare pussy to me. I lowered my head, breathing her in, the sweet scent of her arousal mixing with the saltiness of the seawater that had clung to her since her swim earlier in the evening.

I nibbled my way down the inside of her thigh, pausing at the apex before breathing heavily against her as I avoided the place where she desperately wanted my mouth, and nipped the flesh of her other leg down to her knee.

"Nate," she breathed, my name sounding so fucking dirty as it fell from her lips.

"Yes, Juniper?" I trailed my fingers down the path

my mouth had just run, stopping where she wanted me and snatching my finger away with a tut as she bucked her hips. She wasn't shy, not in any way at all, and I cursed myself for

"What do you want, Little one?" I asked.

"You."

"Yes. Clearly." I eyed her pussy, licking my lips as I dropped my fingers down to her folds, causing her to wriggle as I used my finger and thumb to part her lips, gifting myself with a better view of her wet cunt glistening under the moonlight. "Stay still, and tell me again."

She did as she was told, her body unmoving as she exhaled my name and repeated what she wanted. "You. Nate, I want you."

"Again," I demanded.

"*You,*" she panted, my gaze meeting hers. I sucked in a sharp breath as I found a pained expression on her face. I was in for a treat with this girl. She was more in sync with my desires than I'd have ever guessed.

Fuck.

She wasn't some desperate little slut, but she was sure as fuck about to beg like one.

"Oh, Juniper, you can do better than that," I said coldly, betraying the inferno of heat building in my lower stomach.

Her brows pulled together for a moment, then dipped as she pleaded with me. "Please. This," she squirmed, drawing my focus back between her thighs, "It's all for you. Please, take it. Take me."

I pushed my thumb upwards as my finger slid down past her most sensitive nerves, circled, and ran gently through the wetness coating her. I grazed her clit with my thumb as I pulled away, causing her to whimper. The sound was followed by a loud gasp as I pushed my finger between my lips, and sucked. She tasted so sweet, and I hummed my enjoyment.

"One rule," I said sternly, "You do not come without my permission."

I waited for her to back out like so many of the other women did, and I didn't often care, my tastes weren't for everyone. Except as I waited for her to answer me, I felt my stomach slowly drop. I *wanted* her to agree. But I never let that show.

A smirk slipped across her lips, "You seem very sure that you can actually get me there. So, we'll see about that."

I knew what she was doing, but I couldn't stop myself. The moment she had put the challenge out there, I was gone. My face buried between her thighs, my tongue lashing against her clit as I plunged my fingers inside her. She gasped and squeaked and moaned as I viciously feasted on her and pumped my fingers. I wasn't wasting my time with teasing anymore. I was going to prove a point, and I was going to prove it faster than she could ever fucking imagine.

She tightened around my fingers in a clear sign that she was almost there, and I chuckled as I pulled out of her, spread her wide and sucked hard on her clit. I raised my head, my fingers replacing my tongue without skipping a beat. Her nails were carving deep lines in the sand beside her head, while her eyes squeezed tightly closed.

"How you doin', Little one?" I asked coolly, my

fingers playing her clit like it was my new favourite instrument. And I was already a fucking pro.

"I'm gonna-"

"No, you're not," I reminded her, and her eyes snapped open, meeting mine and widening as her lips parted and she gasped for air.

"Please, can I?" she begged between pained pants.

"Can you what?"

"Come." She all but screamed, her body trembling as I held her on the edge.

"Yes."

Incoherent words fell from her mouth, and I was certain I heard her thank me as she came apart. I watched her face as she came hard. Her legs shook, her eyes tightly closed, her head thrashing in the sand while more words escaped her perfect mouth. I slowed my fingers, then just as her movements slowed, I plunged them inside her, dragging a blissful moan from her that echoed through my head. She wasn't begging me to stop. And as her eyes fluttered back open and landed on mine, I knew she was ready to take so much more.

A fact that she confirmed as she moaned three demanding words.

"Fuck. Me. Now."

5
Juno

My breaths came in short, sharp pants as Nate's long fingers worked their magic inside me. I hadn't come like that in… well, ever. And there wasn't a chance in hell that I would be letting the night end with only one orgasm. I wanted this man to ruin me. I wanted to be walking funny in the morning, and I wanted my daydreams to be consumed with the filthiest memories of what this man was capable of.

    The tide was coming in though, and as much as I loved the sea, I wasn't sure that I wanted to fuck in it. I was shocked that no one had heard us and had come running down to investigate, especially as I was pretty sure Nate had made me scream at one point. Not that I was completely sure, my head was spinning with how rapidly he had brought me to the edge. I had thought he might be all talk, but I had been proved wrong. So fucking wrong.

Thank fucking god.

"We-." I moaned loudly as he struck that perfect spot inside me hard. His fingers curling and his dark eyes dancing with mischief as his other hand pressed down on my lower stomach.

"Should-" A scream – I'm certain this time – left me. My back arched as he pressed down hard, pushing my ass into the sand as his fingers violently fucked me.

"*Fuck.*" I managed. It wasn't the word I had been looking for at all, but it was all that I had. My brain was malfunctioning as another orgasm ripped through me, one that I had zero control over.

"Yes, we should," he said with a low, rumbling chuckle.

My vision had turned spotty around the edges, but I didn't miss the way his lips turned up in the ghost of a smile.

"But before I let you take me home, Little one, you're going to show me what else those perfect lips are good for."

My jaw dropped. Words failing to escape, catching in my throat.

"It's that, or I bend you over my knee. Afterall, you just came without permission."

"I couldn't-" I began to protest but he had already moved away from me, sitting on his knees with his thumbs tracing the line of his waistband as his questioning eyes locked on mine.

This man didn't play fair.

"Not my problem. So what will it be?" He tilted his head, his black hair barely out of place, all apart from a single curl that fell down across his forehead, landing just below his eyebrow, the one I knew to have a single freckle sitting above the peak. Not that I had his every feature memorised or anything…

"I get to choose?" I asked, weighing up my options. So far, I wasn't sure which I'd prefer. Choking on his cock sounded quite nice, but I hadn't seen it yet. There was always the chance that there wouldn't be much to choke on, although with the way his fingers and tongue worked, I could probably get over that pretty quickly. My gaze dropped to his hands. Huge, palms with long fingers. Five large silver rings, one on each pointer and middle finger and one on his right ring finger. I stared at them, falling into distracted thoughts about how the cool metal had felt pressed up against me when he had pushed deep inside.

Did he know how good it felt?

"Of course not." He shook his head. "I'm just curious about which one you would pick."

I could see where his thoughts were going, whatever I picked, he would do the opposite. Keeping true to his cold, arsehole act. Oh, I was on to him.

"I want you to spank me," I decided, pouting and widening my eyes in that way that my sister had always been jealous of. I had mastered doe eyed innocence, while she was more of a seductive siren. We each had our strengths, and luckily always had different taste in men.

"Come here then." He dropped his ass to balance on his heels and patted his thigh.

I attempted to hide my shock but failed. He laughed under his breath and crooked a finger at me before pointing to the floor at his knees.

Pushing back my disbelief that he had managed

to, what, triple bluff me? I shuffled over to him, licking my lips as I moved closer. When I was kneeling before him, I leaned forward, pressing my nose to his as I stared into his eyes.

"So, you really want to suck my cock then, do you?" he whispered, his breath hot against my lips.

"How did you know?" I pushed closer, my tongue darting out to lick his upper lip.

"Because you were *trying* to read me. It's ok, Little one," He raised a hand to my face, cupping my cheek and running the rough pad of his thumb under my eye as his fingers pushed into my hairline. "We have all night. You'll get what you want in due time."

His lips met mine, a breath later our tongues were tangling, and his hand was wrapping around my ponytail again. He pulled hard, breaking our kiss too soon, then used his grip on my hair to guide me into position. My stomach resting on his knees as my cheek rested on the soft sand beside him.

"Are you going to take your punishment like a good girl, Juniper?"

I nodded and blinked the sand out of my eyes.

"Words."

"Yes."

"Good."

A cold breeze blew over my ass a second before his palm struck, heat burning its way through the sting, a muffled squeak held behind my lips. Another hard strike had me letting out a small moan, and a third had my body shaking.

"Good girl," he praised with a deep growl, "Now get up, and take me home."

I did as I was told, not bothering to search for my discarded bikini bottoms. I took his hand and ran, racing across the sand with my dress catching in the breeze and his shirt billowing wide open. A laugh bubbled from my lips, and as I looked over my shoulder at Nate, I found that he was struggling to keep his own laughter at bay. The sight of him like that had me certain about one thing. I was going make this man happy, one way or another. Even if just for a while. I had no idea how many years this man had been broken for, but I was more than up to the challenge. And I didn't care if it all ended in tears, I was about to do anything it took to hear joy in his voice and see a real smile painted on his face.

Maybe I could save this one.

I stumbled as we made our way up the stones. Nates arms wrapped around me before I could fall, his grip tight as he allowed me to regain my balance.

"Thank you," I said quietly, and he nodded, his chin rubbing against the top of my head as he slowly released me. Something in the way he touched me sent a flutter to my stomach, and a moment later, when he lowered his mouth to my ear and spoke, the butterflies descended lower.

"The only time I want to see you falling is when you fall to your knees with your mouth wide and waiting for my cock."

My ass involuntarily ground against him, and I gasped as I felt his hard, *not small,* length press back. He stepped to my side, and I took his hand, silently rushing across the road, up the hill, and to the front door of my tiny bungalow.

The moment my door closed he was on me again,

slamming my body hard against the solid wood, his fingers wrapping around the backs of my thighs, effortlessly lifting me as his mouth trailed hot kisses down my neck.

I wrapped my legs around him and moaned vague directions to my room as his fingers dug painfully into my flesh and dragged up to my ass. I fell down onto my back, bouncing on my plump mattress as I stared up at his toned body, taking in each muscle as I was given a clearer view than when we were on the beach. My gaze dropping from the dark hair dusting his chest, across his carved abs, to the lines that pointed down towards his cock. A frown pulled my brows as my gaze lingered on the dark denim hiding the view that I was so desperate to lay my eyes on.

He noticed instantly. "Sit up, tongue out, and I'll give you what you crave."

I did as I was told, then slipped the straps of my dress off of my shoulders for good measure. Letting them drag the neckline of my dress lower so that the fabric barely covered my black bikini top. I watched Nate as he sank his teeth into his bottom lip, his eyes narrowed as he sucked in a long, slow breath.

I kept my eyes locked on his, losing myself in the darkness of this man, until movement close to my chin caught my attention and I dropped my gaze to find his cock springing free, the tip so close to my tongue I could almost taste the salty bead of precum that he smeared around with his thumb, knocking my tongue with his knuckle.

"Eyes on me, Little one," he growled.

Once again, I followed his command, enjoying

how little I needed to think as I waited. Moments passing between us, saliva running down my chin, my mouth aching to close and swallow, but I didn't. I waited. I waited so patiently while his thumb circled the head of his impressive cock, and I listened as his breathing became heavier, and his next command was finally spoken. "Wider."

He wasn't gentle, forcing his way down my throat, giving me no time to adjust, and causing me to choke around him. It was like nothing I had ever felt before, the way his thick shaft filled my mouth as he slid deeper and deeper. I exhaled through my nose as I worked on relaxing my throat for him, and as my chokes turned into moans he groaned loudly, cursing and winding my hair around his hand before slamming in and out. Harder. Fucking my throat. His hold on my hair keeping me in place until tears started to stream down my face, and he stepped back, his cock falling from my mouth, coated in strings of saliva.

I closed my mouth, swallowing hard and wiping the tears from under my eyes as I grinned up at him.

"Nate," I asked, angelically batting my lashes.

"Yes." His voice was even lower now, a rough whisper that matched the intense look in his eyes.

"Can you please fuck me now?" I cocked my head, smiling sweetly.

His eyes closed and he clicked his tongue loudly while fisting his cock. I took the chance to surprise him by quickly wriggling out of my dress and tugging the tie of my bikini, tossing it aside with an audible thud as it landed.

Nates eyes snapped open, and his jaw dropped as

he looked down at me laying back on the bed, completely bare, with my legs spread and my nipples pinched between my fingers and thumbs.

"You shock me more and more with each second that I spend in your company. I thought you were a sweet girl," he rasped, squeezing his cock hard while drinking in the way I slowly toyed with my nipples. Putting on a show just for him.

"I *am* a sweet girl. Most of the time." I pinched hard, releasing a breathy moan. "Am I going to lay here playing with myself all night, or are you going to get that delicious cock over here and fill my tight little hole?"

"You're going to kill me woman," he groaned, tipping his head back. When he met my gaze a moment later his eyes were pitch black and predatory.

He climbed onto my bed, forced my knees wider apart, dragged his cock through the centre of my soaked pussy, then plunged deep into me. I grabbed the duvet as he filled me, stretching me out in one single thrust that had me shrieking and laughing headily as his hands landed on either side of my face. He bent his head to pull my nipple between his teeth, nibbling gently before sucking hard, pulling out of my pussy, then slamming back in. I shrieked again, and this time his mouth covered mine, his tongue darting, teeth clashing, and cock thrusting in a rapid rhythm that had me seeing stars before I could even comprehend that I was actually fucking him.

"Ple-" I began, breaking away from him to follow his rules. He nodded and collided with me once more, moaning into my mouth as I writhed beneath him.

Nate held me tight through my orgasm, and as my

legs stopped shaking, he rolled onto his back, pulling me with him until I was seated with him deeper than before. It took me a moment, where my hand pressed heavily down on his chest, to get used to the new angle. And then I was riding him, his long fingers clawing at my hips as he guided me. My name fell from his lips, not Juno – *Juniper,* over and over as he watched me. Never breaking eye contact. Even as his brows raised, and a strangled groan escaped him as he shot thick ropes of cum deep into my pulsing cunt. He filled me up, then pulled out, holding me close as his cum dripped from my pussy onto his stomach with every spasm of my lingering orgasm. My body trembling and tears of joy filling my eyes as I bathed in the moment, happily fucked, completely satisfied.

"I'm so fucking sorry," he whispered into my hair, stroking his hands up and down my back as he rocked us gently from side to side. "I'm sorry."

"For what?" I finally managed.

"This," he murmured, kissing my hair.

"You can make it up to me in, what, an hour?" I joked, raising my head enough to look him in the eye. I didn't care that he hadn't lasted very long, he had made me come three times already, which was two more than anyone else ever had.

He searched my face, his brows lowering to shadow his eyes, the expression so familiar to me after a week of seeing it so effortlessly painted on. "Sure," he said, rolling me off of him and getting to his feet, "Where's your bathroom?"

"Good morning, Mr Grumpybum," I sang as Nate appeared in the doorway to my kitchen in nothing but a pair of boxers. His sleepy eyes squinting at me as he leaned against the frame and yawned loudly.

"What's so good about it?" he asked, scratching his neatly trimmed beard.

I laughed lightly, then reached up on tiptoes to grab the flour from the top shelf above the kettle. "Well, I woke up beside a man who delivered the best orgasms of my life, and I'm making pancakes. Those reasons good enough for you?"

He huffed and crossed his arms. "I don't do breakfast."

"More for me then. Coffee? Tea?" I asked, pouring flour into the bowl and mixing it in to the milk and eggs.

Nate turned his back on me and took a step back towards the bedroom.

"You're a coffee man, black, no sugar. You hate mornings, but you'll sit with me while I eat my breakfast and tell you stories that you don't give a flying fuck about, because I'm about to promise you a quickie in the shower once I've eaten."

He paused, turned back to face me, and scowled. "You think I'll stay because you're offering me sex?"

"Yes. You like fuckin' me, you made that very clear around 4am when you declared that you'd happily *die* buried inside me. And I like fuckin' you. So stay and enjoy this. Why deny yourself somethin' you want when it's being offered to you on a silver platter?"

"I don't think I can argue with that," he said grumpily as though he desperately wanted to find a way to as he sat at my small oak table, and I placed a black coffee down on the orange coaster.

He sat silently, running his finger around the rim of the bright pink unicorn mug, and glaring at me as I made my pancakes, poured a tall glass of orange juice, and told him stories about some of the important people in my life.

"Do you have any siblings?" I asked after I had explained in depth what I understood of my sister's current drama.

"Yes," he said sharply.

"Brother? Sister?"

"Sister."

"What's she like?" I asked, pushing a huge forkful of syrupy pancake into my mouth.

Nate pursed his lips and sighed. "I don't want to talk about her."

I nodded, then dropped my fork down onto my empty plate and stood up. "Fair enough. Come on then, oh patient one." I offered him my hand. He stared at it blankly, and I wondered if he had forgotten my promise.

As a gentle reminder I lifted my baggy t-shirt over my head, tossed it on the table, and slid off my underwear. His eyes fell to my chest, then he stood and dragged me to the bathroom. The moment the warm water hit my back he was inside me, and as I gasped his name I knew, I knew I'd never be able to get enough of him.

I searched the bar for his face, but I came up short. There was an hour left before we closed for the night, and I was starting to give up hope that he'd show.

When he had left this morning, I had asked him if he'd come. He'd given me a noncommittal shrug in response before stealing my breath with the perfect parting kiss.

It was clear this man usually only usually spent single nights with women. Yet a small part of me hoped to be the exception, that he would come back for more. He seemed to think that he knew me, pinning me as the cute young barmaid with the bouncy hair and the wide, innocent eyes. He no doubt thought that seeing me again would set me up for a broken heart. But that was not me at all. I had tried to prove that to him last night. I had shown him the side of me that no one ever expected to find. The side that lusted, but didn't love. I was a girl who wanted to enjoy herself as much as she could with a man who had enough experience to make her feel like a sexual fucking goddess.

And *holy shit* did he do that.

I sighed heavily, and continued to pour pints, plastering a smile onto my face for the men whose eyes repeatedly narrowed in on me, scanning me for signs that I was hurting. My friends knew me well, they'd have known I had spent the night with that man. But they also knew that as a rule, not a lot could really break my spirit. So why should he be an exception?

Yes, I was disappointed to not see his face again. I wanted more of him, and I wanted to work my magic too. But I knew better than most that you cannot force people to do things that they just don't want to do. I had tried in the past, and I had learned that people with strong enough wills will not budge.

By the time I was closing up I had pulled myself together, and the laughter that fell from my lips when Hadley made another awful joke was the most genuine it had been all night.

"Want one of us to walk you home?" he asked as I twisted my key in the lock and breathed in the fresh sea air.

"I'm good. Thanks though." I hoisted my bag over my shoulder, and waved off the guys, strolling at a leisurely pace as I listened to the gentle crash of waves as they rolled in and out. Wondering if maybe a midnight dip would be a good idea.

While deciding if I was too tired to go home and come back out, a tall figure standing on the stones a few feet away caught my attention. I tightened my grip on my bag, slipping my hand inside the outer pocket where I kept my keys along with a keyring that the twins had bought for me, it was one that had been put together specially for girls walking alone at night. I was probably being dramatic, but still my fingers wrapped around the small can hanging from a chain and I readied myself to run. The figure stood completely still, and I was almost certain that it was a man. Broad shoulders, narrow waist, head tilted slightly. In the dark, from this distance I couldn't see his face, but I could feel his eyes on me.

I tightened my grip on the can and picked up my

pace. Moving as far away from the edge of the stones as I could. It was only when I was perfectly in line with him that it hit me. A light breeze filled with whiskey and pine.

My feet stopped moving as I turned to face him. He remained still, not turning to face me, not even as I stepped onto the stones and spoke his name so softly that I wasn't sure he had even heard me.

"What are you doing out here?" I asked, closing the space between us and craning my neck to look up at him. His usual loose linen shirt had been replaced with a red and black checked one, his glasses were sitting on his face rather than hooked in his collar, and his gaze was fixed on a spot in the distance.

"Nate." I pushed, placing a hand tentatively on his chest.

His head finally dropped, and his eyes locked on mine. My mouth turned dry at his hollow stare. Before I could stop myself, I reached up and ran my thumb across his brow before pushing that single curl of hair back from his face.

"What did you do to me, Juniper?" he asked, his low rumble sending a shiver down my spine.

"What do you mean?" I flinched, pulling back, my hands falling to my sides as anger flared bright in his eyes, burning away the emptiness I'd seen just a second ago.

He didn't speak. He simply shook his head, pushed past me, and stormed off along the beach. Leaving me alone on the stones with a cold sense of dread washing over me. But it wasn't for me, it was for him. I had met a man with that look before.

Something was wrong.

I tried to forget about my encounter with Nate on the beach, but no matter what I did, no matter how many happy moments filled the following few days, I couldn't get that sense of worry to leave me for long.

Jeremy and Hadley spoke in unison, and for once I didn't laugh. "Somethin's bugging you," they declared.

"It is," I confirmed, nodding, and placing my chin on my fists as I leaned on the bar.

"It's that man, isn't it?" Hadley snapped. "He's got to you. I knew he'd mess you around,"

"It's not like that." I batted his chest across the bar and pushed myself upright. "I'm worried about him."

"Why?" Jer asked.

I filled them in on what had happened the other night, and Hadley snorted in disgust. "You didn't do anything to him, you're lovely, Juney."

"I know I am." I grinned. "Which is why I don't understand what he meant. I can't work it out. And the look on his face, it didn't make sense."

"Forget him," Hadley huffed, "You know, Gloria's sister's son will be visiting in a few weeks, maybe he could take your mind off of the grumpy old bastard."

"The doctor?" Jer asked, and the two men fell into an animated conversation as they spoke about Hadley's wife's family. I rolled my eyes and disappeared off to my office, not wanting to hear about how the med student – not doctor – would a better fit for me for the hundredth time in the last few years.

It was the middle of the day, and the twins were the only two people in the bar. I closed the door and slumped down in my chair, twisting it from side to side as I contemplated my worries.

Nate hadn't been back. He hadn't taken any more midnight strolls that I was aware of, and even though I had put my number in his phone, he hadn't called. Maybe he didn't want to see me again, or maybe there was something else.

I didn't like the thought of something else.

I spun myself in a circle three times before I pushed up, grabbed a set of keys, and flung open the office door. I flew past the twins, tossing the keys towards them and asking them to watch the place until Hannah arrived in an hour.

Ten minutes later I was walking up the stairs of the building that housed multiple offices full of rows of cramped desks. One of the few things I had learned about the man I had spent a perfect night with was that he worked here, I didn't know his role, I didn't even know his last name, but I knew I should be able to find him in this building.

"Do you know where I could find Nate?" I asked the woman closest to the doorway, hoping that there weren't multiple Nate's here.

"Nate didn't come in today," she said and the worry swirling in my stomach intensified, "Can I help you instead?"

"I just, I'm his, I, I really needed to see him, erm, I don't suppose you can tell me where he is?" I bit my lip and widened my eyes, hoping my concerned expression could sway her into no doubt breaking some rules for me.

She gave me an unsure once over, then gestured for me to come closer. I crouched beside her chair, and she tapped at her keyboard. "Now, I can't *tell* you anything, but if you just so happened to be the curious type who can't help herself, then I might accidentally open something on my screen…" She tapped again. "Now."

I quickly scanned the screen as she pulled a tissue from a box beside her and made a big fuss of blowing her nose. I read over the first line of Nate's address and stood up, having everything I needed.

"Thank you," I whispered and squeezed her shoulder.

The woman looked up at me and smiled. "It's nice that someone cares about him."

I returned her smile, wondering what she had meant as I hurried back through the door and out of the building. I knew the road where he lived well, and it didn't take me long to find his flat and jab my finger repeatedly at the buzzer.

The door made a high-pitched sound as he let me in without asking who was there. Maybe there was a camera, or maybe…

"You're not the pizza guy," he snarled as he leaned over the banister.

I ran up the stairs, making it to his door before he could close it, and shoved my way inside. He slammed his shoulder into the wall as he stomped past me through an archway and went and sat down on a plush, grey sofa covered in takeout boxes and broken glass.

I leaned against the archway and watched him for

a moment. He was still in the same shirt he had been wearing three nights before, the red and black one, only now it had stains on it and was heavily creased. The top three buttons were undone, and his jeans had been replaced with comfy looking grey joggers. His hair was a mess, the black curls dropping across his forehead, and his beard was longer, also messy. He looked so much older than he had a few days ago. He was a mess. But nothing worried me more than the look in his eyes.

There was nothing there. There had been anger when I first walked in, but in the last minute it had vanished, replaced by an empty, hollow stare. He looked so tired, so done.

I stepped over a pile of plates and dropped to my knees before him. He leaned back on the sofa, putting distance between us, but not bothering to move. His head dropped against the back of the sofa, and he ran his hand over his face. That was when I saw it. The deep cuts oozing blood covering his knuckles. And when he dropped his hand to his lap, palm facing up, he revealed even more narrow slices.

"Nate, can I clean those please?" I asked gently, placing a finger on his hand.

He nodded slightly but didn't look down at me. Instead he curled his fist, trapping my finger, and cleared his throat. "Kitchen, cupboard above the microwave."

His voice made me shudder, and I swallowed hard as I took in the lack of feeling. What the hell had happened?

I slipped my finger out of his hold and navigated my way through the mess of trash and broken items until I located the kitchen and pulled a first aid box from the cupboard. I ran some warm water into a cereal bowl and carried them back to the lounge.

"Can you tell me what happened?" I asked as I entered the room.

Nate shook his head, once.

I held my questions for a while, but I knew there wasn't a chance in hell that I'd be letting this go. I wanted answers, and I wanted them today. Even if it meant sitting here in this mess until he finally chose to speak. Everything else could wait, this man needed someone.

Me.

6

Nate

Juniper held my hand firmly in place as she soaked cotton balls and wiped away the blood that was still seeping from my split knuckles. She was using warm water, and I wanted to thank her for being considerate enough to think of that, but the words were stuck in my throat.

How had she even found me? Why?

She shouldn't be here. What we had was supposed to be a one-time thing, she shouldn't be tending to me. Witnessing the aftermath of a rage fuelled episode. This sweet girl who was cleaning my wounds didn't need to get sucked into my problems. She didn't need to know this side of me. It was fucking embarrassing.

This was why I had avoided her. Although I hadn't, not really. No. When I had arrived back home after our unexpected night together, I had felt a weird pull. Something about her was drawing me in. It was a feeling I had experienced once before, and it scared the absolute shit out of me. I knew I wouldn't be able to stay away. But I needed to try.

I was trying, I was doing the right thing.

I locked myself away in here, hid from the outside world. I knew this attraction would pass if I just waited it out. But waiting it out meant being alone with my thoughts for long enough to spiral. There was no winning option. Day one had been a blur of nothingness, time had been too fast and too slow all at once. On day two I had been dragged out of the blur, but my emotions were like a dog with a toy. I was being shaken from side to side, one minute I wanted to cry, and I thought it would never end, the next it stopped, and I was fine. Happy even. Painfully happy.

I didn't know that was a real thing until a few years ago. To feel pain with happiness. But it soon became a standard sensation for me. I'm not a person who can be *just* happy, and I'm never *just* sad. I don't feel a single emotion on a basic level. It's all or nothing. I'm drowning, or I'm flying. I never stand on solid ground for very long.

"Nate," she murmured sadly as she turned my hand over to clean my palm. "Are you hurt anywhere else?"

Everywhere, Little one. I hurt everywhere.

I couldn't tell her that. She wouldn't understand. No one ever did. So I settled on placing my other hand palm up on my knee, showing her the embedded shard of glass. She shouldn't be here, but I was out of fight. I was too weak. Too tired from my outburst just before she had arrived.

A sharp breath hissed through her teeth, but she

didn't comment. She simply nodded and continued to wipe away the blood.

We sat in silence for what felt like an eternity, and I was shocked to find that I wasn't bubbling over with frustration. A strange part of me wanted her to ask me about this, all of it. But I also didn't want the silence to break. It wasn't deafening. It was... fine.

My thoughts didn't feel like TV static, and they weren't too loud. They were just there. Tears stung the backs of my eyes as I realised that I had never felt like this after an episode before. The self-loathing and shame were there, *they were always there,* but the hurtful thoughts weren't aggressive. They were pleading.

I cleared my throat. "I'm not well," I stated, keeping all emotion from my voice. My head was telling me to do this, to share something. But I also needed to protect myself. I would not break in front of her.

"I'll take you to a doctor," she offered, glancing up at me through her long lashes. "This hand looks fine, but I'm not sure I feel safe removing the glass."

"That isn't what I meant," I snapped pathetically, then sighed heavily, shaking my head in an attempt to stop my tongue from throwing sharp words at her like it wanted to every time anyone misinterpreted what I was saying.

Juniper wrapped a thick bandage around my hand, encasing my swollen knuckles tightly. She secured a knot as her eyes locked on me, then she quickly averted her gaze down to my other hand. Whatever she had seen on my face hadn't been easy for her to look at.

She shifted along the stained carpet on her knees and began to clean around the glass, taking her time with me while chewing on her lower lip. "I'll wrap this in place, and we can go get it removed when you're ready. And if you want to, you can tell me what you meant."

Her voice was shockingly calm. Soft. It was like being wrapped up in a tight, caring hug, not that I had much experience of that. But it was how I imagined that might feel.

Sighing again, I let my head fall back and focused on the lightbulb in the middle of the room, the one without a shade surrounding it that I never liked to switch on. "Three years ago I was diagnosed with a mental health disorder."

"What was it?" she asked as though I was telling her what I'd eaten for lunch, not like I had just told her I was a crazy person.

"Doesn't matter," I said flatly, keeping my focus on the bulb. "It isn't just one thing anyway, it's more of a buy one, get five free kinda thing."

They are also like family heirlooms, I'm sure I inherited some of mine from my mother, from what I remember of her.

She hummed in amusement, and I knew that if I looked down, I would find a smile lifting her perfect lips. "Can you tell me about any of it?"

"Not really." I bit my lip. "I could try, but there's so much I could say, and too much of it is just confusing. I guess, if I keep it simple, I struggle to control my emotional responses, I feel big, and I ruin everything. I saw a therapist for it once, she taught me a few skills that might help to manage some of my traits, but after three months of seeing her, I had to stop. I was growing attached to her in an unhealthy way. Since then I've not found another therapist who will work with me. I get it. *I wouldn't want to work with me. So, this is my life. This is why you can't be a part of it. I can't love. I can't give you what you need."*

I'm too much, and not enough, at the same time.

I swallowed hard and an uncomfortable sensation swirled in my stomach as I realised that I had just told her so much more than I had intended. More than I had ever told anyone else. Anyone except for *her*. My therapist – Talia. The woman who, even though I was a fully grown man, spoke to me like a mother should. And abandoned me too, just like my mother had. She *knew* what leaving could do to someone with borderline personality disorder, but she had decided that it was in my best interest. Sometimes I could see that, on my more logical days. Other times I hated her for it.

Juniper secured another bandage and released my hand. I finally pulled my gaze away from the lightbulb and lowered my head, a shadow falling across my face as I spoke directly to her. "You need to leave."

"Absolutely not," she scoffed, shifting onto her ass and crossing her bare, tanned legs. "For a start you're injured. Secondly, there is broken glass on the sofa that needs to be cleared up. *And* you've just opened up about somethin' difficult. I'm not just going to walk out of that door."

The determination in her eyes caused a laugh to break free from my lips. Her brows dipped in confusion, and I laughed louder.

"What's so funny?" she asked, clearly unsure about how to take my rapid shift in mood.

"The look on your face when you're trying to be

stubborn. It's cute, it makes me laugh," I explained. And as her face relaxed and a smile bit her lips, I felt my body slump with a weird freeing feeling. Forgetting that only half an hour ago I had been smashing glass and screaming for everything to just stop.

She was taking in everything I said, everything I was showing her, and she still sat firmly on my living room floor and didn't make a single negative comment.

My chest suddenly tightened, and my breath caught in my throat. I flung myself forward, my head dropping between my knees as I felt the familiar rush of panic. I gasped for breath, not understanding why I was reacting this way until my thoughts caught up with my body.

In the end, she's going to hurt me so much more than anyone else has.

"Leave," I choked the word out, "Just go."

My fingers pushed through my hair, my short nails clawing at my scalp as internally I screamed for her to listen, to do as I asked. To just leave me now before I let her in.

It's too late. She's already in.

No, it's fine. I can push her out if she just leaves now.

Juniper was simply a splinter in my thumb. She was there, embedded, but she wasn't too deep. I could grab her between my teeth and yank her out as long as I took deep breaths and focused. She hadn't buried herself under my skin. I could make it out with discomfort, rather than pain.

Oh, who was I kidding. I would feel pain. I would feel pain if she had walked away from me that night at the bar, the night when I had devoured her on the beach and fucked her all night long. This girl, with her huge eyes and her disgusting optimism had captivated me the very moment I had laid eyes on her.

I needed her to leave.

"Go," I hissed through clenched teeth. My nails scraping, hair snapping.

"No," she said quietly, the word sounding so unsure as her voice wobbled. "I'm staying."

She reached out for me, grabbing my wrist and pulling sharply. My head shot up as I snatched my arm away from her. My eyes boring into hers, warning her. *Begging* her.

I had accepted long ago that I would forever be alone. I knew my fate. She needed to stop looking at me like I deserved her, because I fucking didn't.

She ignored me completely. Pushing forward, gripping my chin between her thumb and forefinger, she kissed me. Her soft lips pressing hard against my dry mouth. My lips pressed into a firm line, but she didn't react. She pulled away with a small smile, then stood up, grabbed the nearest stack of plates, and disappeared towards my kitchen. Moments later she appeared with a bin liner, wearing yellow rubber gloves, and began to pick up the trash scattered around my living room.

I watched her with narrowed eyes, my jaw ticking as I held back the scream burning my lungs. She shouldn't be doing that.

She needed to go.

Silently, she moved around until every surface was clear of anything that didn't belong.

"Shirt." She finally broke the silence with a soft

command. "Please give me your shirt."

I twisted my head, resting one side in my hand as I spat a single word at her. "Why?"

I cringed at how harsh my tone had been, but she didn't flinch, or look offended. The sweet thing was made of so much more than she showed the world. She just gestured to the glass covering the sofa. "I need to get rid of that, I'm not putting it straight in this bag, so please, give me your shirt, unless you want to find me somethin' else?"

I considered her reasoning for a minute, then sat upright, tugging my shirt open, earning myself an eyeroll as the secured buttons pinged across the room.

"Really? I just tidied up." She laughed lightly, bending over to pick up a button that had landed by her foot.

"Really," I said sarcastically, *childishly*. "Here."

She took my shirt from my outstretched hand, her gaze lingering on my chest as her fingers curled around the fabric.

"Did you have an ulterior motive?" I snarled, glaring at her.

A wide smile creased her eyes, and I felt my own expression softening. I dropped my gaze to the floor, leaning forward again, my elbows resting on my knees as my head dropped between them once more.

"You're hard to ignore." The sound of glass clinking together followed her words. "But I'm sorry. I shouldn't have let myself get distracted like that. Time and place."

I squeezed my eyes closed. "It's fine." I couldn't believe she was *apologising*. She was acting so mature. If anyone should be saying sorry, it was me. But if I apologised, I would allow her to stay, and I just... couldn't.

She needed to go.

"I'm taking this out." I looked up to see her pointing to the bin bag. "Then I'm taking you to see a doctor."

"I'm fine, just go."

"Bullshit. Stop being such a stubborn ass," she gently scolded, then grabbed my key from the coffee table as she left the room.

Smart girl, I wouldn't have let her back in.

"Go and clean your face, get dressed, and toss me your phone, I can reply to your messages for you. I'm sure you have people who are worried." She held her hand out as she appeared back in my living room.

"I don't," I said, standing and tossing my phone at her anyway. "But you can put it on charge, it's been dead for days."

I left her to go and clean up, washing the blood that I had smeared on my face and pulling a random t-shirt from my wardrobe, not paying any attention to which one it was, then slipped a pair of black trainers on and slumped against my front door as I reluctantly waited for her. Entirely unsure about why the hell I had just done as I was told. *What the hell was up with this girl?*

She poked her head through the archway to my living room and smiled. "Let's go then."

I opened the door, my head low as I stepped through it, then lead the way downstairs with no idea how I felt, and no idea what to do. I was a mess, and she didn't care.

"Why are you doing this?" I asked as we walked back to my flat hand in hand. Her grip on me featherlight as she ran her thumb across my bandaged knuckles.

"Because you deserve kindness," she said simply, "and I like you, ya big grump."

She bumped her side against mine playfully and wrinkled her nose as we continued to walk.

I pursed my lips. "You're wrong."

"I'm never wrong."

The smug look on her glowing face had me stifling a laugh.

"Never," she repeated. "Do you have any pain pills, or shall we stop to get some? Oh, and food? Do you want to cook? Shall I cook? Takeout? You tell me what you want to do."

In the space of a couple of hours this girl had placed herself in the middle of my life. And as much as I wanted her to save herself from me and force her back out, a tiny part of me was warming to the idea of her being around.

She's going to destroy me.

I'm going to ruin her life.

I pushed back the intrusive thoughts, clinging to the few little lessons Talia had taught me. 'Challenge those thoughts' she'd say. 'Your thoughts are not facts.'

"You should go back to the bar," I said softly as I screamed at myself, hating that I couldn't just *try*. Having her close felt good, why couldn't I allow myself to feel good?

Juniper shook her head, "I've already asked Hannah to close up tonight, which is kinda scary for me, but I'm gonna roll with it. Give her a chance to prove that she can handle it."

"Go home then."

"Give up, grumpypants, I'm not leaving you tonight." Her eyes sparkled as the sun caught them, and I groaned loudly. Caving.

"Fine. Takeout. Chinese."

She scrunched up her face, "I don't like Chinese."

I stopped dead in my tracks, and she burst out laughing.

"Are you insane?"

"Maybe." She batted her lashes. "There's probably somethin' wrong with me."

No shit. She wanted to spend time with me.

"Apparently so. We're getting Chinese, and I'm changing your mind about it," I declared, determination filling my voice as my mood shifted for the millionth time today.

"I look forward to seeing you try."

"Good morning," Juniper sang, and I blinked hard. The bed had been empty when I had woken up, and the feelings that had hit me were ones that I was all too comfortable with. Disappointment, pain, and honestly, a little relief.

But she was here. And those feelings melted away

the moment she pushed through my bedroom door.

She placed a bowl of cereal on the bedside table along with a steaming cup of coffee.

"You're here?" I whispered, blinking again.

"Sure am."

"*Fuck,*" I groaned, half annoyed, half...

I snared her arm and tugged her down on top of me, then rolled across the bed until she was on her back. An adorable giggle escaped her, and I stole the sound away with a brutal kiss. My teeth sank into her lower lip, punishing and praising her for staying in the only way I knew how.

And as I tugged down my boxers, pushed her panties to one side, and thrust myself deep inside her I knew that every bad thought I'd had would come true. And I would let it.

Something had changed, I felt out of control. It was wrong, but I would selfishly cling to this girl. I'd let her shower me in the feeling of being wanted for as long as I could, even if it meant that I broke her in the end.

She knew I was no good for her.

And she was far too fucking good for me.

7
Juno

Nate leaned over the bar to whisper in my ear. "When I get you alone, Little one, I'm going to show you exactly what I think of that little skirt."

A deep heat spread across my face, and I batted his chest. "I can't tell if that means that you like it or hate it," I laughed.

He didn't respond. Instead he slowly sat back with a sexy smirk on his face as he hooked his ankle over his knee and glanced up at the clock behind my head. There was one hour until close, I already knew this because I had been watching that clock for the last two hours, willing time to pass faster so that I could show Nate the new underwear I had bought. Although with the way his gaze kept raking over me, I was sure he would be admiring them on the floor rather than my body.

An hour later he was locking the door from the inside, folding his glasses, hooking them in the collar of his shirt, and prowling across my bar towards me. It only took ten seconds – I counted – for him to bend me over, flip up my tartan skirt, tug the lilac silk panties to one side, and bury his face in my pussy. Ten minutes later I was screaming his name as he slammed his thick cock inside me over and over, until I was momentarily satisfied, and dripping his cum onto the sticky floor.

    He helped me to clean up, *then* cleaned up the bar. And once we were back at my place, he showed me again what he thought of my little skirt. Shockingly, he managed to take a moment to admire my underwear properly, with a complimentary groan and bite of his knuckles, before he viciously tore them from my body and fucked me until I passed out.

    I was slowly growing addicted to this man. And I was under the impression that he was feeling the same way. He would arrive in the bar each evening after dinner if I was working, except for the weekends. He'd pick me up when I closed on those nights, and on the nights that I took off – now that I trusted Hannah so much more – he would take me out. I guess we could say we were dating, we were getting to know each other. There were no strings, no expectations, just fun. I had managed to make him smile and laugh. He had stopped trying to keep me at arm's length, and the daily temptation to smugly tell him that he had been wrong about the type of man he was, was getting hard to resist. But I resisted. I kept it to myself, because I knew now that his mental health was a rollercoaster. I had already decided that I was happily going to strap myself in for that ride, but I wasn't going to make things worse. I was going to make everything good, better.

"How do you eat a twister?" I asked.

Nate frowned down at me from his usual position, leaning against my kitchen counter. I was stuffing a slice of jammy toast into my mouth while he sipped his coffee.

"A what?"

"You know? The ice cream."

He considered my question for a moment, then his lips formed an 'o', and he stalked towards me, leaning over me and whispering in my ear. "I take my time." He breathed heavily against my lobe then dropped his head, his lips pressing to my neck. "I lick all of the white stuff first, making sure I get my tongue *deep* into the swirl, and I don't stop until it's all gone. Then I devour the rest with messy, greedy bites. And finally, I lick the stick until it's clean."

A shiver ran down my spine and I giggled as his short beard grazed my neck.

"I have a craving for something else that's sweet. Something else that I can lick."

He took a long swig of coffee, and placed the cup on the table, dropped to his knees at my side, and twisted me in my chair. He parted my legs, holding me firmly in place, eyed my bare pussy hidden beneath the white button-down that I'd stolen from him, licked his lips, and lowered his face. His tongue – still warm from the coffee – ran slowly up my centre and he groaned happily before lapping at me until I couldn't breathe, and my knuckles had turned white as I gripped the back of the chair, begged for release, and fell to ruin.

Nate's thick hair fell over his face as he rolled over to face me, silvery strands that showed his age peeking through the dark, lose curls. His eyes squinting as he groaned. He had made that same noise every morning for the last three weeks. Three weeks straight of me and him, in this bed every single night. We never stayed at his place, and I never pushed to. I knew that he wasn't happy there. He was happy here, and when he woke each day, so was I. My bed had become his safe place.

"What's on your mind, Little one?" he asked, his voice rough with sleep.

I brushed his hair away from his face, enjoying the feeling of the silky, curls between my fingers for a moment, allowing it to ground me, push away the fear that I hid so well every single day.

My morning thoughts weren't usually something that I shared with anyone. But he had asked, and as each day passed, I realised there was very little I wouldn't do if he asked. This morning my head had been filled with various thoughts, some good, some bad. I pushed away the bad though, knowing that now wouldn't be the time to share my haunting memories, and decided to spill my happiness out between us.

"I've not told you about my dream, have I?"

Nate shook his head slightly, his brows dipping low, as usual. "Do you mean sleepy dream? Or life dream?"

"Life," I said quietly.

"Go on."

He pulled me close, pressing his nose to mine and making me go cross-eyed.

I spoke into the space between our lips, pushing forward from time to time to kiss him softly. "The bar, Kim's, it used to be a restaurant. It belonged to my Dad, and it's named after my mum. Well, when they died, everything was left to me and my sister. I took it on. She didn't want it, she had her own dreams, ones that have come true. So I took it, along with the house, which I sold. My sister and I agreed that neither of us could step foot in there again without missing our parents, so it was best to let it go. I kept some money aside for her from the sale, even though she insisted she'd never need it, I wanted her to have a safety net. But I didn't keep a big enough one for myself. I put everything I had into the bar, and…" I paused, not ready to tell him about where else the money had gone. "Stuff. The bar was a huge project. It's come along well so far, but it's also nowhere near where I want it to be. I want to turn it into a proper music venue, one where bands and artists from all over will perform. I want new talent, big names, everyone. I want everyone here to see how incredible life is with music. I know I don't look like the type of girl who would want to own a music venue, especially when you compare me to my sister, but I do. It's all I've ever wanted."

I sighed, pressing my lips to his again. "But it has come to a bit of a standstill. We do fine financially, but it's not enough to push any further yet. One day though. One day it will be perfect."

I drew back, taking in the ticking jaw of my moody lover, and wondering why he was reacting that way to my confession.

"You're angry?" I asked, my voice a whisper as I swallowed hard.

"No," he said, his voice cold, betraying his single word. "Yes."

"Why?"

He scrubbed his hand over his face. "I'm angry that your dream hasn't come true yet."

"I'm young, it'll take time."

"Use the money you kept for your sister?" he suggested.

"No," I blanched, sitting upright.

Nate followed, placing a hand on my back gently, but his tone was still so sharp. "She doesn't need it, she never will. Why are you holding onto it, she can't take it to the grave, so use it. Juniper, your dream is incredible, and I believe you'll succeed. You just need that final push."

I shook my head, bowing it as my fingers twisted in the white cotton sheets. "I'll get there."

"You could do it sooner rather than-"

I twisted and cut him off with a fiery kiss, pushing him back down into the mattress, my hands roaming his chest. "I appreciate your passion, but I'm doing it my way."

"Fine," he groaned, sucking in a sharp breath as my fingers ran down lower, wrapping around him and pumping slowly. "But you better never give up on that dream, Little one. Promise?"

"Promise."

The sea felt amazing as it lapped over my feet. Cooling me down instantly. I couldn't wait to get out in it. I needed a little water therapy. I hadn't slept last night, not after I had received a call from my sister. I had calmed her as much as I could, but I wished I could be with her. Nate had woken up when I climbed back into bed, blotchy faced and sniffing. He had stayed up with me all night, he never pushed me to explain, instead he sat and played beautiful slow songs on his guitar to me, singing in gentle whispers until I was smiling again and started to talk. Telling him about happier things. Happier things like dreams, and my perfect vision for Kim's.

I glanced over my shoulder at him, a fluttery feeling washing over me as he buried his face in a book, the sunshade covering him in shadow. My dark, moody lover. The only light he was ever comfortable under was a spotlight on a stage. He was an entirely different man when he was up there, and I was starting to see all of his sides. The grumpy, happy, sad, broken, excited, wild. All of him. I never knew which side I would get, and I didn't care. I could handle them all, and I could see each day in his eyes that he was trusting me more and more. The sad days were becoming less frequent, in fact, they were often only lasting minutes or hours. I was making him happy more often than not, and that was what I had wanted. I wanted to change this man's life, give him a reason to not... to not end up in a place he'd never come back from. He fucking deserved to be happy.

This had all started as fun, but there had been a

shift, one that I was embracing. I had never intended to feel this much, and I wasn't sure if it could be love, but I was happy. What we were doing wasn't a one-sided effort. He made *me* happy.

I stepped into the water, wading out until it reached my waist, then dove under, ignoring the chill that shot through my body until it had faded away and I was comfortable. I swam around for a while, then floated on my back, closing my eyes and relaxing into the motion of the waves.

"It's getting late," Nate called out. "The old dudes will be waiting."

It was Sunday, so he was right. They would be waiting, and they'd no doubt have some snarky comment to make when we arrived. As usual. I thought that after the last month they would be different. But my friends were not warming to Nate at all, and I couldn't understand why. He wasn't hurting me; he wasn't making me sad. We were good for each other, and I just wished they could see that. Carl seemed to hate Nate the least, but I had a feeling that was more down to the fact he begrudgingly enjoyed his music. Nate was performing every week without fail. He still didn't come down on Saturdays, and I still didn't know why, but that was fine. He didn't need to tell me everything, I still kept things from him, and space was healthy.

I made my way back up to where he was sitting on a towel. He handed me a spare one, and I quickly dried off and sat down between his legs. He pulled my hair back and twisted it into a braid, securing it with an elastic that he tugged off of my wrist. Nate always wanted to do my hair for me, and I never complained when he did. He also liked to fuck me senseless after he had done it, but this time he would have to wait. I had some old*er* men to look after, and the beach wasn't anywhere near quiet enough to risk doing anything. Although that didn't stop him from wrapping the braid around his fist, pulling me back, and kissing me. His tongue brutal against mine, sending the flutters down below my stomach and making me moan happily into his mouth.

"Better get dressed," he said breathlessly as he pulled away.

I did as he said, then peered up over the top of the stones, spotting the men standing outside of Kim's, patiently waiting for me to open up. I held my hand out to Nate, but he didn't take it.

"I think I'll hang back here, I'm not feeling great, and I don't think I can hold my tongue today." His face twisted in that way it always did when he was holding it all in. His temper was explosive, like a raging inferno, or so he had told me. I was thankful that I had never been on the receiving end of it. He internalised so much of his emotion, and it hurt to watch him battle with it, but this was part of who he was. I just needed to trust that he wouldn't do anything stupid.

"Can I help?" I asked, unsure what exactly I might be able to do, but offering nonetheless.

"No, Juniper, you can't. But I know where you are if I need you, now go on, don't give them any more reasons to hate me," he urged, and I leaned down to kiss him, nipping at his lip in a playful way that I hoped might perk him up a little. The look on his face told me it hadn't worked, but his lip twitched, and I knew he was thankful for my attempt. And that was enough.

"I'm fine!" He yelled.

"Yeah, it sure seems like you are," I snapped, then winced at my tone. This wasn't me; I only ever spoke to anyone this way when I was defending my sister. But maybe he needed me to be hard on him. Maybe I needed to learn to speak up like this. Like he kept telling me to.

I just didn't expect to have to speak up to him.

"I am." Louder, his face turned red as his eyes shimmered.

I took a step closer to him and grabbed his hand, turning his palm in my hand to inspect his wrist. "This." I grimaced, "Is not fine."

He snatched his hand away from me, glaring down at me as he spat venom. "What the fuck would you know? You're this little ball of sunshine. Always so happy, aren't you, Juniper. You haven't experienced life yet. You don't know pain, you don't know how *this* feels." He jabbed his finger into the side of his head, "You don't get it."

"I do," I protested but he shook his head, laughing at me as he turned his back on me and paced his kitchen.

"Just leave."

"No," I said, stealing strength from the anger radiating around him. "You don't get to push me away just because you're having a bad day. I get it, Nate, I know it hurts, I've been in pain too."

"Oh sure, what happened? Your milk had turned sour when you poured it in your tea?" he sneered, his lip pulled back in disgust.

"You *know*, Nate," I said bluntly, pushing all emotion from my voice. "I've lost people I loved, and I've…" I closed my eyes, not sure that now was the right time to tell him about it. He knew about my parents, but he didn't know what had happened after, and telling him right now might actually push him away. I was trying to stop him from doing that to me.

"You've what?" he asked, and as my eyes locked on his I swear I saw them soften, just a fraction, just enough for me to see that he cared. Even if he couldn't show it right now.

"This isn't about me," I said softly, mask coming up, hiding the fear from my voice. "Tell me why you did it."

He held his wrist, his gaze scanning over the bloodied lines carved into the pale skin, and I gasped as a single tear rolled down his cheek.

"I don't know," he breathed, his body trembling as he fell to his knees on the kitchen floor. "I don't fucking know!"

"Tell me what happened then. Everything from when I left you on the beach until now." I dropped down to the floor, resting my back against the freezer door. Keeping my distance. Unsure what he needed, and not wanting to fuck this up. I could help him. I could… *this wouldn't be the same.* I had researched. He had finally explained in detail what his illness truly was, and the moment he had, I had gone diving straight in the deep end. I ignored every negative search result – there were so many – and I focused on everything that was factual and helpful. I knew that what I was seeing was all part of the deal when it came to him, and I knew that without the right help that things could become this dark. I pulled on that knowledge, using it to keep me calm, and patiently waited until he spoke again.

"I came here. I ate, and I watched some TV. Then I pulled out my guitar and started playing. I played a song," he squeezed his eyes closed and hunched further over, hiding his face. "This isn't helping, Juniper. Just leave me alone."

I remained on the floor, silently holding my ground, waiting for him to reconsider. It only took him a minute.

"Fine. The song made me sad. Then I was angry. Then I looked at the time, and I was supposed to be leaving to pick you up. But I couldn't, not like that. I couldn't get the feelings to go away. And it just… happened."

He curled himself tighter, his face tucked to his knees. I knew he was crying, and I knew that he was too proud to show me that. I stood up, switched off the light, then sat back in the same spot.

"Thank you," he muttered; his voice choked.

I could still see his silhouette on the floor, the glow from the hallway light enough to highlight the shaking body of my broken man.

"Maybe," I spoke slowly, "it was just a way to find a quick release. I'm not saying it was right, but maybe you needed it." I inched closer, not touching him, but making sure that I could if he needed me to. "Maybe you need to find another way, train yourself to act differently when that urge to hurt yourself strikes."

"Or I could just stop letting it happen," he snapped.

"I'm not sure that's realistic. We all feel emotions, you can't just stop. But you can stay safe. That's all I want you to do, Nate, you can scream and shout and let it all out, but you cannot hurt yourself like this again. We will find another way."

"*I* will find a way," he corrected, lifting his head. I couldn't clearly see his face, but I knew there would be a frown set deep in his forehead.

"No. We. You have me. I'm not going anywhere."

He growled, his throat bubbling with emotions that he refused to show. Then he was on me, his lips crashing into mine in the dark. His hands roamed my body, but a second later everything stopped, and he fell limp, his hands resting on my hips as his face fell to my chest and he sighed loudly.

"I'm a mess," he confessed, tightening his hold on me. I laid back on the cold tiles, repositioning until we were cuddled up on the kitchen floor.

"Yes, but you're my mess," I whispered, stroking his thick curls, "You give me whiplash, but I kinda like it."

"You're a masochist, Little one."

"So are you."

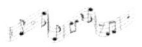

♫

"Dance with me." I demanded as Nate entered the kitchen. He smiled, and shook his head, pushing his glasses up his nose with a low chuckle, his mood brighter in the morning light.

I took his hand and laughed as he played along and pulled me close, swaying us from side to side as he hummed a familiar tune. I rested my head on his chest and tightened my hold on his hand, ignoring the bandage on his wrist as a giddy smile spread across my face. He slipped his other hand lower and groped my arse, squeezing hard then releasing to spin me under his arm. He pulled my back flush to his naked torso, and I sighed happily as he began to kiss down the side of my neck.

He was ok.

"Thank you for staying," he said as he reached my shoulder, then painted his way back up to my ear. "I'm sorry you had to witness me like that, again."

I turned to face him, cupping his chin and snaring his gaze in mine, "No pity party allowed Mr. We're going to move forward, ok?"

I gave him a stern look, but the corners of my mouth lifted too quickly, I guessed it was my bright side shining through. Never allowing the bad feelings to sit for too long. Luckily, he seemed to like it. Something that was clear by the way he kissed me, leaned over to flick the oven off where I had started cooking us – me – breakfast, and dragged me to his bedroom.

♪♫♪♫♪

Laying in his arms, my fingers raking through the dark curls on his chest, in a blissful post-fuck daze, was becoming one of my favourite states to be in.

"You said you'd help me to change how I cope," he said quietly as he sat me up and started to twist my hair, parting it down the middle and gently repositioning my head so that he could work the perfect plaits into my hair.

"I will. But you've got to lead here, baby. I can't help if I don't understand."

"So, I need to open up. Seems like a dumb thing to do." He laughed, then sighed heavily, securing my second plait quickly and pulling me to rest my head back on his chest. "I guess I could start with the childhood trauma, but I dunno, it's ancient history, is it really necessary?"

"Tell me whatever you want, whenever you want."

He made a thoughtful noise in his throat, "How about I tell you *my* dream, since you told me yours. It's connected to why I started to spiral last night."

"I would love to hear about your dream," I whispered, smiling wide at his choice to open up with so little persuasion from my end.

Nate began, starting off with a brief explanation of where his love of music had come from. It was actually a lot to do with his childhood, and the fact that growing up he had no outlet. But music spoke to him, he took comfort in the lyrics of sad songs, then began to appreciate how other things made him feel. Like the way a piano piece would feel so different from a violin. And then he fell in love with guitars. When he was thirteen, he brought a second-hand guitar with the pocket money he had been saving up for a whole year, and began to write his own music. Apparently, it was awful, but something about the way he explained his passion to me made me think that he was full of shit.

"I would probably be mortified if I ever heard those songs now. But back then I thought I was the next Clapton. I lived and breathed music. I even studied it, going against my father's wishes. My sister labelled me as a fuck-up because I wouldn't put my focus on an academic course, but that was one of the nicer things she had said to me in my life, and I was happy. Then in college I met this guy, Christopher, and we hit it off instantly. We had these big ideas for our futures. We wanted the same things, and we knew that together we could make them happen. All we wanted was to make it." Nate sighed, a sense of longing in his breath. "We wanted someone to notice us, so we worked hard to give someone, *anyone,* a reason to. We formed band after band that failed miserably, but over the years the failures only made us more determined. It was four years ago that we finally created a group that gelled properly. Everything was perfect and our dreams were only just out of reach. We knew it would be a long journey to the top, but Christopher and I knew it would all be worth it in the end. Every late night, every missed day of work because our lives revolved around the music, it would be worth it."

Nate paused, trailing lazy circles around my shoulder. I remained quiet, waiting patiently for him to continue. Whatever came next, he was struggling to say, and I hoped that he would be able to gain the strength to tell me.

"I had a breakdown," he finally said, his tone flat, the excitement that had been in his voice before was gone. "The stress, the lack of support, it was too much. I was scared of failing, scared I would never be enough. I had pushed everyone in my life away, and I was starting to push the band too. Christopher had me committed for a short period, thirty days, and it seemed to have helped. I felt more confident after that, and I thought that we were back on track. And we were, we got noticed by the right people. The people who I had always hoped would see that we had this talent. We were something special. They wanted to sign us, and I was over the moon. I was about to live my dream."

His voice broke slightly, a wobble that he cleared away with a loud cough. He didn't need to hide his emotions from me, but I knew he would. "They didn't want me. They would only sign if I agreed to leave. Apparently, my *behaviour*," He spat the word stiffened, anger radiating from his entire body. "It wasn't going to be good for the band's image. The industry had too many unstable types already, and my level of unstable wasn't *cute* or *sexy*. It hurt, and I thought the guys would tell them to get fucked. It was all of us, or none of us. But they didn't. My closest friend of twenty years tossed me aside like I was nothing. I was handed a cheque from the label for my silence on the matter, forced to sign an NDA, and not so subtly threatened by the woman at the top. I'm in breach by telling you now, but fuck it, I don't care anymore. I lost it before I left, trashed the studio, broke our drummer's nose. I'm sure you heard how it was twisted in their first interview."

I sighed, the pieces falling into place, realising which band he was talking about. Six months ago Hand That Feeds had their breakthrough, and during their first interview their drummer had a broken nose and black eyes. The media had spun this story that he had been attacked by a guy who had attempted to assault a woman. He had been painted as a hero for something that I was now learning he had never done.

"Last night I played one of our." He paused and corrected himself. "*Their,* songs. And it hurt me more than ever before. I moved here because I needed to get far away. I needed somewhere quiet and disconnected from that world. Little did I know I would end up wrapped up in a woman who reminds me of the one thing I truly love every single night."

I sighed again, snuggling closer to him, not sure if I should apologise for being that person, or if I should ask the question sitting on the tip of my tongue.

The latter won. "Is it still your dream? Or do you have a new one?"

He snorted. "Dreams are for upbeat little angels with bright futures, like yourself. I'm past it. I'm done with dreams."

"What if you could have it though? What if someone realised you were talented enough alone?"

Nate hummed and kissed the top of my head. "No one is going to do that. It's ok, I know that I'm not enough."

"You are more than enough," I whispered determinedly, pressing my lips to his arm.

He shook his head but didn't argue. I knew he didn't believe me, and that was fine. I didn't need him to believe me. I just needed his honesty, and now that I had it, my thoughts were rushing like busy little bees, an idea forming that might just make him happier than he could imagine. It wasn't a coping mechanism, but it was something good. And surely that was better?

8
Juno

"He's coming tonight?" I asked, my phone jammed between my ear and shoulder as I hauled barrels around in the cellar.

My sister's sarcastic response had me rolling my eyes and laughing. "You're the best, Bumble. I love you. Always and forever."

"Always and forever, Bug," she said, sniffing. "I'll visit soon, promise."

I placed the barrel down and shoved my phone in the pocket of my denim shorts, wiping my hands off on them too, and noting that I definitely needed to go home and change before tonight.

Jeremy was sitting in the bar when I finished up, an excited look on his face as I approached him.

"Spit it out, Jer. Why do you look like an overexcited husky?"

He beamed at me, slapping his hand down on the

bar with a twinkle in his eye, "Guess who's coming to visit next month?"

I hummed thoughtfully, playing his game as I rounded the bar and unstacked the dishwasher. "A bear? The ghost of Elvis? The Queen? Gosh I hope not, all of my fancy frocks are at the cleaners."

Jeremy snorted, shaking his head and bouncing on the barstool. Jer wasn't a small man, and for a brief moment concern for the stability of my stool hit, but then he got to his feet, rounded the bar, and shoved his phone under my nose.

"Woah, I can't see anything that close." I took a step back and squinted at the screen. Standing proudly, in a long black robe, was a tall, handsome man with perfectly styled golden blonde hair and startling blue eyes. I tutted and batted Jeremy's shoulder, "I've told you; I'm not interested in Hadley's Nephew. I'm seeing Nate."

Jeremy scoffed, and shoved the phone in my face again, "*This* young lad is much better for you than that worn out, washed up, waste of nice hair. Come on, Juney. You can't genuinely be happy with the miserable bastard?"

I frowned at his weird comment about Nate's hair, then glanced at his thinning grey hair and receding hairline, biting my lip to stop myself from laughing.

"I'm happy," I insisted, just like I seemed to do almost daily. The old dudes weren't buying it, and I was starting to grow tired of repeating myself. I couldn't understand what they saw in Nate that I didn't. I had been gifted him in his rawest form, and I was still in, all fucking in. Not that I had actually told him that. But my actions were saying it pretty loudly, and so were his. Why could they not understand that? Why, after two months, were they still so against us?

Jeremy continued to ramble on about his twin's nephew, and I forced a smile as I pretended to listen and continued on with my list of jobs. When Hannah finally arrived, I tossed her my keys and batted my lashes at her as I asked her to watch the bar for a while so that I could head home to change. The night was set out to be a big one, I hoped, so I needed to look, well, not like I had been rolling around in a vat of beer and dust.

I was back at the bar faster than I expected to be, and apparently looking even better than I realised, if the wolf-whistles that greeted me were anything to go by. I curtsied in my black dress, and twirled my hair into a messy updo, securing it with a silver claw clip and revealing the open, strappy back that subtly showed off the tattoo that trailed up the length of my spine. A delicate, slender string of flowers that Nate often traced as I fell asleep.

I was always asleep before him.

Hannah smirked as I joined her behind the bar, "Looking hot. Boss."

"Coming from you," I laughed. Hannah was beautiful in the most haunting way, with her cool, pale skin and deep emerald eyes. It was no surprise that we had a bigger crowd on the nights when she worked. It was mostly eighteen-year-old guys attempting to get into her knickers, a place they'd never end up. Hannah had high standards, *and* her heart was set on marrying 'rich, old and hung,' – as she put it. I had told her time and time again that Kim's was the wrong place to find someone like that, but she disagreed.

"You found yourself one." She would say. And I would remind her that my guy was missing one of the things she was looking for. Rich guys don't drink in places like this. Also, Nate wasn't *that* old.

Nate came storming in with a face like thunder, his mood hitting me like a gust of wind as he growled at me over the bar. "I've had the day from hell."

I grinned, ignoring his mood and brushing off the tiny twinge of doubt over what I had planned for tonight. "Need an angel to come and turn your day around?"

His lips twitched, but he supressed a smile. "You might look like an angel, but we both know you're not." He leaned over the bar and quickly kissed me, then gestured to a bottle of whiskey and tilted his head. I pulled it down, poured him a small measure, and giggled as he frowned into the glass. "Where's the rest of it?"

"Later, I want you sober for now." I winked, and quickly bounced to the other end of the bar before he could question me.

I had no idea when my visitor would be arriving, but I hoped it would be sooner rather than later, especially with the way Nate was now glaring at me with a confused quirk in his brow.

I avoided him for as long as I could, but eventually he got up and positioned himself in front of me.

"Juniper, what is going on?" he asked, clear annoyance in his tone.

I shrugged just as Hannah gasped loudly and tugged my arm. I turned to her, her eyes bugging out of her head as drool practically fell from her gawping mouth. "Who the fuck is that beautiful beast?"

I followed her line of sight and found a man moving to sit at one of the tables near the door. He looked to be in his mid-fifties, dressed in an expensive looking royal blue suit. He had salt and pepper hair, slicked back away from his deeply tanned face. He pulled a phone from his pocket and held it to his ear just as he turned to face us, raising a hand and beckoning one of us over with the slightest flick of his fingers.

Hannah audibly moaned and I laughed lightly. "Go serve our special customer, Han."

She clamped her mouth shut, a scarlet blush spreading across her cheeks, "I..." she spluttered.

"Go on babygirl, work your magic," I urged, prodding her in the ribs then repositioning her sleek black hair. She swallowed hard, then glanced at the bottle of vodka I had stashed behind the bar, I quickly poured her out a shot which she tossed back with a wince, then confidently approached our interesting customer.

"Once again, Juniper, what is going on?" Nate asked as I turned my attention back to him. His brows pinched even more than before.

"I'm just really excited about you performing tonight, and I *might* have a little surprise for you after." I half lied. I had a backup plan. On the almost impossible chance that the guy in the fancy suit didn't like Nate, I was going to keep it to myself and treat him to a night of living out the fantasy he had confessed to me last week. The one that involved a clifftop and his car.

Nate leaned closer, "What's the surprise?"

I laughed, pressing my hand against his firm chest and telling him that surprises didn't work that way. He scowled, but I could feel his mood lifting just a fraction – not enough to bring out even the hint of a smile, but enough to stop him from looking like he might legitimately murder the next person who breathed too close to him.

Hannah came back behind the bar, snatched the most expensive bottle of bourbon we had, and poured out a large measure. She grabbed a clean cloth, swiped it around the rim of the glass, then pulled a lighter from her tight jean pocket. I watched her with amused curiosity as she lit the flame and circled the rim of the glass twice.

"I saw someone do it at a bar up in London this one time, she said it added to the flavour. Could be complete bullshit though." She frowned, then slid the glass over to Nate, "Be my guinea pig?"

He sipped the liquor and hummed appreciatively. "I like it, but I have awful taste." He smirked at me, and my jaw dropped in mock outrage.

"Fine, no surprises for you then." I turned my back on him, hiding my smile, as I watched Hannah make another drink. Once I was composed, I turned back to Nate and quickly changed the subject. "You wanna go up first tonight?"

He glanced around the room, then shrugged, "Sure. And I didn't mean it, Little one. You're one of the best things in my life."

I sucked in a sharp breath and bit my lip, my face heating instantly. That was possibly the most genuinely nice thing he had ever said to me. Sure, he complimented me all the time while we were fucking, but this was something else, this seemed to mean something more.

"You are too, Baby."

He rolled his eyes and grumbled, "Why the hell do I let you get away with calling me that?"

"Because I'm adorable," I stated with a grin. "So adorable that I could probably get away with calling you my cute cock-womble, if I wanted to." I fluttered my lashes and pressed a quick kiss to his stubbly cheek. "I'll let Carl know you'll be ready in what? Five?"

"Sure."

Nate stepped up onto the stage, and I glanced over at the suited man. He met my gaze and I nodded sharply, indicating that this was the guy he had been asked to come and watch. My sister, the wonderful little bean that she was, had managed to pull some pretty hefty strings, and had managed to convince this bigshot to come and see my man play. Ever the perfectionist, she had scoured through every contact she had until she found someone who she thought might be a good fit.

Shane Hudson.

He leaned forward, resting his elbow on the table and his chin on his fist. I tried to keep my focus on Nate, attempting to ignore Shane as he watched him play the song that I had hoped he might play tonight. For the past week Nate had spent countless hours working on it, a soft song filled with pain and passion. He closed his eyes and sang just like he had yesterday morning when I brought his coffee to bed. He had looked so delicious, toned naked body sitting on my bed, the crumpled white sheets not covering a single inch of him as he rested his favourite acoustic guitar – Lola – on his lap and excitedly announced that he had finally nailed the riff. I sat on the edge of my bed and listened intently as he showed off his hard work, and I couldn't help but think that maybe the words he sang were meant for me. Not that I would ask.

But one line had felt personal.

"You never walked away, I never wanted you to stay, but you did, I'm so glad you did."

He sang the words, his eyes opening just enough to meet mine, a slight lift to his lips. I swayed from side to side, ignoring the guy who I could see out of the corner of my eye attempting to get my attention, and quietly thanked Hannah for stepping up, even though I knew that her focus was elsewhere too.

When Nate finished, I squealed and cheered, setting off everyone else in the bar. They applauded my man, and I gave him a squinty eyed smile before turning my attention to Shane. He was sitting back in his chair now, his lips pursed as he folded his arms, the fabric of his suit straining slightly with the movement.

"Han," I said hesitantly, attempting to push the worry from my voice, "Can you please go and top up Mr Hudson's drink?"

"Who?" she asked, and I nodded at the man. "How did you know his name?"

"Doesn't matter, can you just make sure he has everything he needs please."

She did as I asked, and I turned to fill a glass for myself, topping off a single measure of vodka with lemonade just as Nate shouted over the bar for his usual.

I pulled myself together, smiling as I continued on with my shift, keeping my focus on working rather than keeping tabs on Shane and wondering if he was going to say anything, or if we would have to wait to find out what he thought. Although his silence so far didn't feel promising. In my head I had built up this fantasy where

Nate would stand up after playing and Shane would get to his feet, shove through the crowd, take Nates hand and offer to sign him on the spot.

Instead, he remained seated until the last amateur performance of the night, then approached the bar while Nate was in the men's room.

"Your man, he's good. I'm sick of all of these twenty-something kids with their bouncy love songs, no offence." He turned his gaze on Hannah rather than me, and I stifled a laugh as she turned red once again, which was no surprise from the way the man blatantly undressed her with his intense green gaze.

"None taken," I said, even though it hadn't been aimed at me, I needed his attention for just a moment longer. "What does this mean then?"

"It means." He tore his gaze away from the raven-haired beauty beside me. "That I'll call in the week. No promises. But he's good. I just need to have a few discussions before I can offer anything. Oh, and this place, it has potential, fix it up and I'll see if I can throw some better names your way. Your sister was right to push me."

"Thank you so much," I gushed, then reigned myself in as I felt the urge to jump over the bar and hug him. He didn't seem like he'd appreciate that one bit. Not from *me* anyway.

He nodded, then reached over the bar, grasping Hannah's arm gently and pulling her closer. I stepped away to give them the idea of privacy, even though I was not so subtly attempting to listen in, and I would be grilling her the second he left. Hannah and I had been growing closer over the last couple of months and it was nice to have someone other than the old dudes to talk to, and someone who *actually* approved of my choice of companion.

"Want me to stay and help you ladies close up? Or shall I steal your keys and go warm up the bed?" Nate asked as I passed him by on my way to clear an empty table.

I paused, leaning into his warm body and running a finger down his chest, "I have a surprise, remember. So stay and help, please."

He removed his glasses, hooking them into his shirt and giving me a suspicious look. I kissed him before he could ask me *again* what the surprise was and went to stack glasses.

When the last patrons had left, I hurried through the clean down, and once she had filled me in properly on what Shane had said, I shooed Hannah off home. We locked up, Nates fingers pinging the straps down the back of my dress impatiently as I fumbled with my keys, then pulled *his* car keys from my bag and dangled them in front of his face. He gave me a confused look, no doubt wondering how and when I had lifted them from him, then his eyes lit up, and he snatched them from me.

"Where am I taking you then?" he asked as he put the key in the ignition of the sleek, red Mazda. I directed him away from the road where he usually parked his car, and eventually we reached the edge of a cliff that overlooked the sea some way away from home.

I stepped out of the car and Nate followed me to the edge of the cliff where I stood and stared out at the moonlit sea.

"I love this view," I whispered. It had become

somewhere for me to hide out when I had been deep in the mess of what had happened after my parents' death. And when Nate had confessed his ultimate fantasy, this was the place that had sprung to mind.

His arms wrapped around me from behind, his chin resting softly on my head, "I've seen so many beautiful things in my lifetime, but this, I think it's pretty high up there."

"Lifetime," I laughed, "Shit, you sound old."

"Sometimes I feel like I'm a million years old," he said sadly, "but then I look at you, my little one, and I feel like *I'm* twenty-four again. I might not know who I am, or what I want, and I may not always trust my feelings, or even show them, but the ones I get around you are different to any I've felt before. You're the good in my life, I hope you know that."

"I do now." I smiled, twisting my head to look up at him. He pressed his lips to my forehead, his short beard scratching my skin as I nuzzled into his lips. Committing the moment to memory.

"Whatever happens between us, I need you to know something else," Nate whispered against me.

"What is it?"

"You inspire me."

My heart somersaulted, skipping beats, feeling like it might jump out of my throat if I opened my mouth and let it. My breath stuttered, and I spun in his hold, his arms tightening as I pushed up onto tiptoes and crushed my lips to his, stealing the air from his lungs, fisting his hair between my fingers as tears pricked the backs of my eyes.

The perfect words that were leaving his lips made

it feel like all of the difficult moments had been worth it. I was happy, he was happy.

I hadn't expected us to end up here, but here we were. Being more.

"You in this, for real then, Nate?" I finally asked.

"Damn right I am, Baby," he teased, dipping me low as he kissed me again.

I laughed against his lips, the taste of sweet cola lingering on them, then dragged him backwards towards the car. When the backs of my knees hit the front of the hood I smirked, released him, then climbed up onto the front of his car, hanging my legs off of the edge and wriggling with my hands beneath my dress. I slipped my knickers down to my ankles and grinned at Nate.

He dropped to his knees on the stony ground, and removed the lilac lace, pulling it down over each foot, then pinging it up at me. I caught it with a laugh which turned into a sharp gasp as the tip of his tongue painted a line from my knee, up under my dress, and straight to my pussy. His hands slipped beneath my dress too, grabbing my ass and tugging me forward, pressing his face hard against me as he lapped at me and hummed loudly against my clit, sending sparks flying throughout my body.

He had me pleading to come, and exploding in record time, slamming my hands on the hood of the car as I fell back, mumbling his name with a million slurred curses.

"Up," he commanded, getting to his feet and holding his hand out for me. I took it, righting myself with wobbly legs, smoothing down my dress, and tilting my head in question.

Nate grabbed my hips, turned me sharply, and sank his teeth into my neck, biting me so hard that I yelped. But I refused to move away, knowing the pain would be chased away with the most intense pleasure. His fingers looped under the straps of my dress, sliding it down, the fabric bunching around my tummy as his fingers pinched and tugged my nipples. He released me, the cool air of the turning season harsh against my sensitive nipples. I felt him fumbling behind my ass, heard his zip slide down, followed by the clanging of metal, his belt, his trousers falling down to his knees. I knew what was coming, yet as he pushed me down over the hood of his car, my bare breasts pressed hard against the cold steel, a gasp fell from my lips. A scream fell next as he brutally slammed inside me.

He groaned loudly. "Take me, Little one. Take every inch, my perfect little slut."

Fuck. I shouldn't like that, should I?

He slammed in again. A moan. Again. Louder. His fingers skating up my spine gently, the contrast in his touch setting my skin on fire. I clenched around him, but I knew the rules, always the same rules. His fingers slid past the nape of my neck, into my hair, gathering it messily, wrapping the long curls around his fist. He pulled, my head lifting, back arched, his cock hitting me so much deeper. It was torture in the best fucking way. He *knew* I couldn't take it, but I would try. I would hold on until he granted me permission, because I wanted so badly to give him whatever he needed.

"Beg, Juniper. Use your words, otherwise you will never get what you want," he growled, his cock punishing my soaked pussy.

I spluttered, a strangled noise following. My back arching more, my breath barely there. "I want to come." I managed to force the words out.

"More."

Another tug on my hair, my chest peeling away from the car. I braced myself, my hands slippery against the hood of the car. Nate wasn't holding back, and this was my favourite way to have him. Raw, unapologetic, fuelled by needy desire. I felt my hold on my orgasm begin to slip. If he continued on that way, I would be going home with a glowing ass. And as much as I loved it when he made it painful to sit, I also loved the way he praised me when I was good for him.

"P-pl-please." My eyes squeezed shut, my jaw clenching. I swallowed down the deepest lungful of air I could manage and screamed. "Let me come, Nate!"

"Fuck."

I tightened, my grip like a vice around his cock, he pushed through, his rhythm only slightly slowed by my body.

"Let go, Little one. Come for me."

I fell flat, his body crashing down on top of my trembling form as I detonated, milking him as he joined me in an earthshattering release. Filling me up with my reward, pulsing inside me as our breaths evened out and my body stopped shaking.

He stood up, pulling out, then dropped down behind me, his fingers parting me as he praised me quietly and watched his cum drip from my pussy over the hood of his car. I closed my eyes, a blissful smile on my lips as he kissed my ass, gently rolled me over, and lifted me as though I was the most fragile thing in the world.

He spoke soothing words against my cheek as he sat down on the ground and cradled me.

"You're far too good for me, Juniper."

I nuzzled into him, and sighed, "You are more deserving than you think."

9
Nate

Five days. I had spent five entire days feeling uninterrupted happiness. Until I looked in the mirror and *realised* that I had spent five days feeling that way. I knew that it couldn't last, and fear instantly kicked in. I leaned closer to the mirror, resting my head on the cool surface, and closed my eyes as I wondered what I would feel next. How I would get there. And if I was about to lose everything that I had.

Work was fine. I was writing music in my spare time, and I was even considering setting myself a new goal. Juniper had shown me so many things about myself, my ability to care and comfort, my desire to make her happy, and my capabilities. Every song that I had written recently was better than the last. I wasn't lying when I said that she had become my inspiration. She was everything. I had fallen, and I…

I was about to push her away, wasn't I?

My eyes snapped open. Panic building beneath them as I stared at my reflection with the thought echoing through my mind. I couldn't. No. Not again. I was getting better.

Please. No.

I needed to get a fucking grip, and quickly. Pushing her away was probably the dumbest thing I could do. I needed to make sure that I didn't do it. She was good, good for me. Too fucking good for me though, and one day she would realise that, wouldn't she?

I should have walked away months ago.

"Nate." Juniper knocked on the bathroom door. "You're going to be late for work."

I dropped my gaze, inhaling a steadying breath, dispelling the panic and schooling my face into a simple frown, the one that I wore so well. I opened the door and found her leaning against the cabinet in her hallway with two travel mugs in her hands and a wide grin on her face. The one *she* wore even better.

"Ready to go?" she asked, handing me the black mug with the subtly inappropriate slogan on it.

"You're coming?" I asked, confused.

If Juniper was leaving the house in the morning it was usually for a swim, and from the looks of her, in a pair of short denim shorts and floral cropped cami, no bra, she wasn't going in the sea.

She nodded. "I need to grab a few things from town, so I might as well walk down with you, otherwise I'll never do it."

She scrunched her nose up in that adorable way she always seemed to do whenever she didn't like something. The first time I had seen it was when she tried a dumpling from the local Chinese. She *hated* it, and it solidified her opinion of Chinese food. She had refused to try anything else and had poured herself a huge bowl of coco-pop's when we had arrived back at my place.

We walked down to town with our fingers loosely linked together as Juniper told me yet another random story about something crazy her mum had done when she was young. I was finding out more and more about the wild, free spirit who raised her. The incredible couple who had forged her beliefs and outlook were so different from the man who had influenced mine.

My mum had walked out when I was three. Emma was barely one. I don't even remember the woman's name. I wouldn't want to.

I knew my face was set in that blank way it always did when I thought about her and what she did, how my sister and I had been left with a man who had no idea how to be a parent. His expectations of the pair of us were far too high for a man who have taught us zero skills. It was a wonder that I hadn't ended up on the streets, or in prison. Luckily, I had always been able to somehow get myself out of any situation, but my temper and my outbursts were irrational and uncontrollable. It hadn't been easy.

It still wasn't easy.

Dad had ignored it all. Ignored *me*.

"Maybe one day you'll tell me about your family," Juniper said, smiling up at me as we stopped outside the small office block.

My stomach twisted. I *wanted* to tell her. I wanted to let her in, deeper than I had ever let anyone before. This girl had clawed her way under my skin and was refusing to budge. The bouncy little thing who couldn't say no to anyone had said no to *me*. She had stood so firm with me. I just wished she could do that with other people. I wasn't the type of man to care much for other people's wants and desires unless they benefitted mine. *Selfish.* But I wanted this girl to succeed. She had a strong backbone, she showed it to me constantly, but never anyone else.

I'm in way too deep here.

"Maybe," I murmured, knowing that it wasn't likely that I would even give myself the chance to share it all. I needed to get out of this now before both of us ended up getting hurt.

Except… I didn't want to.

Her smile didn't budge, her pretty pink lips tilting up slightly higher on one side. "Have a great day, Baby."

I groaned. I wouldn't have a great day, and I was sure that I wouldn't be her 'baby' for much longer. I wanted so desperately to smile at her, and to ignore every stupid thought racing around in my head, but I couldn't. So I did what I always did when I wanted to hide things from women. I grabbed her face in one hand, my thumb holding her jaw firmly as I dropped my head and kissed her like she was my reason for breathing.

The distraction worked. She gave me a soppy, dazed grin as she walked away, and for a moment I believed that things could be fine. That maybe she really *was* my reason for breathing, and that I would be able to get the fuck over myself and my bullshit.

Walking into the bar with a heavy weight sitting in my chest was the hardest part of my day. I fully intended on breaking her tonight. And I *really* didn't want to. I was still desperate to make her happy, but no matter how I pushed and poked my thoughts around in my head, they just kept screaming at me to run.

I was a coward. I knew it. I had been this way since I could remember. Always leaving when shit got real. The only time in my life that I had stayed through the fear, was when I had thought that Hand That Feeds were going to make it. Getting what I had always wanted had terrified me, but I had pushed through. Sure, I had ended up going off the rails first, but I made it through.

Then I lost it all.

Had it all ripped away from me.

That's what would happen here too, wouldn't it?

It was best to walk away, save myself.

I had been kidding myself all day, tricking myself into believing that I was doing it for her. But deep down I knew it was all for me. Selfish. I didn't deserve someone like her. I didn't deserve anyone at all. She would end up with someone worthy of her. Not some washed-up, wannabe rockstar who didn't know how to properly love anyone but himself.

Hell, I didn't even do that.

I sat in my usual spot at the end of the bar and watched Juniper laugh at something that one of the twins had said with her head thrown back. The sound leaving her lips made my stomach churn violently. She wiped a tear from under her eye, then noticed me. Her entire face lit up, her ocean eyes sparkling as she squealed, ran around the bar, and threw herself at me.

"I'm so happy you're here. I have some incredible news," she rambled, her voice a whole octave higher than usual.

The churning got worse, my stomach feeling like it was on a fucking spin cycle. I needed to keep her at a distance tonight, until she was done here. Except, my arms instinctively banded around her, and my lips found hers like we were fucking magnets. I couldn't stop myself.

"Do you want the news now, or later?" she asked, placing her hand on my chest, putting a small amount of space between us, giving me a clear view of her beautiful face. Making me wonder how the fuck I'd be able to tell her I was done.

"Erm." I inhaled slowly. "Now I guess?"

I shouldn't have come in here. I should have just gone home and met her after she had closed up.

"Great, because later wasn't *really* an option." She spun on her heels, taking my hand in her tiny one, tugging me up from my stool and away from the bar. She made a beeline for a man in an expensive suit. He stuck out like a sore thumb in this place, and my interest was instantly piqued just as my protective wall shot up.

Juniper stopped before the table and cleared her throat. The man looked up at her, deep creases around his eyes as he smiled at her and glanced at me.

"You've told him?" The man asked, his voice loud and excitable.

She shook her head, then pulled out a chair, shoved me down into it and stood behind me, her hands on my shoulders, her body practically vibrating behind me. "I thought I'd let you do the honours."

What fucking honours? What is this?

The stranger chuckled then drew his attention to me, placing his hands on the table, his tanned knuckles adorned with gold rings. He appeared to be a slightly older opposite of me. "Natha-."

"Nate." I cut over him, crossing my arms, tucking my silver ringed fingers beneath my biceps.

"Of course, she did tell me that." He glanced up at Juniper quickly, sharing an awkward smile with my girl.

Not my girl for much longer.

"Nate, I'm sure you didn't notice me, but I came in here earlier this week, and I saw you perform. You're talented, aren't you."

It wasn't a question, but he still paused, and I got the feeling that he was the dramatic type. But I didn't pander to dramatics, I just wanted him to get to the point.

"She also told me you're a grumpy bastard," he laughed as my frown deepened. I wasn't mad about her calling me that, but I didn't really understand why it was relevant. "So I guess if you take me up on my offer, you'll be... *fun* to work with."

I raised a brow and stayed silent, was this a job offer? I had a job. I didn't need another one. Ok, I hated my job, but I wouldn't be leaving it for *another* stuffy office job. I almost got up and walked away, having no patience for the man, but Juniper's hold on my shoulder was so tight I was sure if she moved, she'd rip my shirt, and I quite liked this one.

"I'm Shane Hudson." The name sounded familiar, but I couldn't place him. He held his hand out to me. I glanced at it. He pulled it away a moment later, brushing me off with a shrug and another laugh. "I own

'Limelight'. I'm sure you've heard of us."

My brows instantly shot up and my mouth turned dry. *Limelight.* Fucking Limelight. This guy was *the* Shane Hudson, the guy who discovered Leo Birch. He had *seen* me play.

I glanced up at Juniper, who looked like she might burst any second. She squeezed me tight and blew out a long, shaky breath, just as I did the same.

"I've heard of you," I confirmed, meeting Shane's eye and biting down on my lip. I must have been dreaming. There was no way this was real.

His emerald eyes twinkled, and he nodded. "Well, Nate, I'd like to give you a shot. Shall we discuss this over a drink?"

My heart skipped about twenty fucking beats as I nodded like a manic puppy. Juniper bounded away, grabbed us the most expensive bottle from behind the bar and placed it down on the table with two glasses and a little too much force. She muttered an apology, then groaned as a huge group of guys came wandering through the front door.

"I guess I'll leave you to it." She pouted then kissed my cheek. "I'm so proud of you, Baby."

Her words felt like being punched in the stomach, and I cursed under my breath as I watched her walk away to deal with her new customers. She was *proud* of me. No one had *ever* been that, not of me. I had never in my life heard those words. The sick feeling from when I had arrived came rushing back, and I turned and grabbed the bottle, pouring whiskey into the glass closest to me and quickly tossing it back. Shane did the same with a huge smile splitting his face.

"What are your plans for next week?"

I knew what I needed to do. Sunday night arrived and I knew. I had just been avoiding it. I hadn't told Juniper what Shane had offered me on Friday night, partly because I was struggling to say anything to her in general, and partly because I wasn't even sure what I was going to do. I had left him hanging, and I had taken her home and fucked her all through the night to avoid talking, to avoid thanking her for what she'd done – because I *knew*, she had made that happen – and avoid leaving her.

I was so unsure about everything.

Walking up to Kim's seemed to take so much longer than usual, my feet felt like they were made of lead, holding me back, fighting with the rest of my body. My heart was screaming, begging me to not do it. My head was winning though, shouting so much louder.

Juniper would leave me one day, and it would destroy me. The choice there was clear.

Shane had made me an offer with no promises. The taste of fame on my tongue had been so tempting. The choice there had not been quite so clear.

I stopped just as she came into view, locking the main door. Alone. Juniper was never alone on a Sunday night. Those men, the ones who hated me, were always there with her. They usually stayed until I arrived, making snide comments to me before hugging my girl and reluctantly leaving her in my hands.

They had been right to not trust me.

"Oh." She gasped softly as she turned to face me. "I thought I'd have five minutes to pull myself together." She sniffed, swiping at her face. That was when I noticed, in the moonlight, her face was wet, she was crying.

I took a step closer, then stopped. If I was going to do this, I needed to keep my distance. I couldn't be there for her. But how could I do this while she was crying? How could I add to her sadness?

My feet took control, and before I knew it, I had closed in on her and she was in my arms, her face buried against my chest, nuzzling me and sniffing as she let out a small, unsure laugh.

"What's wrong, Little one?"

She craned her neck, resting her chin on my chest as she gazed up at me with watery eyes. "It's just a day, a day that marks a day that I would like to forget. I'll be fine in a minute."

"Will you?" I cocked my head, not believing her. Juniper didn't cry. The only time I had seen her with tears in her eyes was when she was happy, or taking pity on someone, and those tears never fell.

These ones were. Fuck, they weren't stopping.

I brushed my thumb across her cheek, wiping away the fresh tear that was rolling down to the corner of her mouth.

"Thank you," she whispered, her voice bubbly with emotion. "I will. Just give me a moment. I'll be ok."

She pulled away, and took my hand, silently leading me away from her bar. "Yours or mine?" she asked, but she knew the answer already. Hers. Always hers. We only stayed at mine if we really had to, usually when I was having a 'moment' – as she liked to call it. It was cute, the way she saw it. *I* saw it as more of a breakdown.

She had pulled herself together by the time she put her key in the door. Or so I thought. Walking in on her in her room crying after she had disappeared to 'freshen up' was not what I had expected to find. I had gone in search of her with the intention of starting the uncomfortable conversation, the one my brain was impatiently forcing me to rush into having. But one look at her and I knew I wouldn't be able to do it then. Not while she was sobbing into her pillow.

She flinched as I placed my hand on her back. I pulled away, but she rolled to face me and caught my hand before I could right myself. She pulled me onto the bed, wrapped herself around me, and cried.

"Juniper," I soothed. "Tell me what it is."

She hiccupped as she attempted to tell me that she couldn't speak. My fingers twisted in her hair, and I coiled small curls around each finger as I patiently waited. Eventually she spoke. The words falling from her lips so quickly I was sure that she hadn't inhaled once. She explained everything. The secret she had been keeping. The one she had tried so hard to get buried. The anniversary of the event that still haunted her. She confessed that she had woken every day the past week with images of that morning stuck in her mind. And she had forced them away before I rose each day.

I listened without judgement. How could I judge her? None of it was her fault. But I understood, it was a heavy thing to carry. My jaw tensed painfully as she spoke of her sister, telling me that she was the main reason that it needed to remain a secret. She didn't want to hurt her sister's career by association.

It wouldn't though. Bea was huge, and respected, even if she did have a bit of a reputation. Nothing could really paint the girl in a bad light. But Juniper couldn't see that. Her love for her family was so much stronger than logic.

"Thank you, for just listening," she whispered.

"Of course." I uncoiled her hair from my fingers and smoothed it down, pressing my lips to the top of her head. "But you've got to know that it doesn't matter, it doesn't define you, and it shouldn't make anyone think any less of you. You couldn't have stopped it from happening."

She nodded, sniffed, then climbed on top of me, straddling my lap and smiling weakly at me. "I think I do know that, deep down. Thank you."

"Stop thanking me," I chastised gently. It was hurting me, the way she was being so nice to me while I knew what I needed to do to her.

"No," she giggled, then dropped her face to mine, our lips connecting, her tongue pressing to the seam of my mouth, asking so softly to enter.

I gave in, my heart taking over as I allowed myself this moment.

Just one moment.

It couldn't, *shouldn't,* go any further.

Her hands roamed my body. I pulled away, but the moment her hand slipped below my waistband that tiny bit of decency that I had, vanished. I was addicted to her, and I couldn't stop myself from taking one last hit.

She palmed me, wriggling happily as she felt me grow rapidly against her warm skin.

"Thank you, Baby." She whispered with a playful grin, but I wasn't in the mood to play. I knew I should be gentle with her, but I couldn't do it. Just like I couldn't walk away yet.

I threw her off of me and she landed on her back, bouncing on the mattress with wide eyed excitement. Her hair fanned out around her, making her look so angelic. A pang struck my heart, but I ignored it. Rolling her onto her front, grabbing her hips and pulling her ass up. She gasped loudly and clutched the sheets as I flipped her skirt up and ripped her tiny black thong off of her body. The scrap of fabric tossed over my shoulder as I shoved my trousers down, grasped my cock, and teased it over her pussy.

I needed this.

She needed this.

I pushed into her slowly, gently, as her back arched and she raised her head.

"What are you doing?" she panted, wiggling her ass impatiently. "Fuck me, Nate."

I paused. Met her gaze. Then thrust hard. Filling her tight little cunt with my thick cock. The smile that she wore as she moaned my name was something I would never fucking forget. It was devilish, so unlike the girl she showed everyone else. This girl was just for me. And it might be the last time I ever saw her.

I swallowed hard, wondering if I should stop or continue. But she made the choice for me, rocking forward and slamming back against me, impaling herself on me over and over until I was cursing her name as she clawed at the sheets and began to beg.

    I couldn't listen to it. The moment that first plea left her obedient lips I granted her permission to come. I didn't want her begging me this time. I wanted her to take what was rightfully hers. It was the fucking least I could do.

    I filled her for the last time and cleaned her up as she lay in a dazed, satisfied puddle. I held her close with tears in my eyes, and once hers were closed, and her soft snores filled the room, I slid my jeans on, grabbed my shirt, and ran.

    No looking back. No bittersweet goodbyes.

    I just fucking ran.

10

Juno

Something was wrong. Very fucking wrong.

The moment I opened my eyes, I knew. The feeling wasn't the same as the other mornings, and I was thankful for that, for only a second. Because it only took me a second to realise that my bed was unexpectedly empty. I strained my ears, listening for any sign of my man, but all I was met with was the beating of my own heart. A loud pounding in my ears.

Gone.

I inhaled sharply, rolling over in my bed and clutching his pillow.

Where the fuck is Nate?

The pillow was too cold, unused. No dip in the mattress, only the feintest scent of him lingering deep in the fabric. He hadn't got up early and gone out. He hadn't even stayed.

He was gone.

Bolting upright in bed, my breath came in panicked, rapid pants. Had he gone because of what I had confessed? The secret I had finally shared with him.

I had kept it to myself for so long, knowing the judgement I might receive for that night, and the following morning. But I thought that Nate of all people would understand. I *never* judged him for anything he had done. I had stayed, no matter what. I knew he wasn't a bad guy; he had just been dealt a shitty hand that he didn't know how to handle. Could he not see the same in me?

Where the fuck is…

I snatched my phone up from the bedside table, scrolling down to his number and pressing call. It rang. And rang. And fucking rang. Twelve attempts. No answer.

Where the fuck…

Making a snap decision, I jumped up, threw on the first dress that I saw, grabbed my keys, pushed my feet into flip-flops, and flew out of the door. Colliding with my neighbour as I ran down the steps, I called out an apology, feeling a pang of guilt for not stopping, but I couldn't. My head was spinning with a whirlwind of thoughts. Mostly that he was leaving me, but a scarier one crept in as I rushed down quiet streets. Nate was unstable, just like *him*. And the unthinkable had crossed my mind so many times over the last couple of months. What if I found him in a state he couldn't come back from? What if I had to live through…

Nate didn't hurt other people, he only ever seemed to hurt himself. What if my past had upset him, what if it had given him…

Suddenly I was praying to find that he had left town – not the entire fucking world. Ideally, he would be sitting on his sofa, being a grumpy fucker, having just needed a little space. But I had woken for the second time in my life without a single shred of optimism. That ideal seemed like a dumb fantasy. Something was wrong.

Where the...

I typed the code into the intercom to gain access to his building then climbed the stairs, taking two steps at a time. I came to an abrupt halt as I reached the door. I couldn't move. I couldn't breathe.

Where...

The windows were too dark to see inside. A note was taped to the door. Four words. Four fucking words. 'I'm Sorry, Little one.'

Fuck.

Sorry?

My body began to tremble, a dark haze washed over me, and in a single heartbeat my foot was slamming into the door. Over and over. I screamed as I ran at it, pain ricocheted through my body as I alternated between kicking and ramming, desperate to break it down, but I wasn't strong enough.

I searched frantically, my eyes darting between plants and his doormat, until I noticed a stone, a stone sitting in a plant pot. Who put stones in plant pots? Only people who had hidden things. Hidden keys.

I flipped it over, finding a catch on the bottom. Inside was a key. Thank fucking god. I twisted it in his lock and fell through the door, my legs like jelly. I scrambled back to my feet, tears in my eyes as I searched the small flat for my man.

Gone.

Standing in his room with the wardrobe doors wide open staring at the half empty rail. My favourite shirt, gone. The jeans with the ripped hems from years of wear, gone. He was gone.

I span in a circle, my hands twisting in my hair. I pulled it up into a high bun, securing it with the band that he placed on my wrist every night. I turned, taking in his room, again and again. My breathing slowing as I took in my surroundings over and over. Panic subsided.

The moment it was gone, I saw red. My eyes locked on the acoustic guitar in the corner of the room. Not Lola. She was gone. Gone with him. My man.

There was a sharp pain in my chest, pricking and stabbing sharply as I took each step closer to Aly. I didn't like that feeling one bit. I didn't like that he had buried himself so deep under my skin that this was *hurting*. There was no way for me to force a smile and walk out of his empty flat.

At first, I hadn't intended to give up my heart, but over time I had done it anyway. I thought that I was safe, and that even though I had been slowly falling, and we were getting so much closer with each passing day, I thought that I was still guarding myself enough to walk away with happy memories and the knowledge that I had made his life a little better, even just for a couple of months.

He had said he was all in, and so was I. But… I hadn't believed myself. Not really. Not until now.

My fingers wrapped around Aly's neck, squeezing tight as I lifted the guitar from her stand. I admired her with fire burning through my body, burning away the pain. It felt better, and it made me wonder if I would feel even better if I did something stupid. Something completely unlike me.

I slammed her down onto the bedside table, splitting her body with an almighty shriek. I visualised his face as I repeated the motion then spun around, launching her across the room, knocking the contents sitting on top of his dresser across the floor. Glass aftershave bottles shattering as they hit the wall.

My chest heaved, and a manic grin split my cheeks as tears streamed down my face.

"Fuck!" I yelled, gritting my teeth as I searched for another outlet.

I had told him everything. I had let him in. He knew my secret. And then he did this. Left in the middle of the fucking night with a four word note pinned to his door, not even left beside me on his empty pillow, or scribbled on the notepad by my front door. A last second thought as he fled. That was all I was to him.

He used me.

My feet carried me to his lounge and my hands wrapped around the small wooden end-table, my fingers flexing before throwing it towards the T.V. My eyes locked on the flowers that I had bought earlier in the week, a sad attempt to brighten this place up for him. The half dead arrangement of orange roses ended up clutched in my hand and carried into the kitchen. I left a trail of water in my wake as I moved to the oven and lit a burner. I inhaled the flowers as fresh tears cascaded down my face, my vision blurring as I focused on the flame. I blinked hard, swiped at my face, then held the heads of the roses over the flame. Burning the sweet gesture I had made. They caught, fire flicking and rising. I gazed at them, turning the burner off and twirling them in a circle. Hating what he had just done to me.

I dropped the dead, smouldering roses on top of the oven, and fell to my knees. Sadness clawing its way up inside me. My heart beating rapidly, unevenly, as I clutched my throat and attempted to hold back the sobs threatening to tear me open.

I didn't like it. That feeling. That *hurt*.

I liked the anger much better. The anger didn't hurt me. It made me feel strong. Powerful. I needed it. Even though my head was screaming at me to stop, to let it go and just feel the painful shit. I couldn't.

I wanted happy. Not sad.

I would take *anything* over sad.

I sniffed hard, pressing my thumb into the centre of my chest, rubbing a small circle, then got to my feet. Unsure how I was going to hold onto the anger, but I knew that I needed to try.

I slammed my hands down on the counter, then swiped along it, tossing coffee, sugar, and tea bags across the floor. The mess made me smile. I *knew* anger would be better. Anger made me *smile*. Although, I was sure I would lose any reason to smile pretty soon. This was only a temporary fix. I would take it though.

I paced the room, then headed into the hallway, circling until my eyes locked on something on the wall. Something I had expected to be gone, along with him.

Keys.

Car keys.

And beneath them, a long umbrella propped up against the wall beside the coat rack.

My smile dropped as I reached for them both, running my tongue over my teeth as I considered stopping myself from going as far as temptation was leading me. This wasn't me.

Temptation won out, and a moment later I was flying down the stairs with Nate's door slamming loudly behind me, no doubt worrying his neighbours. But I didn't care. I couldn't give two shits about anything right now, because deep down I *knew*.

I felt something – something that I wouldn't name – towards the coward who had left me.

His car was parked on the next road over, he could never find a space closer to his flat. I located the shiny red Mazda, trailed the metal tip of the umbrella along its body, then paused just before a wing mirror. The smile crept back, and I swung as though I was about to play the most aggressive game of cricket known to man.

The umbrella collided with the mirror, knocking it clean off. I ran to the other side and repeated on the other mirror, then with a wild, freeing laugh, I smashed into each window. I struck each one repeatedly until it shattered, then climbed up onto the hood. I focused on the driver's seat as I stared through the windscreen, the seat where Nate had sat earlier in the week, holding my hand on top of the gear stick as we drove through the night in blissful silence. Nothing but smiles on our faces and joy fluttering inside my heart.

It had all been a game to him though, hadn't it.
Just a bit of fun.
He hadn't felt what I had.
Unrequited.
Fucking bullshit.

I drove the battered umbrella into the window. My entire body trembling as I fell forward. Sharp stabs of pain registered in my brain, but I was growing numb. I couldn't feel it, not really.

"Oi, what are you doing?" I heard someone shout. I blinked hard, rolled off of the hood of the destroyed car, and ran down the road. Shaking as I turned the corner, fingers brushing at my dress as I sucked in heavy, slow breaths.

Twenty minutes later I was sitting in the swivel chair in my office with a bottle of vodka. No tears fell anymore. I had managed to skip over the sadness that I was avoiding. My lips tipped up for barely a second, a snort leaving my nose.

He fucking did this.

I glanced in the small compact mirror sitting on my desk, taking in the cold look in my eyes. He told me they reminded him of the ocean. What would he say now? Ice cold glaciers?

I swallowed a mouthful of vodka. I knew it was far too early, but I wasn't intending on working today. Not anymore. I would rather not open at all than stand behind that bar and pretend I had not just lost something I didn't know I needed.

Because that was the painful truth, wasn't it. I *needed* him just as much as I had thought he needed me. He had filled that little space in my heart, the one saved for a special type of person.

I was a fucking idiot.

I had let this happen, without even realising.

Fuck.

11

Juno

One-hundred-and-thirty-four. That was how many hours had passed since I had woken to that empty bed. I had cancelled the haircut I had scheduled for that afternoon, called Hannah, asking her to handle the bar for a few days, and had sat and stared at the walls of my bedroom for almost the entire time.

Seventy-one. That was how many times I had cursed his name, as I replayed the last two months in my head. Each time coming to the same conclusion. What I felt had been real. And what he had done was an entirely awful dick move, and one that I should have seen coming.

Twenty. That was how many times I had told myself that it was my own damn fault for forcing my way into his life, and for trying so hard to give him what I wanted to give to every angry, broken person in the world. A reason to smile.

Four. That was how many bottles of vodka I had consumed on my own in the last five days. Was I standing behind the bar in a slightly tipsy state? Yes. Did I particularly care? No. Vodka was easier to swallow than the fact he wasn't coming back.

One.

I had left him one message. I had only called him a single time, on Tuesday night, when another moment of anger had pulled me out of my numb state.

"You're a fuckin' coward Nathaniel." I had spat, knowing those words would bother him more than telling him that I was hurting.

I had nothing else to say to him anyway. What *could* I say? That I had fallen in... No. I couldn't. He didn't need to know that truth. I didn't want his pity. I didn't want him to come back and look at me like I was some sad little girl who fell like a dumb teenager. *If* he even came back.

I knew where he was now. It hadn't been all that hard to work out, and one call to Shane Hudson had confirmed it. Nate hadn't told me he had been offered a chance to join 'Jamie O' for the final week of his UK tour. Shane had explained it all to me when I had called. He told me that if Nate was as well received as he hoped, then there would be a higher chance of him getting signed by his label. His partner was having some trouble coming around to the idea of signing my... *no* – Nate. She wasn't too keen on the idea of having someone so much older than their usual names. But Shane wanted him, and he was going to do everything he could to make it happen.

"Didn't you know?" *he asked, his voice dropping as I sniffed and cleared my throat.*

"Nope. He didn't tell me."

It stung that Nate had kept that from me too. I would have celebrated with him if he had told me. I would have sent him on his way with a smile, and…

That didn't matter. Because he hadn't wanted that, had he? He had decided to keep it from me for two days, making vague comments whenever I asked and – I finally realised – distracting me with sex. Then he left me in the middle of the night. Just after I had fully opened myself to him and had told him my secret. I was a fool. A fool who let it all happen. My friends had warned me, they had seen him for what he really was. How had I been so blind?

I glanced up at Hadley, catching his eye and quickly averting my gaze. I was leaning against the dishwasher, standing in the same spot I had been in for the last half an hour. Kim's was reasonably quiet for a Saturday night, which was something that I should have been upset about. But I wasn't. I was fine with it, I could avoid speaking to customers, and I didn't need to plaster a smile on and pretend that I wasn't hurting.

It wasn't just him leaving that had pushed me into the painful state that I was stuck in though. No. That had simply been the start of my unravelling.

On Wednesday I had woken in a panic, sweat coating my entire body as my body shook and I gasped for air. The nightmare was playing over and over, except this time it wasn't quite the same. This time it wasn't just *that* morning that had haunted me for all these years. It was a montage of every painful memory that I had squashed down into a cute little box, tied a bright yellow bow on top of, and had pretended was actually full of sweet little things.

My optimism was a lie. And it made me wonder if Dad's had been too. I hoped that it wasn't, that he had genuinely been the laidback and happy man I remembered. But I was his daughter, and I had been putting on a show for too long. If he was here now, would he still be smiling? Or would he have finally given up exhausting himself with that shit too?

"Juney," Hadley called out, walking the length of the bar until he reached me, leaning over and placing a huge, gnarled hand on my forearm. "Juney. Give us a smile, little lady."

I closed my eyes, turning my head to one side as I swallowed down the bitter words sitting on my tongue. *What have I got to smile about? Give me one good fuckin' reason.*

As if reading my mind he tightened his grip and spoke softly, as if coaxing an injured wild animal out of hiding. "You have friends who love you, a sister who wouldn't be half the woman she is today without you, this place, a dream. Juney, don't give up just because some pathetic prick with a guitar messed you around."

So close.

He had been *so* close to forcing a small smile to my lips, but the moment he mentioned Nate the urge was gone. Hadley didn't get it. Neither did the other men. None of them understood that I had real feelings for him, they were too blinded by their own intense dislike towards him that they couldn't see that I wasn't just angry, I was heartbroken.

Hannah could see it though. When I had called her on Monday afternoon and had asked her to open the bar for me, she just knew. She had raced down to Kim's, took my keys, wrapped me in a huge hug, and had walked me home. Hannah knew that I wasn't ok, and she hadn't tried to force me into doing anything I couldn't bring myself to do yet, like smiling. She had taken charge and had run the bar while I had drowned myself in self-pity. She had also checked in on me every few hours. No pressure, just making sure I had eaten, slept, washed, all the basics. And when I wasn't doing it, she would scold me, tell me I could be as angry, sad, numb, whatever, as I wanted, as long as I did the little things.

She treated me the same way I had treated him.

She stood her ground, just like I had. And I let her, just like he had.

My eyes stung, but tears didn't fill them. I wondered if I was all out, if I had used up my allotted amount for him. And maybe that was a sign that I needed to move onto the next part of this process. Except, I wasn't sure exactly what that was. I wasn't sure how to live without him. Even though it had only been a couple of months, they had been so intense, so full on, that I couldn't remember what it had been like before. I had woken to his face pretty much every morning. I had eaten meals with him, spoken to him about my day and listened to him tell me the occasional thing about his. My home was constantly filled with music, *his* music. I had grown addicted to him, and I had thought that he was just as obsessed with me.

Now, when I arrived home, I would be met with deafening silence. There was no one to talk to, no one to share myself with. My home was empty.

I was empty.

"Smile for me," Hadley coaxed again, but I still couldn't.

He removed his hand from my arm with a heavy sigh just as Jeremy approached. He shook his head at him, and the twins shared a concerned look. I hated that I was making them worry, but I also hated that they weren't fucking getting it.

Before either of them could try again I took a step back and snapped, "Stop. That's enough."

Hannah abruptly turned to face me too, from the corner of my eye I could see her worrying her lip between her teeth, but I continued on.

"I am not ok. And telling me to smile isn't going to change that. Can you not see that? Are you that single minded that you can't fucking see that I am hurting. This was not just a little fling, this was real. What I had with that man was real for me, and I will not just smile and get the hell over it. He's gone, and right now I think I'm entitled to be *at least* a little pissed. So stop. Just leave me the fuck alone."

I shoved past Hannah, my skin prickling with heat and my head spinning as my emotions took control.

He had done this. He brought this out of me.

I slammed my office door closed, threw myself down into my chair, and screamed. I didn't care if anyone heard me, I was so far past acting. I needed to feel. Even if feeling hurt like crazy.

I twisted the chair from side to side as I dug my nails deep into the squishy armrests. My knees clunked against the wooden desk over and over until they hit with enough force to nudge the mouse of my computer, waking up the screen and drawing my attention.

I knew I shouldn't do it. Do the same thing I had done since I worked it out. But my fingers had minds of their own, and before I could stop myself, I was dragging the keyboard closer, opening the internet browser, and bringing up a page I knew I should be avoiding.

There he was.

Live, on stage, looking even more heart stopping than usual. I leaned back in my chair, propping an elbow on the arm and resting my chin on my fist as I glared at the screen.

I watched him until he walked away, my gaze fixed on his dark eyes as he finished his set, thanked the crowd like a fucking pro, and pushed his fingers back through his thick hair. My fingers twitched with the urge to replace his hands with mine, and a fresh wave of anger crashed over me.

I shouldn't want him. I fucking hated him.

"I hate you," I snarled at the screen, but he was gone. Not that he could hear me. Still, I repeated those three words over and over again as I closed down the computer, grabbed my phone, and pulled up his name.

I typed the words, my thumb hovering over the send button. But I couldn't do it.

A small part of me knew that I was stronger than this, more mature. I had always been mature, and even though the urge to act out again was almost impossible to ignore, I did. He could be the weak one who left like a scared teenager, I didn't need to act in the same way.

I deleted the three words, locked my phone, and grabbed my bag. Opening the office door and finding Hannah hovering outside.

"Boss." She nodded. "You want me to close up?"

"Please," I said through gritted teeth, then winced as I caught her eye. "Sorry," I whispered, but she simply shook her head, shoved her hand into my pocket, pulled out the keys, and smiled.

"I got this, go home. I'll call you later?"

I nodded and made my way out of my bar with the knowledge that Hannah was probably the only person here I could count on entirely. The thought brought tears to my eyes, and this time, they fell. They fell because they weren't for him. They were for me. For my loneliness. In that moment I only wanted one thing.

I wanted my sister.

"Why didn't you tell me any of this sooner?" Bea complained as I finished explaining everything to her.

"Because you've been through so much recently," I sighed, feeling like a deflated balloon now that I had let my feelings out to the one person that I felt entirely safe with. "I didn't want to-"

My sister barked a laugh, "You never change, do you, Bug? Can you please stop putting me first and start letting me be there for you."

I dropped my phone onto my bed, tapping the speakerphone button and flopping back against the plump pillows. "I'll try."

"No. No trying, just do."

"Do or do not, there is no try," I sighed, quoting my sisters favourite film to her.

Bea's laughter rang out in my bedroom, and I

closed my eyes as the first real *happy* smile I had managed in days lifted my lips.

"I wish I was there, Bug," she complained.

"Me too," I confessed, squeezing my eyes tight to hold back any more tears. "I miss you so much."

"I miss you too. I'm so sorry, I wish we hadn't agreed to add these extra dates. Also, we're on in five minutes, shall I call you after?"

"No, I should be asleep by then," I lied, biting my lip and hoping she couldn't hear it in my tone.

"Bullshit." She laughed, "We'll be home next week, I promise. No more extensions, no more delays. When we get back, I'm all yours."

"Looking forward to it."

"Love you, always and forever."

"Always and forever."

With that she was gone. It didn't take long for the emptiness to creep back in, twisting its way inside of me. I slowly sat up, reached over to my bedside table, and pulled out the fresh bottle of vodka. Maybe I *would* be asleep by the time she finished her set, but it was far more likely that I would black out instead.

Blackouts were preferable anyway. Because tainted with vodka, my dreams didn't twist into nightmares. They were messy, and uncomfortable, but they didn't scare me.

Not like the memory of *that* morning did.

To everyone's surprise, when mum and dad had died, I had handled it worse than my sister. She had always been the reckless, carefree one. But *I* had stolen that role in that first week. I refused to accept that they were no longer part of my world. I couldn't smile, no real ones anyway. And I couldn't get through a single day without tears streaming down my face, leaving my eyes red and puffy. My head constantly hurt, but it was nothing compared to the pain constricting my chest and clawing at my heart. That was when I had found the beauty in alcohol. I had never really been drunk before, only a little tipsy from alcopops at teenage beach parties. But by the end of that first week, I had found a new love, two new loves. Vodka and Tequila. Did they complement each other well? No. Did they make me feel like shit the following morning? Yes. But I didn't care about that, because a hangover beat heartbreak any damn day.

Except for that day.

The day that I woke up beside *him*. I had met him the night before, and we had hit it off instantly. He hadn't tried to make me smile, he wallowed in my self-pity and encouraged me to drink away everything. Every stupid feeling. So I did.

He was so broken, and when I looked at him, I saw a project. A distraction. I poured myself shot after shot, and he matched me drink for drink. It seemed that it was only logical to take him home with me. In the morning, I would focus my energy on him. Redirect my pain into something good. My pathetic drunk ass was on to something.

Until we woke.

No. *I* woke.

I woke beside a cold, lifeless corpse. A pool of vomit between us, soaking into my hair. His face, twisted. His nostrils lightly dusted with a white residue that I later found out had been cocaine. But that was barely the start of what had taken him. A note, poorly written, a messy scribble, laid on my dining room table, but I hadn't seen it for hours. Not until an officer shoved it in front of me as I sat on my sofa, cross legged with a cold cup of coffee nursed between my palms. I didn't move. I scanned the note, then proceeded to lean forward and hurl on my carpet.

Julie,
Sorry. I didn't want to die alone. Thank you for everything.
Max.

He hadn't even got my name right, and it had taken months to prove that I wasn't involved. Not really. That it was suicide, and I was just the poor soul who had been dragged in to spending his final moments with him. I wasn't charged, but I couldn't truly bury the story. Newspapers had taken it upon themselves to label me as a something I wasn't. My life was a fucking mess.

But now it felt as though it was so much worse. Because I was haunted. Haunted, broken, and done.

A gentle breeze ran through the bar, cooling the back of my neck where the stray hairs that had fallen out of my bun were sticking to my damp skin. In typical English fashion the weather was having serious mood swings, where it *should* be cooling off as the seasons changed, we had a sudden burst of heat.

I flopped down onto a barstool, dumped the paperwork on the bar, and took a sip from the tall glass of water I had placed on a beermat. I was finally sober after a messy blur of a weekend. Hannah had taken the reins, allowing me more time to wallow in my meltdown, but now I needed to be a responsible adult. Afterall, I had something important to do, a goal to achieve. I knew I shouldn't let that man get in the way of turning my bar into the place of my dreams. I just needed to find the energy and motivation to push forward.

    I sighed loudly, drumming a pen on the bar, then froze as the sound of footsteps made their way through the door. I didn't need to turn around to know that it wasn't one of the old dudes, these feet were not clad in heavy boots. It wasn't Hannah either, there was no clack of heels.

    "What the fuck have you done?" His voice hit me, cold and deadly, full of venom.

    My spine straightened as I felt a fresh stab of pain, but it was quickly followed by rage. *How dare he.*

    He stopped behind me, the anger vibrating from his body as his hand landed on my shoulder. I shrugged him off, dropping my pen and turning to face him with the most disgusted look I could manage painted on my face.

    "*Me?* What the fuck have *you* done," I snarled, my hands shaking as I met his gaze.

    His brows were drawn tight, shadowing his eyes in the way I was so familiar with. But the way he was looking at me was new. Nate had never thrown his rage *at* me, until now. Towering over me, he looked more intimidating than I could have imagined, but I wasn't scared.

    I was fucking outraged.

"No." He shook his head, his tongue pressing into his cheek. "You went too far, Juniper. Trashing my flat is one thing, although the burnt flowers were a little psychotic. You crossed a line with Madz. What the fuck were you thinking, destroying my car? Who do you think you are? Carrie fucking Underwood?"

"Madz?" I scoffed, "You named your car too?"

He took a step back as he spoke through his teeth, "What does that have to do with anything?"

I got to my feet, clenching my fists to stop my trembling fingers as I closed in on him, "Nothin'. Just another thing that I can add to the list of stupid shit you've done. What the hell Nathaniel? You really couldn't tell me you were going?"

He flinched, then bent down, pushing his nose against mine as he spoke. "Don't call me that."

I pushed harder, our noses pressed painfully together. "Why not? It's your name. Or does it make you feel *old?* It's a shame you don't act it. Maybe if you had been more mature, I wouldn't have acted out. I was just following *your* lead."

He growled, his breath hot against my lips, tempting me in. I refused to back down though, no matter how badly I wanted him, how badly I wanted to forget how I had felt over the past week. I could close the gap so easily, start fresh with the man I lo-.

No.

I slammed my fists against his chest, shoving him away as I swallowed down the lump that had suddenly risen in my throat. I would not fall into his trap and allow him to play me again.

"You should know by now that this is who I am,"

he snapped, pushing his fingers into his hair as he started to pace.

I wanted to pull him close, hating the space that I had forced between us. It was necessary though.

"No, Nathaniel,"

He froze, his entire body convulsing with ripples of rage. "Don't call-."

"No." I grabbed my glass of water from the bar and launched it. The sound of shattering glass giving me a boost of confidence. Allowing me to not break, even though the look on his face was damn near tearing my heart into pieces.

12

Nate

"You do not get to play the whole '*this is me*' card. Hold yourself a little accountable, you're almost Forty."

    She looked so fierce. So strong. Stupidly fucking hot. I cursed myself for even having that thought. I had gone away and came back to a fucking nightmare, and although it should have been a good thing, I couldn't stop myself from coming here and losing my shit. I *knew* I should have taken her reaction as a blessing. I should have packed up the last of my things and left for London like I had planned when I was making my way back home. But when I had seen those burnt roses on top of my oven something snapped, and my feet moved of their own accord. Pausing in horror as I passed by my car had sent me completely over the edge. I knew my car had been vandalised, but I had no idea it was this bad. I had ignored it all while I was away. I had presumed it was kids, but kids wouldn't leave *my* umbrella behind.

I may have hurt her, but *that* was too much.

"Exactly. I'm almost Forty, and you're young, too young to understand any of this shit," I seethed.

She rolled her eyes, leaning back against the bar. "You're unbelievable. Clutching at silly straws to justify what you did. It was a dick move, *Nathaniel.*"

I hated the way my name sounded as disgust curled her lip, it sounded dirty, but not in the way I was used to, the I wanted it to.

"Well, well," I smirked unkindly at her, redirecting our focus as I hid the realisation that she had a point. It *was* a dick move. One that I really couldn't justify. I left her because I was scared of how I felt about her, of how those feelings would destroy me. I got out first, leaving so that she never could. I did it in the worst way because I was – *am* – a coward. But I would rather throw myself in front of a bus than *ever* admit that out loud. "Look who finally grew a *real* backbone. Does it feel good, Little one?"

The words burned my throat as I forced them out, but it was worth it to see the look on her face. The way her eyes had momentarily flickered with something softer as her breath stuttered.

She still cared. And as selfish as it may have made me, I needed to know that.

"Don't," she said sharply.

"Don't what?" I took a step towards her with a tornado of rage and need battling in my core.

She straightened her spine. "Don't call me that."

"Why not?" I pressed. I had no idea what I was doing, and as usual, I couldn't stop myself from acting before fucking thinking. Stepping closer. Placing my hands down on the bar, caging her in. She didn't back down though, she stood tall, her nose pressed back against mine once more as she stood her ground.

"Stop," she commanded in a venomous whisper.

"Make me."

Fuck.

Something evil was taking over me. A side of myself that I fucking despised. But maybe she needed to see that.

Her gaze dropped to my lips for a second, then she locked them on my eyes as she spoke slowly, clearly. "I hate you."

I lost all control. My lips crashing into hers. A deep growl filling my throat, escaping into her mouth as she parted her lips with a frustrated moan.

All too soon she tore herself away, panting needily with a furious look in her tempestuous blue eyes.

"Yeah, I fucking bet you do." I gave her my cockiest smirk.

She closed her eyes shamefully and turned her head.

"Get out," she whispered with far less strength than before. My stomach clenched at the sound. I hadn't wanted *that.* I just wanted to… I wasn't sure what. Not that though.

I pressed my lips to her flushed cheek, readying myself to apologise before I left for good. But as I pulled back, her lost strength reappeared.

"Get the fuck out!" She roared, her head snapping around, eyes wild as she shoved me. "I'm done with your games."

Games?

I blinked in bewilderment. What the hell had she meant by that? I wasn't playing any games.

She shoved me again and screamed in my face. "Leave!"

Huge fingers wrapped around my shoulders and panic filled her eyes as I was suddenly dragged out of her bar.

"Wait. No. I…" her voice was cut off as the main door to Kim's was slammed shut and one of the twins stepped in front of it.

I guessed it was the other one who was holding me. I thrashed around until his grip on me loosened and they spoke in unison.

"You heard her, leave, and don't come back."

"But…" I began to protest. The look in her eyes, those cut off words, it was making my chest feel tight in a way that I didn't truly understand. The only thing that was clear to me amongst my whirlwind of emotions was that I wanted to go back inside and make sure that she was ok.

I didn't believe that she hated me. There was no way she would have kissed me back the way she had if she did. She cared. *I cared.*

"Go now, if you know what's good for you," the angrier twin growled.

A breath later a fist collided with my stomach, a satisfied sigh leaving the twin as I bent forward, wrapping my arms around my middle and choked in pain as I gasped for breath.

"You don't get to come back here and hurt her all over again," the other one said.

He was right.

Even if she didn't hate me, I knew that the twin was right. I was still leaving. I was chasing down my dream. And there was no way that I could justify hurting her again. I had to go, and leave them fix the damage I had caused by stepping foot in there in the first place. It didn't matter how I felt.

I straightened up and stepped back before either of the men could strike any other blows. I gave them both one final cold glare, then turned and stormed away. Only stepping foot inside my flat to grab my still packed bag and Lola before calling a cab, climbing in, and leaving Lyme Regis for good.

I was done.

"Don't hang around after your set tonight. I need you on the road straight away if you're going to support Hive in Glasgow tomorrow *and* get enough sleep."

I rolled my eyes at my phone as Shane continued to repeat, for the millionth fucking time, my schedule for the week.

It was my busiest week so far since leaving Lyme Regis. Shane had me supporting so many different artists that I was starting to lose track of who was who. Not that I cared much. There were only two things that interested me at the moment; getting up on a stage, and writing my own music. I wasn't doing any of this to make friends, and I never hung around after my set anyway. Not that there was much point in reminding Shane of this, since he had barely let me get two words in during the entire ten minute – so far – call.

"Lynda isn't anywhere near as annoyed about this anymore. It's all falling into place." Shane's voice was as excitable as usual.

"Great," I said flatly, rifling through my case for a set of strings. I was going through them like nobody's business, and I was trying to kid myself that it was from my talented fingers. But I knew deep down that it was rage and pain that had me snapping them so frequently.

She hadn't fought for me.

"Always a pleasure to chat with you, Nate," Shane said sarcastically. "Talk again soon."

I jabbed the button to end the call without saying goodbye. I didn't dislike Shane or anything, I just wanted to keep things simple, professional, between us. If that meant being even more closed off than usual, so be it. I wasn't going to let anyone in and allow them to hurt me. It was bad enough that he essentially held my future in his hands. And even though those hands were allegedly very safe, I couldn't trust him yet.

I'd had this dream pulled out from under me before. This could end the same way too. But Shane knew this. He knew that failure wasn't an option for me. This was it. My last chance. So maybe I should have been a little nicer to the man who was giving me a shot. Maybe.

I got to work restringing my guitar as I skimmed over the words that I had written earlier in my notebook. The string of possible lyrics laced with the usual pain that I felt whenever I wrote. These words, unlike the ones I had written yesterday, were inspired by an unsupportive family. They pieced together a life full of struggles and fights, being pushed and 'toughened up' until they reached a brutal breaking point.

With my freshly stringed guitar sitting on my lap and a couple of hours to spare, I began to sing gently under my breath while plucking and strumming. Playing with compositions, rearranging the words until something close to a chorus fell into place. I then worked on the verses, frustration building as I couldn't work out how to let it all out.

After an hour, I placed Lola on the bed of the hotel room I had been staying in, and grabbed a blank piece of sheet music, scribbling down everything I had worked on and hoping that during my journey that night I might find that more of it fell into place.

This was the eighth song I had started to write since leaving my life behind. And it was the first one that had nothing to do with her. The rest, somehow, even very loosely, had her essence embedded into them. Whether it was songs of regret, anger, lust, loss, or love. They all held a little part of her. My Little Juniper.

No. not mine. Not fucking mine at all.

I flipped to the back of the notebook, reading over the one piece I had been working on the longest. It was one that I had started the night Shane had asked me to come on that first tour. Back when Juniper had still been in my life. The words showed more emotion than I had been capable of expressing to her face. Unfinished lyrics, messy chords, no riff. If I ever finished this piece, it would likely remain in this book. No matter how big I might make it in this world. The words hidden in the back pages were too raw to ever make their way out there.

I yearned to finish it though, but I had no idea

how. Things with her, with us, felt so incomplete, even though we were nothing anymore. I wasn't sure how I could make the words work. And even though I wanted it done, I knew that it was fear that was holding me back.

How appropriate.

This was me. That stupid emotion was the biggest obstacle in every aspect of my life. It sucked having moments like these, ones where I was crippled with self-awareness.

I scribbled down another line. A line with no place. Needing to get the words that were beginning to buzz inside my head onto paper before they were all that I could think about. This had become a daily ritual. Work on the songs I was writing for the world to hear, then put everything else in the back of this book. It felt as though it was keeping me sane. And a little bubble of pride filled my chest as I realised that I had been actively doing something good for myself.

That bubble burst before it had a chance to swell though, and self-doubt came bouldering through, with his best friend imposter syndrome sitting firmly on his back. Those fuckers always had to show up whenever I started to feel anything good. The only time I was able to banish them was when I was standing on a stage with a mic inches away from my lips. Nothing could touch me up there. But I wasn't up there right now. So they would get their shining moment. And I would close the notebook, launch it across the room, and lay on the bed staring at the ceiling until I needed to pack up my shit and leave for tonight's show.

"Ladies and Gentlemen, welcome to the stage, Nate Cook."

I strolled across the dark stage, making my way towards the stool that had been placed before a microphone where a single spotlight was shining. I hoisted Lola over my neck, and perched on the edge of the dark wood, taking in a lungful of thick, sweaty air before I spoke. The venue was smaller than the last two I had played in, and it was a hell of a lot warmer. Even for an icy November evening.

"How are ya'll doing tonight?" I asked, hating the cliché opening but not having anything smarter or wittier to say. All I wanted to do was play, but Shane had explicitly said that I needed to work on my people skills. Apparently, Lynda would be more open to me if I was showing improvement on the skills that I was lacking.

"You don't have to be perfect, just show her that you're willing to listen and try."

So I was. I listened to every complaint that she had made during the dinner I had attended a fortnight ago, and I tried like hell to make the changes that she needed to see.

I was starting to look at myself as more than a musician now. I was an actor. And up on the stage I was putting on more of a show than I had ever done in my life. Every time I spoke, I was pretending to be someone I wasn't. But luckily, my music was still mine. Lynda's only compliment during that dinner had been that I was a talented songwriter.

No one had tried to take that away from me. I was singing the way I wanted to, the words I wanted to. I was just smiling more and talking more and being, well, more.

I went through my script, the one I had perfected for opening shows. It had a little flexibility in it to tailor it to whoever I was supporting, and so far, it seemed to grab the attention of a large portion of the crowd. That was my job really, to entertain while they waited for the headline act. And maybe one day, the headline act would be me.

My heartbeat slowed as I finished, and as my fingers found their place along Lola's neck, I felt all of my discomfort wash away. As my thumb glided over the strings, and words fell from my lips, I was lost and home, all at once.

"Underneath it all, I'm but a broken beast.

A failure in their eyes, the one they want the least.

But they don't see the pain, the struggles and the fear.

How could they, when I won't let them near."

I bowed my head as I played an intricate solo, my eyes gently closed. This song had been the first one that I had completed in the last month. Shane had allowed me to use the studio to record it and then upload it to my own socials. As long as the labels name wasn't on it, I could get away with sharing it with the world. And the world seemed to love it. Not that I could really keep up, it was a social media hit, and I fucking despised social media. Luckily, Shane had convinced one of the interns at Limelight to take over that side of things for me behind Lynda's back.

I should really learn to be nicer to the guy. He was going to extremes for my sorry ass.

After my final song I announced the band that would be taking to the stage next, then disappeared into the darkness. The backstage area was small, set up with a couch and a cooler. I grabbed a bottle of chilled water from the cooler and swigged until the plastic bottle crinkled in my hand and the last drops slid down my throat. I slipped Lola's strap over my head, grabbed my jacket, and found the stage manager to announce my leave.

Leaning up against the wall outside the venue with my packed bag, I waited for the Uber that I had booked to take me to meet the bus that would be passing through in an hours' time.

"Hey tall, dark and moody," a rough female voice purred, and a slender, pale woman emerged from the shadows. She closed in on me until her chest was pressed to my arm and her fingers trailed down my chest.

I tensed under her touch and glared at the woman. She was hot, with her red lips, heavy eye makeup, and revealing black dress. But that didn't matter to me, I wasn't interested. I hadn't been interested since…

"Don't fucking touch me," I snapped.

"Oh, he's feisty too." The woman laughed, her fingers continuing to explore my chest. "I wonder if that sharp tongue is good for anything else."

My stomach churned. My sharp tongue unable to force any words out. The girl I had left behind used to get excited about my tongue, and there wasn't a single person who I wanted to use it on anymore. I had accepted that I wasn't going to be showing any woman any of my skills for quite some time.

"How about you show me," she rasped, leaning

closer to my ear.

"No," I finally managed. Grasping her wrist and removing her from me as I stepped to the side, looking out for my car.

The woman wasn't put off that easily though, stepping closer again and laughing in her throat. "You really are exactly my type."

"I'm not," I insisted firmly. Stepping again.

"You really are, so now I want you even more. And I always get what I want."

I locked my eyes on hers, the cold, dark orbs mirroring mine. Take me back six months or so and she would have been exactly my type too. Broken, empty, just looking for a toy to play with for a single night. But since then I had met *her*, the woman who had changed that pattern and made me feel so much more than momentary lust.

My car pulled up, and I hoisted my bag higher on my shoulder, shoving past the woman and tapping the boot of the car until the driver popped it open. I shoved my bag inside and gently placed Lola on top, ensuring she was safe and secure before closing the boot.

"Where are we going then?" The woman asked, leaning against one of the back doors.

I moved to the other side, "Nowhere."

She slid into the car at the same time I did, and I groaned at her, my fists clenching and jaw tight. "Get out."

"You all good back there?" the driver asked, placing his hand on the passenger headrest and turning to face us.

The woman smiled seductively at him, then

leaned close to me, pressing her lips to my ear as she whispered. "You know I could show you a good time, come on, just for one night."

I tightened my fist, my knuckle cracking painfully. I wasn't even slightly interested in her, but as I looked into her eyes once more, a realisation hit me.

I would have to rebound someday. Maybe it was better to just get it over with. Do it with someone I wasn't even slightly in to. Afterall, that was the safest way, right?

"Fine," I growled, then turned my attention to the driver, nodding at him. He gave me an unsure cock of his brow, but still turned back to the wheel and started the engine.

I checked my phone, working out that I had about enough time to sit through an awkward hand job in the back of the car, then quickly fuck this woman down some alley as I waited for the bus to arrive. I might even have enough time to find an off-licence and grab a bottle of whiskey before hitting the road for the long haul.

"So, it's Nate, right?" she asked, her fingers fumbling with my belt buckle.

"Yes," I said, not bothering to ask her name in return. It didn't matter to me if her name was Clare or Doris, hell, her name could be fucking Steve for all I cared.

"Thought so, I'm-."

"I don't care." I cut her off, shoving her hand away as I unbuckled my belt and popped open the button at the top of my trousers.

She scoffed, but apparently I hadn't put her off one bit. She pushed her hand under my boxers and wrapped her long fingers around my flaccid cock. She pumped her hand a few times, then squeezed as though frustrated at my inability to respond to her touch so quickly.

"What's th-."

"Nothing." I snarled, pushing my hand down to join hers, encasing it as I used her in the way I liked, and let my thoughts wander away from the backseat of the car.

I managed to get hard just as we pulled up to my meet point, and the woman let out a sigh of relief.

"Get out," I commanded, and she did as she was told.

I thanked the driver and got my things from the boot, but as the cool winter air hit me and I turned to face the woman, bile rose in my throat.

"Get back in the car," I said, trying to hide the panic in my voice.

"What? No," she said, propping a hand on her hip and pouting.

"Get in the fucking car. I don't want this. I don't want *you*."

Panic was rising. I needed to get her the hell away from me. What the fuck had I been thinking? I wasn't ready to do something like this. I was forcing something that I wasn't ok with at all, and for the sake of what? Ripping off a band aid that I was quite content to leave on for a while longer. It didn't need to come off, it could stay.

I tore the door open, leaning in and barking a command to the driver to take the woman back to the venue. I paid him up front, and ducked back out of the door. She still had her hand on her hip, but it didn't stay there for long as I grabbed her arm, pulled her harshly, and shoved her into the car, not caring one bit that she was complaining, that I was hurting her. I just needed her gone.

I needed to be alone.

I slammed the door behind her, and the car sped off. The window opened and she screamed out of it at me, calling me a pathetic waste of space as she turned a corner and disappeared from sight.

My fingers were raking through my hair, and my breaths were coming in short, sharp pants that I couldn't gain control of. It was only when I spun around for the fifth time that I noticed the fluorescent sign above the corner shop window and heard the distinct ding of the door opening.

Moments later I was walking out of the shop, having grabbed myself a bottle of whiskey, just like I had originally planned. I perched on the side of the road with my guitar safely propped against a lamppost as I swigged from the bottle and let the burn calm me until I was able to breathe easily, and my head finally fell silent.

13

Juno

Seasons changed, and so did I. Most days my smile was fake and forced, I wasn't the upbeat young woman I had been before him. I had become more *like* him, and I hated that. I wanted to just forget him. But I couldn't, because aside from our new similarities, I couldn't get the morning he had come back out of my head.

He was gone for good though. Someone new was living in his flat, his battered car had been moved, all trace of Nathaniel Cook was gone. If I wasn't so angry, bitter, and heartbroken, I'd have wondered if I had made him up. But he had been real, and so was the mark he had left on me.

My friends acted as though it had never happened and that he had never existed though. They pretended that I hadn't become someone that they didn't recognise. They'd have all made wonderful actors if they chose to come out of retirement. Hadley was probably the least convincing though. Occasionally I would catch him watching me with pity in his eyes, but he never said anything about it. In fact Hadley was putting the majority of his energy into pathetic attempts at convincing me to give his nephew a shot.

"He's visiting this weekend," he repeated as I dropped the paint can onto the table and plunged a butter knife under the lid, wiggling it until it popped open.

All of the energy that *I* had was being thrown into doing up Kim's. I still couldn't afford to do much to it, but I was going to try my best to work with what I could. I'd had so much pent-up energy, and my daily swims weren't doing a lot to release it like they usually would have. Painting wasn't doing much for me either, but occasionally, when I was alone in the middle of the night, I'd walk down to the bar, sit on the pathetic little stage, and take in everything I had accomplished. Those moments, though fleeting, were able to calm me enough to get through another day.

For now.

I started to stir the paint as Hadley went on and on about all of the wonderful qualities the young 'doctor' possessed. Sure, he was actually a real doctor now, but that didn't really add anything to his appeal. I had met Simon once before, a few years ago when we had both just turned twenty-one. We shared the same birthday, and Hadley had attempted back then to set us up by bringing that fact up over and over. Simon seemed to be a nice guy. A little cheeky, very smiley, and full of curious questions.

Simon simply wasn't my type though.

And if he had not been my type back then, he

definitely wasn't it now. But as my friend rambled on and on, and my head began to pound with the beginning of a headache, I realised that I might just have to do something I really didn't want to. My need for him to shut up causing me to make a frustrated decision.

"Fine," I snapped, slamming my fist on the table. Hadley instantly stopped speaking, his eyes wide as he leaned back in his chair and stared at me in bewilderment.

"Fine?" he questioned, quirking a silver brow.

I ran my hand over my hair, pushing the loose strands away from my face and smoothing my ponytail as I exhaled slowly and forced my expression to soften.

"Fine. I'll go on *one* date. But do not get your hopes up. And Hadley." I met his gaze, planting my hands on my hips. "If I do this, then you will stop pushing me. Agreed?"

The grin that split his face was sickening, and as he nodded vigorously, I felt my stomach flip. I didn't *want* to do it. I didn't want him to get his hopes up, but this was the only way. If I pretended to try, I could satisfy his need for a while, and maybe I'd manage to avoid any more attempts to push me until the end of the year.

Although that felt like extremely wishful thinking. My friend would no doubt become even more overbearing over the festive period. But he'd have to find some other willing *young* guy first. Maybe luck would be on my side and not a single one of those would cross our paths.

Yeah fucking right.

Kim's crowd was getting younger by the week. All of those barely legal guys chasing Hannah around like needy little puppies, completely oblivious to the fact that my friend – I guess I can call her that – was crawling into bed with a man older than her father every single weekend.

Her and Shane were getting on like a house on fire, and I was thankful that my friend never mentioned Nate when she spoke about what she had been up to. I knew she would have seen him at some point, what with Shane still working hard on getting his business partner to sign him to their label. Nate was gap-filling on tours for their other artists, and from the occasional late-night, when self-loathing had really kicked in, I had scrolled the internet and had learned that he was writing his own music, and that there were rumours that another label had their eye on him. He would be as successful as I had once hoped in no time. And I'd have to live with the fact that his name would likely ring out in my bar again, that someone would request one of his songs, and that on open mic night, someone would cover one too.

Depp down, I wanted to be happy for him. But I just couldn't.

If he hadn't left the second time, maybe things would be different. Sure, the twins had dragged him out of Kim's after he had kissed me. But I didn't want him to go. Even though I had told him to, I was sure he had heard me before that door closed. The moment of panic where I knew I might lose him for good. I had been angry; I had acted in the same way he probably would have. I didn't want him to leave. I wanted him to come rushing back inside, force his way through that door and stand his ground, just like I always did with him.

I wanted him to fight for me. Prove me wrong.

But he left. He walked away like I was nothing, again. And I needed to forget him.

I had told him that I hated him, but I hadn't meant it, not back then. Now though, I clung to it. I believed that it was true, because I fucking needed to. I still had a dream, and although at times it was tempting, I wasn't going to give up on it over heartbreak. So to keep myself going, I let myself hate him. But I also needed to heal. Forgetting seemed to be the only way to do that.

"He's going to be over the moon, he's always said you seemed like such a sweet girl, Juney. You can prove him right." Hadley bounced his knee as his excitement radiated around him.

Sadly that energy didn't quite radiate far enough to touch me. But I still forced my lips to lift for a second before I turned to the wall and started to paint around a light switch, neatly lining it with black before I came back around with a roller on the rest of the wall.

Hadley sat and spoke softly to me for a while. I wasn't sure that I had actually listened to a single word he said, but the sound of his low rumble was keeping me from listening to any of my own thoughts. Soon enough he was replaced with Jeremy, who – unlike his brother – silently helped me paint.

"Well, haven't you been a busy little bean," Hannah cooed as she came strolling through the front door for her shift. She was going to be opening, and I was planning on hiding myself away for the rest of the day once I had roped off the freshly painted wall and exchanged the keys with her.

"D'ya think it's the right choice?" I asked her, stepping back as Jeremy dropped his roller and glared at me.

"It bloody well better be, young lady. I hate paintin'," he huffed.

I cocked my head, taking in the new colour. Hannah came and stood beside me, mirroring me with a smile on her face.

"Yes. It looks great. Are you doing all of the walls black?" she asked.

I glanced around at the mix of exposed brick and pale blue walls. "No. I think I'll do some white and leave the brick," I decided.

Hannah smirked and nodded, "I love that idea."

A genuine smile spread across my face, and she nudged me before whispering, "It's all coming together."

I turned in a circle, taking in the re-waxed tables and chairs, the new layout, and the small touches, like the new glasses and black napkins. It really was coming together. The whole place already looked so much better than it had two months ago. All I needed was that extra cash so that I could upgrade the stage to an *actual* stage. Carl had moved his 'sound booth' – as he liked to call it – to the darkest corner and had even built a false wall up around it with a blacked-out window. He said it gave a more professional feel to the venue, but honestly, I was almost certain he had done it so that he could hide in there and eat all of the bar snacks without getting caught. The wrappers he left behind kinda gave him away though.

"It's lookin' more and more like I've always wanted," I murmured, still smiling.

Hannah stepped around the bar and poured me a glass of water. I frowned at it but sipped anyway. She was trying to steer me away from my good buddy, vodka. And as much as I insisted that my friendship with the burning liquid wasn't toxic, I knew that it was kinda heading that way.

"I still don't underst-"

"Don't start with the I don't understand crap, Han," I cut her off. Somehow, Hannah had found out about the nest egg of money that I had stashed away for my sister, and she had taken it upon herself to continuously push me to use it.

I wouldn't do it though. No matter how badly I wanted Kim's to become more than just a seaside bar. I didn't care how famous my sister was, how much money she had, who she ended up with. That money was for her. Not me.

"Ugh, fine," she groaned, flipping her inky black hair over her shoulder. "Have it your way. But I still think it's fucking dumb."

I raised my brows at her, wondering where the hell my deathly adorable little barmaid had found the freaking balls to sass me like that, then smirked as a little wash of pride rushed through my body. No one would ever fuck this girl around. I was certain of it.

"Want me to stay and keep you company?" Jeremy asked Hannah. She shook her head, insisting that she had things handled as she changed the music station, took my empty glass, and shooed us out of *my* bar. Just as a familiar voice filled the speakers.

My stomach clenched as she closed the door, cursing loudly as she must have heard it too. I gave Jeremy a quick, one-armed hug, then hurried away from Kim's, heading straight home with one thing on my mind.

Him.

The air was cold against my bare arms, but quite frankly, I couldn't give a flying fuck. Simon was at my side, walking in step with me as I took my sweet time getting from the restaurant to the bar that he had picked out for us to finish the night in.

He hadn't offered me his jacket, which was a bit shit. But it was also something I didn't care about; it was more of a passing observation. I didn't want his scent on my skin. I didn't even want to spend any more time with him. Dinner had been just about tolerable. All he had done was speak about himself, which in a way, I suppose, had been a blessing. He hadn't noticed how quiet I had been, and I hadn't needed to uncomfortably open up. Let him in.

I had only agreed to his offer of a drink afterwards because, one, I *needed* one. And two, I had promised his uncle that I would try. The last thing I needed was Hadley moaning at me, saying that I hadn't given his nephew enough of a chance. It was only one evening. Then I could go back to existing with very little joy or purpose.

"And then I said, *well maybe you should have thought about that before you went out wearing something like that,*" Simon explained with a disgusted sneer pulling his top lip. I hadn't been listening to his story, but that last part had caught my attention. "Honestly, this girl had been asking for it. Luckily, I didn't have to deal with her for long. She started crying, so I got a nurse to take over. Which was great, I didn't have to do the boring shit."

I looked up at him with a frown. "What boring shit?"

"I knew you hadn't been listening," he complained, squinting at me with his bright blue eyes. "You really should work on that, Juniper."

"Juno," I corrected. Hating how my name sounded on another man's tongue. I corrected everyone now. Even the man at the bank last week. I couldn't stand to hear anyone say it.

He rolled his eyes, "Whatever. If you had been listening, you'd have worked it out. Unless you're *stupid*. The woman was claiming she had been raped. Honestly, you girls go out dressed like..." he looked me up and down, raising his brows. "Well, that." He gestured to my outfit, a tight-fitting black midi-dress with strappy sleeves and a pair of low heels. "And when you don't like the attention you get, you cry rape. I hope you're not like that, *Juno*."

I stopped dead in my tracks, my jaw falling to the floor.

"You said *what* to a woman who had been raped?" I practically screeched at him.

He paused, turned to face me, and shook his head in confusion as his brows pulled together and he shrugged. "The truth. I bet nothing even happened."

"Are you alright?" I shook my head, unable to fathom the words leaving his mouth. I had thought him to be self-absorbed, but apparently, he was actually a giant fucking prick. "Did you get hit in the head or somethin'?

Because I do not understand how *anyone* in their right mind could let such shit come out of their mouth."

"Excuse me?" he took a step back, but I advanced on him. Repressed anger bubbling away under my skin.

I jabbed his chest with a black, glossy fingernail, "How dare you speak to anyone that way. Especially a woman who has been through that kind of trauma. Do you know how hard it is to speak up about that type of thing? Do you know how many assaults go unreported because of the judgement women fear of receiving if they tell anyone? You're vile. You know that?" I took a step away and began to pace as he watched me with an amused look on his face.

"Do you think your opinion of me matters?" he scoffed. "I'm a *doctor*. I could get any girl I want." He dipped his head patronisingly. "You're not special, *Juno*. I only agreed to this date to shut my uncle up. And then you turned up, and I thought, *fuck it, she looks easy*. I bet you're a complete freak in bed. Come on, let's skip the drinks."

"Are you fuckin' serious?" I yelled, pausing to glare at him. "You think I'm going anywhere with you?"

"Well, I can see that you're angry, but that'll just make it more fun."

He approached me with a wicked glint in his eye, the angelic face he had worn all evening well and truly gone. He grabbed my throat, his thumb digging painfully into my flesh as he ran his tongue over his lower lip. "Don't act like you don't find me attractive."

I attempted to pull away, but before I could, his mouth was on mine, his tongue licking over my lips, up my cheek, and around the shell of my ear.

Bile rose in my throat, and a moment later my knee was slamming into his groin, and I was running to the nearest bin, shoving my head through the small gap, and throwing up the entire contents of my dinner.

"You fucking bitch!" Simon shouted. "Who the fuck do you think you are?" His voice was getting closer, and I knew this man wouldn't take *'fuck off'* for an answer, especially since he had made his stance on sexual assault very fucking clear. I'd either have to hurt him, or run.

I slipped my feet out of my shoes as I lifted my head out of the bin. Simon's hand landed on my shoulder, his fingers painfully gripping my cold skin. He turned me to face him. His top lip was peeled back, his eyes ice cold, and his hair out of place in a way that made him look far scarier than a moment before. He looked unhinged, and not in that sexy way that my ex-lover had. This man looked damn near psychotic as he tightened his grip and attempted to push his body up against mine.

Clearly he hadn't learned from the first time. My knee shot up again, and the disgusting moron released me once more. This time, instead of simply doubling over, he fell to the floor, calling me every awful name under the sun as he clutched his dick and rocked from side to side.

I didn't waste time gloating or making comments back at him. I took my chance and I fucking ran, heading along the beach in the direction of Kim's, where I hoped I wouldn't bump into my date's uncle.

I shot through the door, tears stinging in the backs of my eyes as I searched the bar, my gaze landing on Hannah. She noticed me straight away, and her eyes widened as she took in the urgency on my face.

"What's happened?" she gasped, running around the bar, and grabbing my arms.

I swallowed hard, shaking my head as I caught my breath, then proceeded to explain to her in the simplest way I could what had just happened. My eyes darted around the bar, taking note of every patron watching the band performing on the shitty little stage. I couldn't see any of the old dudes, but I knew that Carl would be sitting in his booth.

"Hadley and Jer left an hour ago," Hannah said, realising who I was looking for. "Do you want me to call them? Or do you want to wait to see them tomorrow?"

I shook my head quickly, then pondered for a moment, gently shrugging her off and walking up to my bar. I sat down on a stool and exhaled slowly while Hannah poured me a shot of vodka. I tossed it back before answering her.

"I guess, maybe, call Hadley. I need to explain why I ran before that vile creature comes up with some awful story that paints me out to be the bad guy."

Hannah nodded, pulled out her phone, and called my friend, asking him to come back to Kim's, and telling him that when he arrived, he would sit and listen before he did anything stupid.

"We all know what his temper is like," she explained after hanging up, then filled my glass again. "I reckon he's going to kill that kid. And if he doesn't, I think I might."

I laughed bitterly. "He isn't worth the energy, or the jail time."

"Nah, but you are." She gave me a gentle smile. And I softened instantly. Hannah seemed to be the only one who could get me to do that these days, and it made me even more grateful to have her. She showed me that I wasn't just a broken, angry woman. I still had some light in me. Even if it was buried down deep.

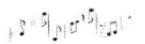

"Do you still think about him?" Hannah asked me the following morning. I had stayed at her place for the night. Not wanting to go home and be alone after what had happened with Simon. Not that I had actually voiced that. She just knew. So she offered up a girly sleepover, and I accepted without hesitation. Hadley had walked us to Hannah's place after I had told him everything. Luckily, he had believed me, and as he left us, he promised he would put Simon in hospital. I told him not to bother, but who knew, my friend had a dark, secretive past. Maybe he did go home and murder his nephew.

    Hannah and I had stayed up most of the night talking about the most random things, like what we would spend our money on if we won the lottery, and which characters we found most attractive in various films. It was fun.

    We had fallen asleep sprawled out across her bed, and in the early hours of the morning, when I had woken up shivering and surprisingly calm, I had pulled her thick duvet up over us both and had stared at the ceiling, allowing my thoughts to run free until she woke a couple of hours later. I wasn't haunted when I was laying in her bed, it made a nice change.

    "Who?" I asked, still staring.

She sat up and looked down at me as she whispered hesitantly. "Nate."

I tensed, not wanting to answer, keeping my eyes trained on the ceiling as I forced my body to relax back to how it had been before she had spoken his name.

"Yes," I confessed simply, my voice void of all emotion.

"Did you think about him last night?" She leaned over, her face hovering above mine.

"Yes," I repeated, relaxation failing, my jaw tightening.

She sat back with a sigh, "Because he would have saved you?"

I sat up, glaring at her, "I didn't *need* saving. I handled it myself. And if Nate had never left, I wouldn't have even been on a date. I thought about him because Simon was unhinged in a way that Nate never was. No matter what, Nate never tried to physically hurt me. He never forced me to do anything. He would never have…" I trailed off, not wanting to think about any of it anymore.

"He did hurt you though," Hannah said quietly. "Do you think you could ever forgive him?"

"Why would I do that?" I snapped, throwing off the duvet and getting to my feet. "He's gone. He's happy. He's touring, writing, making a name for himself. From what I hear he's getting his big break. So why the fuck would I need to forgive him?"

Hannah tilted her head, her dark hair spilling over her shoulder, completely unphased by my outburst. "I dunno. Maybe he isn't as happy as you think."

"Has Shane said somethin'?"

"No. Shane doesn't talk about him much at the

moment. The last time he spoke about him it was just about the offer."

My spine stiffened. "What offer?"

"You're right about his big break." She smiled. "Shane's meeting with him tomorrow."

Why did I care? Why was there a tornado of butterflies in my stomach? Why was I battling so violently between anger and…

Pride.

14

Nate

I burnt my tongue as I sipped my black coffee, but I was too on edge to really register the pain. I was waiting for Shane. He had called me on Friday night saying that when I got back from Edinburgh on Monday morning, I should head straight to the coffee shop down the road from my flat – the one where the owner's dog was always snoozing in a bed in the corner of the shop – and wait for him. He had big news, and I was certain I knew what it was already.

My foot was tapping a rapid beat on the linoleum floor, and I alternated between running my thumb around the rim of my coffee mug and twirling my glasses between my fingers.

I dropped them onto the table as the door flew open and in strolled Shane, his huge frame leaning over the counter as he loudly placed his order, turned to face me, and spread his arms open as he called out my name.

Not that there was anyone else in the shop. The display was completely unnecessary, but I couldn't help but crack a smile as he pulled out a chair, shrugged off a thick woollen coat, and sat down with an excited shimmer lighting up his bright green eyes.

"Cold enough for ya?" he asked, then glanced up at the waitress, thanking her for his coffee as she placed it down on the table.

"It's a damn sight warmer than Scotland." I leaned back, folding my glasses and hooking them into the collar of my thick black jumper. I felt completely underdressed. Shane was dressed head to toe in designer everything. His suit had no doubt cost more than a month's rent in my new flat. I always felt underdressed in his presence though. Apart from that one time we had gone to dinner with his business partner, the woman who was so sceptical about whether or not I'd be able to fit her mould. He had dressed me up in Gucci, not that it really mattered much to me. She had been impressed though, and I was guessing that the meal, along with all of the video calls and arse-licking had finally paid off.

Shane chuckled loudly, brought his coffee mug up to his lips and slurped. I knew what he was doing, and the way he kept wiggling his brows at me as we silently stared at each other just confirmed it. Shane was a dramatic man. He loved to build suspense. I, on the other hand, couldn't stand that, unless it was in the bedroom, and that was somewhere I never *ever* wanted to be with Shane Hudson. Especially after what I had walked in on last month when he had asked me to come over for dinner between tours.

Hannah was a *very* lucky young woman.

I'd have told her that, if I hadn't turned my back instantly and decided to grab takeout on my way back home. I was quietly glad of it though. Hannah was a sweet girl, but she reminded me of what I had given up to be where I am, and that, even though it had been my choice, was something I was still at least just a little bitter about.

I wished that I was a better man. The type of man who didn't run scared when things got too real. But I wasn't. And as that thought hit me my heart rate spiked, and heat flooded through my body.

My vision blurred as I tugged on the collar of my jumper, dislodging my glasses. They clattered against the table, and I quickly pulled my jumper off.

Shane's voice caught my attention, and my skin heated even more. "Can we get a water?"

I blinked hard, clearing my vision and attempting to slow my breaths. The waitress placed a glass down between us and I tossed my jumper to one side then snatched the glass up, gulping down the ice-cold water with shaky hands.

"Sip it, man," he said with a light laugh. "Fuck, what was that?"

I met his concerned gaze and lowered the glass. His kind eyes and uncharacteristically soft tone soothing me enough to speak.

"I dunno, maybe I'm coming down with something," I lied pathetically, shrugging as though I hadn't just had a small panic attack in front of the man who I may have been about to get life changing news from.

"I hope not," he said, but I could tell that he

wasn't convinced. His brows were dipped low, and his eyes searched mine for a while, but I wouldn't give anything away. I kept my focus on my expression, hiding how I felt. I couldn't fuck this up over a silly moment of panic.

Fear wouldn't win today.

He blinked, grinned, and slammed his hand down on the table. "Well, shall we get on with it then?"

Perfect.

"Yes. Let's."

He leaned forward and spoke the words I had dreamed of hearing for as long as I could remember. "Nate, it's time. Lynda is completely on board. You've done it. We're signing you. The contract is being drawn up as we speak, all you need to do is come and meet with us and the lawyers tomorrow, and then we can move forward. Congratulations, man."

He held his hand out to me, and I reached across the table to take it, his gold rings clattering against my silver ones as we shook hands, grinning at each other like we had both just won the lottery.

A hint of panic rose up again, and I grabbed my coffee mug and hid my face in it as I quickly squashed it back down.

"This is good, yes?" he asked.

I peered over the rim of the mug. This man wasn't going to hurt me. He wasn't going to rip away this one thing that I had worked so hard for. This was no joke, no game. No matter how scared I was to lose it all, I also knew that this genuinely was it. I was getting my big break, at long fucking last.

"This is amazing."

Shane had suggested I wear a suit of his choosing tonight, and as I stood in the elevator, making my way up to the top floor, I realised that I fucking hated how it looked on me. I wanted black, he had pushed for blue. I had grudgingly agreed because he was making my dreams come true, and after I scribbled my name down probably about fifty times, we were going for a celebratory drink, and Lynda was joining us.

    I stared at my reflection in the back wall, tightening my grip on the cold, metal bar that ran along it. I pressed my forehead against the mirror, closing my eyes as I pulled on the excitement that had been coming and going like crashing waves since yesterday morning. I felt like I should have been a lot happier about this moment, and I prayed that I was only coming up and down because it wasn't set in stone. When I scrawled my name on those dotted lines it would all feel better. Calmer. Certain.

    I leaned back, still holding the bar as I raised my head and sighed. A silver curl fell out of my perfectly styled do, one that I was certain last month had been black. Shane was pushing me to go natural, claiming that going grey was something I shouldn't hide, and was something that would work well for my image in a few years' time. I wasn't so sure, but he knew best, so I begrudgingly followed his lead.

    Pushing the curl back, I felt my stomach drop. Then a loud ping signalled the door opening. I stepped out, slid my glasses on, and hesitantly walked across the open area to the glass wall. Beyond it I could see Shane, Lynda and a man who I presumed was a lawyer. I wondered for a moment if I should have bought one with me too, but Shane hadn't mentioned it, so I guessed the man was just there in case I had any questions.

"Nate!" Shane's voice boomed through the glass and his smile had me picking up my pace.

I stepped inside the room, and Lynda gestured to the chair opposite her. I took my place and tucked my hands under the table, not wanting anyone in the room to notice that my fingers were twisting in knots as I steadied my breathing.

"I hope you don't mind," the younger woman began, flicking her blonde curls over her shoulder as she ran her gaze over me. "But I have a party to get to after our drink, so can we make this quick?"

"Sure," I said, untangling my fingers and wiping my slick palms down my trousers as she pushed an iPad across the table towards me.

"All digital now," she smirked, handing me a stylus. "Oh, and if you want, you can join me at the party. It might be nice to show off our latest piece of meat."

I hated the way she spoke. Calling me a piece of meat as she pulled her red painted lip between her Hollywood white teeth. Lynda had made her opinion of me very clear the first time we had met. She didn't like me. But she wanted to fuck me. She didn't think I'd be the right fit for the company, but the perfect fit for her cunt.

Sadly for her, I wasn't interested.

In fact I still hadn't taken a real interest in any woman since leaving Juniper. There had yet to be a successful rebound. No taking advantage of the girls I met on the rest of each tour since that night in Kent. I *could* have spent meaningless nights with random cute girls, but the desire to do it still wasn't there.

Deep down I knew why. I wasn't ready to rid myself of her completely. Filling some dark, twisted girl with what belonged to *her* was something I wondered if I would ever want to do.

After the panic I'd had, it seemed unlikely.

Dragging my focus to the iPad before I could dive into memories of Juniper, I skimmed over the contract. Tapping back and forth through the pages as I twirled the stylus between my fingers. Another rush of heat hit me as the words blurred. I dropped the stylus, stood up, and shrugged my jacket off. It wasn't enough though. I fumbled with the buttons on my cuffs, then shoved my sleeves up my forearms, not caring that it was creasing the shirt. I needed to cool the fuck down.

My gaze caught on something on my wrist and my vision suddenly cleared. I ran my thumb over one of the pink scars. My hand flexed, and I dropped my gaze lower to my palm, the place where another deep line sat, this one more raised than any other mark on my body. I blinked rapidly and attempted to refocus on what I was here to do. I attempted to force myself to sit back down, but my head and my heart had already begun their battle. The one that deep down I knew had been coming since the moment I walked away from the twins that morning outside Kim's.

"Nathaniel?" Lynda's voice barely registered, and for once I was too distracted to correct her, scold her, anything. She didn't exist to me. No one fucking did. No one apart from *her*. My little one. *Mine*.

But she wasn't mine anymore, was she? She was gone. She hadn't come for me; she had let me go. I couldn't blame her though. I had fucked it all up. I hadn't gone back to fight for her either. I had walked away just like I had planned. I had torn my heart to shreds out of fucking fear. And now I was standing in the office of one of the biggest record labels in the UK, falling into a goddamn spiral because she wasn't here, and she never would be.

"Ju-." I choked, and then my feet were moving. Running. I was gone, flying through the door, my sights set on the elevator as Shane's loud booming voice followed me.

"Nate!" he shouted as I jabbed the button and clawed at the collar of my shirt. My chest tight, throat constricting, as tears filled my eyes.

The doors opened and Shane followed me into the elevator. I turned to face him, his features a blur as my hands collided with his chest and I shoved him backwards, pushing him out before stabbing the button for the ground floor over and over until his body crashed into mine and I was pinned against the back wall as the doors closed on us.

"Get the fuck off of me," I roared, thrashing around against the wall in an attempt to get the huge man away from me.

He didn't budge, his face pressed against my cheek, a growl in his voice that I had never heard him use before. "No. Not until you calm the hell down."

I attempted to headbutt him, but he simply leaned back and quickly placed his thick forearm over my throat as he glared at me. "Calm down and tell me what the fuck that was all about."

"It's none of your fucking business," I choked, his arm pressing too hard against my neck. "Get off."

He shook his head, leaning even further back to reach the buttons and halt the elevator. We jolted to a stop, and he released me just enough to wriggle free. I threw myself into the furthest corner, getting as far away from him as possible in the confined space.

I dropped to the floor, tucking my head and digging my short nails into the exposed flesh on my arms. My body shook, and my thoughts flashed back to the night she had laid with me on the kitchen floor as I broke down. The night I gave myself even more scars.

She wasn't here. I hadn't let her be a part of this. And all I wanted was to see her smiling face peering up at me as she held my hands and bounced with excitement as I signed on to my future. The future I had always wanted.

I didn't want any of it now…

"I don't want it. Not without her," I whispered my confession. Keeping my head low.

I heard a shuffle and peered through my lashes to see Shane sitting on the other side of the elevator floor, his head tilted back as he stared up at the ceiling.

"Finally," he breathed.

My head shot up, anger burning through me as I snapped at his simple word. "What the fuck does that mean?"

"It means," he dropped his head to meet my gaze. "That you're an idiot who finally realised that he lost the best thing that ever happened to him."

"I thought *you* were supposed to be the best thing

that ever happened to me?" I said coldly.

He barked a laugh. "I wouldn't be here with you if it hadn't been for her."

"What?" I baulked, sitting bolt upright and cocking my head.

"You really think that I just came wandering in off of the beach in the middle of Dorset? That I was on my holidays, and I just so happened to walk in, wearing a fucking suit. Fuck, Nate, I know I dress well, but I do know how to relax when I'm away. She called her sister, who then practically threatened me to come and see you. That girl made this happen for you. So yes, she *should* be here, and yes, you fucked it up. I'm glad you can finally see that."

He rested his head back again. I rolled my tongue over my teeth, taking in what he had just said, and realising that Juniper hadn't overreacted as much as I had thought when she had trashed my place. *My car.* She was even more entitled to her anger than I had initially realised.

"I'm done with your games." She had thought I had been playing her. That I had *used* her. She had given me the life I wanted, and instead of taking her along for the rest of the ride, like I should have, I left. I left her *twice*.

"You have a big decision to make, Nate," Shane sighed, "Because Lynda will only wait around for so long before that offer comes off the table."

"What the fuck am I going to do?" I groaned, slumping back against the wall.

Shane reached up and jabbed a button, sending the lift shuddering back to life as we descended. He got to his feet, and held a hand out to me.

"It's us or her, my friend. When you look at your perfect future with your bigshot career and your perfect young thing, which part makes you smile the most?"

I stood up, running my fingers through my hair as I thought about a life where I had it all. I had never done that before. It wasn't something I ever felt entitled to. It made me uncomfortable. But when I imagined her sparkling ocean eyes Shane laughed.

"What?" I snapped as the doors opened.

"What were you just picturing?" he asked, stepping out.

I followed, telling him that it was her eyes, and asking him why?

"Because I've not seen you smile like that before."

I stopped. Standing frozen in the lobby as my choice became crystal clear. Nothing was worth having if I was without that girl.

She was made for me. Made to handle everything that I was. The chaos of my brain, the harshness of my bitter outlook on life. She was my sun, my rain, my fucking air, filling my lungs and giving me life. Without her I was a shell of a man, barely alive. Music didn't fill me up the way she did. I wanted her. I needed her...

I was in love with her.

15
Juno

My thoughts were consumed with him. Wondering if he had done it. If he had made it at long last. There had been no news though, and Hannah hadn't mentioned him at all since Sunday morning. Every time I scoured the internet, I came up short. I wanted to know, to see for myself that he had finally got his big break.

If he had made it, then it was all for something. He'd have gained something out of his stupid game. He'd have used me wisely. And I'd have been left behind.

If he hadn't though, then it would have all been for nothing. I'd just be that pathetic girl who had seen something in a man that no one else could really see.

Either way I'd have a good reason to cling to the bitterness that radiated through my every fucking pore.

I shook my arms violently, attempting to shake off all thoughts of the man who had let me in enough to hurt me. I was tired, so fucking tired of being sad about it all. I needed to forget all of it.

The bottle of vodka that I had been taking sneaky sips from each day was calling me, her sweet voice like a sirens call, and as I locked my gaze on her, I knew I wouldn't be resisting. I slammed down the lid of the laptop, and snatched her up, flicking the cap off and taking a long swig straight from the bottle.

I quickly put her down as the sound of the main door slammed shut and I wondered who the fuck had just entered my bar. It was 10am, Hannah wasn't even due in today, and the old dudes had been giving me more space unless I asked for help, so it wouldn't be any of them. Who the hell even attempts to enter a bar at 10am? A raging alcoholic no doubt.

I groaned, grabbed the pepper spray from my handbag, and mentally ran through the plan I had in my head ever since I took over this place. The one I had if anyone ever broke in and attempted to hurt me. There was a baseball bat behind the bar, it had moved when I had the new fridges installed, but it was still back there. There was also the small fire extinguisher beside one of the bathroom doors, and then the countless chairs and stools that I could quite easily launch at someone.

Slipping my phone into my back pocket, I made my way out of my office. Not needing to bother pulling on a pissed off bitch face, since I had been wearing it so freely these last few months. I may be tiny, and reasonably cute, but I was pretty certain I had nailed the death stare.

"Right, it's 10am, so whoever the fuck you are, you can get the hell out." I raised my voice as I walked down the short corridor towards the bar.

The intruder didn't respond, and I groaned loudly this time as I leaned against the doorless frame and glared at the back of the man's head. He was perched casually on one of the stools at the bar, his back to me, and his head tilted to one side. He wore a tight, black leather jacket, and his hair was black, speckled with grey. The loose, short curls looking temptingly touchable.

A gasp caught in my throat the moment the thought ran through my mind. My knees buckled and I slammed my hand against the wall to steady myself, stopping my body from crumpling to the floor.

"This place is looking good, Little one."

My heart hammered in my chest as my blood heated in every vein. This was so much worse than some random alcoholic. He shouldn't be here. Why the hell *was* he here?

"What the fuck?" I breathed, my chest tightening as he began to move, twisting on the stool to face me.

The moment our eyes locked I felt it. That intense pull, combined with pure, furious outrage. How dare he come in here, looking so casually cool, and call me fucking *Little one*.

"You look good too," he commented, cocking his head as he raked his dark gaze over me.

I glared at him, my top lip peeling back as I wondered if he was drunk. I was standing here – barely – dressed in an oversized t-shirt and black jeans. My unwashed hair had been thrown up into the messiest bun, and the purple bags under my eyes were now a permanent fixture thanks to the many sleepless nights I had, and mornings where I had woken early in a cold, panicked sweat. Frankly, I looked like shit.

"What the hell do you want?" I snarled, my anger giving me the strength to step towards him. Each step deliberately slow as I glared at him with my jaw locked, my fists clenching and releasing.

He dropped his head, his gaze tearing away from mine. He nodded to himself, then peered up through his lashes. "I'd be an idiot to think it would be this easy."

"No shit." I paused a couple of feet in front of him and leaned my elbow on the bar, still glaring even though he refused to meet my gaze again.

"I want you back, Juniper. I want *us* back," he confessed, looking down at his hands which were twisting in knots on his lap. His posture was no longer laidback. Maybe he realised what he had done to me. That I was no longer that agreeable little girl who fell at his feet because she thought she could fix him. I didn't want to fix him anymore, even though he looked far more broken than when we had first met. I was done with that. I didn't need a man in my life who couldn't see my worth, who used me and played with me like a dog with a chew toy.

"Good for you," I said coldly, *childishly.*

His head shot up, his eyes finally locking back on mine as he pushed his tongue into his cheek and raised his brows. "Really, Juniper? You're going to act like a moody fucking teenager?"

I smirked, the sound of a laugh sitting in my throat as I exhaled loudly through my nose. "Yeah, I am. Are you disappointed, Nathaniel?" My smile widened as he flinched, his feelings towards my use of his full name clearly written in his eyes as they burned into mine. "It's a shame I don't give a fuck about what you think anymore."

It was a lie. I could taste it as the words left my mouth, but the effect it had was worth it.

Nate stood from the stool, closed in on me, and pinned me against the bar.

"Liar," he hissed, his head dropping, his lips so close to my ear that I could feel his breath hot against my lobe. Sharp and heavy. He was angry. But so was I.

But only one of us was really entitled to feel that way though.

"That's rich, coming from you."

"What?" He pulled back, searching my face.

"You lied. You told me that I was one of the best things in your life, you told me I was the *good* in your life. Then you just left. You left, twice. So you lied, I wasn't that to you, was I?"

His jaw clenched, and he stepped away, turning his back on me. "Is that what you think? That I didn't mean every word I said? I thought you could read people, Juniper. I thought you could read *me.*"

A fresh wave of outrage rolled through my body. "Clearly I read you wrong, because I thought you were a good man. A mess, sure. But *good.* Good men don't leave in the middle of the night without a word."

"I was scared," he countered, his voice raising to meet mine as he turned towards me, his brows arched in a way that sent a jolt of sympathy straight to my heart. But that jolt didn't hit my head, and I spoke before I could let it attempt to shoot up there.

"That's no excuse. I was scared too. You didn't even *try* when you came back either. So what's changed now then? Did you get bored? Lonely? Horny?" I sneered, leaning over the bar to grab the bottle I kept stashed behind it. Popping the cap off and raising it to my lips.

"What the hell are you doing?" Nate exploded, advancing on me and swiping at the bottle, sending it flying across my bar. It shattered on the floor, and I stared blankly at the puddle forming on my freshly cleaned floor. "So I leave you and you turn into this?"

Another wave.

"You don't like what you see anymore?"

"I don't like you drinking at 10am."

I raised a brow at him and smirked again. "Well that's too damn bad."

"Juniper." His voice dropped, quiet, soft, *pleading*. His dark eyes fixed on mine, his hand reaching up, knuckle caressing my cheek. "I didn't come here to fight."

I didn't flinch away from his touch. But I also didn't lean in, as much as my heart was screaming for me to. Deep down I knew that everything I said wasn't even close to the truth about how I felt. But I couldn't be this girl who fell back into some man's arms just because he turned up. His life had probably gone to shit, and he was crawling back into my bed. I needed to throw him out and close the door before he could get under the covers.

I slowly pulled away, just enough to break the contact. My cheek instantly cooling, missing his touch.

"Then leave," I whispered, clutching the bar for support.

"No."

"Go."

"No." Firmer this time. His lips twitched, and I

knew that he was thinking about every time I had said no to him when *he* had told *me* to go.

I closed my eyes, blocking him out, forcing myself to stay strong and not become this man's doormat. The air surrounding me grew warmer, and a breath later his lips were on mine, his stubble grazing my chin as his hand twisted into my hair. And for just a moment, I gave in and allowed him to kiss me.

Only for a moment.

My eyes snapped open, and as I pulled back my palm collided with his cheek. The sound echoing around the bar like a whip cracking. His head spun, his jaw dropped, but he didn't shout, he didn't turn to me with fire in his eyes. Instead he dipped his head, and he apologised.

"Leave," I repeated.

"No. I'm not leaving until you hear me out."

I shook my head in disbelief. What the hell gave him the right to come in here after all this time and demand that I *hear him out.*

I jabbed my finger into his chest, forcing him to take a step back, then shoved past him, stepping over the puddle of vodka and beelining for the door. My entire body began to tremble, but I refused to turn back now.

He stared at me, wide eyed as I opened the door, "I am not your little play toy, Nathaniel. You do not get to come back here and do this to me." I met his gaze, taking in the redness in the whites of his eyes as he wrapped his arms around himself, swallowed hard, and stepped towards me, his lips parting to speak, but I was done listening. "No."

"I want-."

"If you want me, you'll have to show me that you deserve me, fucking earn me. But I won't be holding my breath. Goodbye Nathaniel."

I stepped out into the cold winter air with tears filling my eyes. My vision blurring as I walked straight down onto the beach and collapsed on the stones.

Out of sight, I fell apart.

Out of sight, I forced myself to let him go.

16

Juno

I think he's really gone. Gone for good. Although I had thought that twice before, and he had come back both times. It had been just over a week though since he had arrived at Kim's. Since I had walked away, leaving him standing in my bar as I sat crying on the beach over the man who had never seen me sharing his future.

I hated myself that day. Hated the fact that I had let him do that to me. I had cried over him already, and I couldn't stand that it was happening all over again. A small part of my heart was telling me that it was my own fault, and I should have let him speak. Maybe he would have proved me wrong. But if he was going to do that, surely my storming out wouldn't have been enough to turn him away for good. But it sure seemed that way.

Hannah knew what had happened. She had come in the following day for her shift with nervous excitement as she searched the bar and asked how I was feeling. She had thought that I would've caved and taken him back, but I quickly shot down that idea, and she had spent the rest of the evening pouting and attempting to bring him up. After closing, I lost it, I screaming and shouting about him as she stared at me and simply blinked over and over. When I was finally done, she nodded, shrugged, and confused the shit out of me with one parting sentence that she has since refused to discuss.

"You're living the dream, and you can't even see it."

It maddened me that she refused to explain what she had meant by that, but it was hypocritical of me to keep bringing it up when I was also refusing to speak about things regarding the man who had shown up a week ago then disappeared like a ghost.

If it wasn't for her, I'd have thought that I had dreamed it up. Afterall, for the last couple of months all I had wanted to do was scream at him and make him hurt the way he had hurt me. At least I had got the screaming part in. I would never be able to hurt him though. I'd have to mean something to him if I ever stood a chance of doing that.

"Are you sure you don't mind doing this?" I asked, leaning over the bar as Hannah poured a pint for Hadley and slid it down towards him. The glass caught on a dent in the bar and the three of us collectively cursed as it went crashing to the floor.

No wonder it was always slightly sticky.

"Ugh, I really need to get this replaced," I groaned, running my hands along the battered surface.

Hannah and Hadley shared a look, and I knew exactly what they weren't saying. The two of them knew that it wasn't worth mentioning anymore. I had made it crystal clear that I would not use Bea's money. No matter how much I wanted things to change. No matter how badly I was struggling, which currently was bordering on a lot. That was her safety net, not mine. I just needed to hope and pray that things picked up over December. Otherwise I'd possibly end up saying goodbye to everything.

Dream over.

This final week of November had been painfully quiet. Which, although it was not ideal, in a way it was a blessing, as I felt far more comfortable disappearing for a long weekend while things were like this. Hannah *could* handle anything thrown her way, but I still felt a little twinge of guilt for leaving her. Since training her into a higher position, - and that day that I had lost my optimism – I felt as though I was leaning on her more than I should.

"For the fiftieth time, I don't mind," she said with a roll of her eyes. "And I promise, if anything happens, I will call you."

I pulled my lip between my teeth, dragging it in and out while tapping the bar. "It's just that I'll be so far away."

Hadley cleared his throat, "Juney, just go. We'll all keep an eye on her, and Kim's." He rose from his stool and grabbed my case, wheeling it to the door. He held it open, shoved the case outside. "Go on. Get," he grinned then pressed a kiss to my temple as I passed him. I grumbled about it not feeling right, but left the bar nonetheless.

My Uber was already waiting up on the road, and in no time, I had my case loaded into the boot and we were speeding off to Axminster station where I'd be settling in for the long train journey up to London.

Cameras flashed up ahead, and I shook my head as I shoved my half-eaten bag of Maltesers into my pocket and grabbed my suitcase. I had been sitting on the cold bench in the middle of the station for the last fifteen minutes waiting for her to arrive. She had text to say there was a slight delay, and now that she was here it was pretty clear what that delay had been.

"June-Bug," she called out, her voice raising to a pitch that she reserved only for me.

I beamed at her as I hurried through the station, making sure to *accidentally* knock at least one paparazzi with my suitcase as I ran at my big sister and launched myself into her open arms. She tightened her arms around me and nuzzled into my hair, whispering to me that she had missed me, and was so happy I was finally coming to see her.

I never came up to visit her. I never really had enough time to step away from the bar. But during our last late-night call she had insisted that I needed a break, and that maybe after a few days away I would feel a little more optimistic about everything in my life. I wasn't so sure, but I came anyway, mostly because I wanted some quality time with her, and her last visit to Dorset had been cut short because of some drama with one of the guys.

I glanced over Bea's shoulder, noticing her usual

shadows lurking a few feet away. I forced a smile then bit my lip as I pulled back and met my sister's gaze. "Are the rumours true?"

"Mostly," she smirked, "but don't worry, everyone will be on their best behaviour."

She winked at me, then linked her arm in mine and guided me past the men towards the exit, completely ignoring the lights flashing behind us and the shouts for her attention. Before we got into their car – if you could call it that, the thing looked more like a tank – I heard two of the men joining us begin to argue, but one stern look from my sister had them both instantly clamping their mouths shut and climbing in behind us.

"Trouble in paradise?" I asked quietly, and Bea laughed loudly.

"When is there not. How are you feeling? Are you tired?"

I buckled my seatbelt and rested my head on her shoulder, just like I always had done when we were kids. "A little, but nothin' a quick power nap can't fix, why?"

"Because we have friends in town for the night, and they owe me a karaoke night. You game?"

I snuggled closer to her and scowled as the man beside her placed a tattooed hand on her knee. *He was interrupting cuddle time.* I peered around her at him and narrowed my gaze. He grinned back at me, and my expression instantly softened. There was something annoyingly uplifting about this man, and as he kissed my sister's cheek, I felt my heart begin to thaw. That shit was adorable.

"Karaoke sounds fun, but they better not all be as talented as you." I poked her rib, still cuddling up to her, breathing in her fresh, floral scent, the same one that mum had always worn.

"I have it on good authority that at least one of her guys can't sing for shit. And there is also a good reason that these boys never sing with me." She glanced around the car, and I sat back, taking in her four bandmates. The only four people who might actually be closer to her than I was.

"*I* sing with you all the time," one of them said, and I laughed lightly as his face twisted with frustration.

"And your voice could use some improvement." Bea winked at him, and his brows dropped low.

Their exchange made me sigh heavily. I wished that I knew them all better, and that I paid more attention to my sister's life, rather than constantly trying to put out her fires. I only knew a few simple things about them, like which one was the calmest in a crisis, and which one was most likely to start a fight. Deeper than that, I didn't know these men who had been in my sister's life for the last six years. The men who had helped her grieve our parents when I hadn't been in any state to. Who had been at her side on every birthday, half of the Christmases. I should know them better. And I decided right there and then that I was going to make an effort to try. This weekend would be a bonding experience for everyone. Not just my sister and I.

The pretty blonde girl flopped down beside me in our booth, having just screamed her lungs out to a Bon Jovi song with the South African drummer.

"You gonna get up there?" She asked, leaning forward to grab a bright red drink from the table, missing her mouth repeatedly with the straw.

"I think I will soon," I admitted, looking around the small, tightly packed bar, and taking in the drunken states of the people surrounding us. Most of them seemed to be far gone enough to not remember anything in the morning, giving me the confidence to willingly make a tit of myself.

"It's not really fair though, is it?" I started to complain. "I mean, you sounded great, but how is it fair that we're stuck performing with a bunch of legitimate rockstars."

The girl threw her head back and laughed. "Oh girl, you just wait."

She winked, then grinned with the straw between her teeth as she finally managed to get it in her mouth. I liked her, she seemed fun, but sensible, like she had everything all figured out, which was no surprise really when I looked at the people that she surrounded herself with. There was a good balance of personalities in the room. It had a similar vibe to my bar, except this one was a hell of a lot smaller, and it wasn't trying to be something it's not.

That thought hit me like a vicious jab to the stomach, and as I glanced across the bar at my sister, I felt it again. We had both worked so hard, yet here she was, living her dream while I was barely making ends meet. I didn't begrudge her of that, not at all. But it did make me wonder if there was any point at all in pushing forward. Maybe I would be a lot happier, a lot more myself, if I just let this shit period with the bar go on, and just gave it all up. Maybe I should forget about the life that I had wanted – the job, the man, the joy. I could move. I could start fresh. Be closer to the last piece of my family, maybe even build one of my own. Maybe…

"Ladies and Gent's," The lead singer of the band that we were out drinking with had stepped up onto the stage, the microphone held close to his lips as he smiled and wrapped his arm around the guy standing beside him, the one that I was pretty sure was a guitarist, although I was struggling to remember all of their names, Andrew? Aston? Aladdin?

"Ashy baby is going to put on a very *very* special performance for you tonight," he went on. *Ash, that was his name.* "But he need's somebody to join him, ideally a lovely lady, but we'll take a lovely man too." The singer flicked his bleach blonde hair back and searched the room, waiting for someone to volunteer.

"I volunteer as tribute!" the blonde beside me shouted, and the singer gave her a stern look before shaking his head.

"Of course you do," he muttered, and everyone around me laughed. I grinned at their little exchange as she stood up, shoved her middle finger in the air, and stuck her tongue out at him.

"I'm the perfect candidate. I'm the loveliest lady you know."

"That's debatable," he said with a raised brow.

She gave him a sarcastic as fuck smirk, placed her drink down on the table, and made her way up onto the stage, ushering him away as the music started up and Ash started to complain. Apparently, he didn't know the words, but she assured him that he'd be fine just as the opening beat of a song from a well-known musical started up.

As it turned out, Ash was completely tone deaf. Even I could have done better than him. But his voice hadn't mattered one bit, there hadn't been a single person in the room not joining in with them. The atmosphere was so alive that I completely forgot that I had been about to fall into a downward spiral only a few minutes beforehand.

The girl shimmied her shoulders, then kissed Ash on the cheek, leaving a bright red lipstick mark in her wake as she jumped down from the stage and dragged the rest of Ash's band up with her, two of which looked like they'd rather eat glass than sing that song. The other two bounced around, twirling each other as the song came closer to its end.

I clapped along, laughing freely, and finally feeling the urge to get my own ass up on the stage to show everyone that unfortunately I was not as blessed as my sister in vocal range.

Getting to my feet, I made my way over to my sister. She pushed away from the bar and wiggled excitedly as I told her I was gonna get up there next.

"What song are you doing?" Her eyes were wide as she pushed the tip of her tongue between her teeth and smiled.

She burst out laughing when I told her, shaking her head and asking me why the hell I'd pick that out of all of the songs I could have chosen.

"Because, dearest Bumble-bee, if I'm doing it, I'm doing it right."

"Well, for the next four minutes, you're not my sister. Hell, I don't even *know* you."

I grinned as I stepped up onto the stage. I had spent a good portion of the evening debating which song I might do if I managed to grow the balls to perform. The crowd didn't *look* like they'd appreciate the song I'd chosen, one of those guilty pleasures. But with the way they had just reacted to the previous song I was sure they wouldn't judge, some might even join in.

I was not disappointed. And I was thoroughly entertained when a huge guy in black leather boots, and what looked a little bit like a motorcycle gang jacket, stepped up beside me and took on the backing vocals while I repeatedly asked the audience to 'tell me why' before screaming the words 'I want it that way'.

The bar erupted with cheers when I finished, and I spotted my sister bent over with tears in her eyes as she almost collapsed laughing. The rest of the night was filled with people singing their own guilty pleasure songs. And as someone started to destroy yet another awful 90's song a voice echoed in my head. One that made my heart drop.

"How can you tolerate this shit?"

"...because it's fun."

Bea's hand landed on top of mine, and I flinched.

"Wanna call it a night?" she asked, giving me a knowing look. I nodded, attempting to force a smile to my face for long enough to say goodbye to her friends, not wanting anyone else to notice that I suddenly wasn't having a good time. I wouldn't be the wet blanket on this evening, but I was so glad that my sister could read me the way she had.

"Do you want to talk about it?" She asked me

when we were in the back of an Uber. The guys had decided to give us a little space, opting to stay with their friends for the night. I had a feeling that Bea might have said something to them, but I didn't want to ask. Instead I just thanked them and told them that we'd have to all go for breakfast in the morning.

I shook my head, resting it on my sisters' shoulder, just like I had done earlier on. I had explained everything between me and Nate to her months ago, and I was tired of going over it. I didn't want him consuming my thoughts, let alone my words. And the other stuff, the realisation that maybe I needed a new dream, was something I wasn't sure I could say out loud yet to anyone. Especially as I wasn't exactly sober. Those thoughts could easily be long gone by morning.

All I wanted tonight was a stupid amount of snacks and a big cuddle with my sister, while watching a film until we fell asleep. I could organise my thoughts another day.

17
Juno

My nails were still tacky, but the train was pulling into Axminster, and I needed to get off. I awkwardly attempted to place my kindle back into my bag without smudging the red varnish – an attempt to banish a little of the doom and gloom that had been sitting over my head the entire way home. I couldn't bring myself to paint them a bright, cute colour like I used to, but red felt like a good middle ground. I had failed miserably though, pulling my hand from my bad with the nail on my middle finger coming out lumpy and with fluff clinging to it.

  I blew air loudly through my pursed lips, then yanked my suitcase down and moved to wait by the door, hoping that the smudged nail would be the last thing to go wrong today. I had already had a nightmare of a journey home, thanks to the man who had sat opposite me, swearing down the phone at someone who I presumed was his girlfriend, or maybe even wife. He had then attempted to hit on me, and had eaten the most offensive smelling sandwich imaginable. As much as I was dreading going home, I was glad now that I was off of the train. I just wished that I could get on another one and go back to London,

I'd had the best time with my sister and her band. I had felt more and more like my old self the longer I spent around them. The guys were like the brothers I had always wished I had, and watching them argue over the silliest things had been some of the best parts of my break.

Bea had given me a long lecture before I had left her this morning, one that was mostly about money, and the fact that she really didn't need me to hold on to any for her. She said she would rather I spent it on something useful, not let it sit in an account waiting for the day her life turned to shit. I hadn't actually told her about the safety net I had saved for her, but it didn't take a genius to work out who had. When I got home, I was going to give the twins the biggest telling off of their lives.

They hadn't needed to interfere though. I didn't need that money.

I had made a decision about my future on Sunday afternoon, while I was flitting around the band's kitchen, prepping a roast dinner with Maverick. I was going to keep going with Kim's until the new year, then I would look for a buyer. Once someone had taken the place off of my hands, I could pack up and leave. I had spent too many years clinging to something that wasn't going to happen, and I needed to refocus. Move on to something more realistic. I had been an idiot to think that I, single-handedly, might have been able to turn the place into a successful music venue.

The car moved slowly along the seafront, and I closed my eyes as we passed the slope that led down to Kim's. I needed to go down there as soon as possible to check the place over. I was pretty certain that I had left the bar in good hands, I trusted Hannah, but there was still always a chance that something bad had happened, and that she had kept it to herself so that I didn't worry while I was away. Even though she had promised to not do that.

When had I started to think this way? Anticipating the worst.

My head bumped against the headrest, and I opened my eyes, glancing out of the window at the little path leading to the black door that we had pulled up outside.

"Here ya go, love," the driver said cheerily, twisting in his seat to look at me. "Need any help with your bags?"

"I'm fine, thanks."

The smell of salty water hit me as I stepped out of the car, and a small smile tugged at my lips. A second later it dropped, and I wondered if I was being too hasty in my decision to give up. Would I really be able to walk away from the place I had called home for the last 24 years? Giving up Kim's – and my dream – was one thing, but to leave the sea. I wasn't sure that was something I could do.

But could I walk past Kim's every day knowing that it was no longer mine? If I gave it up, I would *need* to leave. My sister's friends had moved to Brighton, that was by the sea, and they seemed pretty happy with their lives. I could move along the coast, travel its length until I found somewhere that felt right.

Somewhere where I could find a new direction for my life.

A place where I wasn't haunted by ghosts and painful memories.

A shiver ran down my spine as I let my thoughts linger on the nightmares I had been having so frequently over the last few months. I couldn't understand why they were happening so often, when I had spent the last five years keeping them mostly at bay. Only ever really having them resurface around the anniversary. Yet, staying with my sister, and that night I had stayed at Hannah's, I had managed to fall into peaceful, dreamless, unintoxicated sleep. It made me wonder if the nightmares were gone, or if they only existed in my head when I was here, in my own bed.

With heavy thoughts weighing on my mind, I lugged my suitcase up the stairs, and tossed it though my front door. I didn't bother to check my pile of post – which was probably only take away fliers anyway – as I snatched my spare set of keys for the bar from their hook and locked back up.

It had been cold when I had left London in the morning, but it was a damn sight colder here. I needed to wrap my coat even tighter around my body to stop myself from shivering as I got closer to the sea. It was a long, puffy one with a fluffy lined hood, although I wasn't actually too keen on the fluff, since whenever it rained it would just drip water into my eyes. I was thankful that the sky was clear today, a beautiful shade of blue that surprisingly lifted my mood a fraction.

But with each step along the seafront my mood was starting to plummet again. It was frustrating to not be able to cling to that happiness like I used to. As I became aware of it, I thought of Nate, and realised that if I was finding these small ups and downs so tiring to keep up with, it must have been completely draining for him. My chest tightened as I felt a pang of guilt for how I had last spoken to him, and the fact that I had *hit* him. He didn't deserve that. But I also didn't deserve what *he* had done either.

I shoved the feelings deep down. Nate was gone, and I needed to continue on with my life without letting him creep into my thoughts as often as he did. He was my past now. I had to let it, along with many other things, go.

I frowned as Kim's came into sight, wondering why my 'A' board wasn't standing outside like it usually was. Even when we were closed, I would keep it out, mostly for the tourists, even if it was no longer the right time of year for them to be around. Surely Hannah hadn't decided to make any changes like that in the last four days, and as far as I was aware, there were no weather-related reason for it to not be out.

I liked to think that she had a good reason, so I hunted in my bag for my keys and phone, pulling them out together and dialling her number as I shoved my key into the lock and twisted. I pushed the heavy door open as the line rang out, and instantly froze in the doorway as an array of completely unexpected things hit me.

The smell – fresh paint, new wood, and varnish – filled my nostrils first, then my eyes adjusted to the scene before me. My bar top was no longer a battered, black slab of marble, but was now a glossy, smooth mahogany surface. The small, square, patchwork mirrors behind the shelves of liquor were replaced with one single mirror that ran the entire wall, the name 'Kim's' scrawled in the centre.

I managed to take a step forward, my phone dropping from my shoulder to the floor as my lips parted and I stared down at the light wood laminate beneath my feet, following its pattern until it changed to black. The area leading to the stage finally suitable for people to dance on.

I choked on a breath as I took in the stage. Higher up and deeper than it had been when I left, with a faux wall built to one side, giving the illusion of a backstage area. The platform was no longer constructed from leftover wood. It looked like a real stage, one with a drum kit set up to the back, and amps scattered along the front. It was ready to be used. All it needed was a performer.

It was perfect.

Everything I had ever dreamed it could be.

Only one other person on this earth knew how perfect it was, and when I stepped up onto the stage, peering behind the faux wall, I fell to my knees. A shuddering sob tearing from my throat as I looked down at the sleeping man, wrapped up in a single blanket, with a black hoodie shoved under his head. Tears streamed down my face, blurring my vision. I could just about make out Nate shooting upright, and the next thing I knew his arms were wrapped around me and I was being cradled against his firm chest. The warmth that radiated from his body, mixed with his familiar pine scent, soothed me in a way I never believed it would again.

I thought I was done with this man. I thought he

had left, realising that what I needed from him was too much. I had truly believed that he would never return, because I wasn't what he wanted, and I wasn't worth earning, fighting to keep.

I blinked hard, craning my neck to look up at him. My chin on his chest as I studied his face and attempted to understand what dream I had just walked into. I knew it was mine, but I wasn't asleep.

"Did you do this?" The words bubbled in my throat, but he had understood me.

He nodded. Releasing me but keeping a hand on my back while gazing into my eyes. He looked so tired, as though he hadn't slept in days, and as I looked around my bar, I realised that he probably hadn't.

Nate liked to take the easy way out of things, but there was no way that he had done that this time.

What did it mean?

"Do you like it?" he asked sleepily.

I bit my lip and nodded slowly, but as my gaze landed back on him, I flinched away. A different realisation hitting me.

"Why did you do it?" I asked quietly, praying that the words that I was expecting didn't leave his mouth.

"You know why," he said matter-of-factly. Standing and stretching with a loud groan, before jumping down off of the stage. He picked his glasses up from a nearby table, pushed them up his nose, and made his way to the bar like he owned the damn place.

And that was what I feared now.

What if he knew? Maybe he had seen the defeat in my eyes when he had me pinned against the bar. He could have seen that I was giving up, even before I was certain of it. And this was him using me one last time. Taking advantage of me being out of town and doing this place up just so that he could swoop in and take it away from me. Afterall, it was what he was best at. First, he had stolen my heart, then my optimism, and now, my bar.

"Actually," I straightened up, pulling myself to the edge of the stage and letting my legs drop down, taking a moment to marvel at the fact my feet only just brushed the floor from this new height. It was incredible, but I couldn't let myself enjoy it too much, not until I knew what the hell it all meant. A wall quickly erected itself around me, and I released a strengthening breath. "I have no idea why. So tell me, Nathaniel. Why did you go to all this trouble?"

I cocked my head, my eyes fixed on his, hiding all emotion from the annoyingly beautiful man leaning against my bar, sipping water. His simple black t-shirt was distractingly tight, but I forced myself to focus, because if I was about to have something taken from me before I was ready, I'd do it with a clear head, not mixed up with filthy thoughts about the man who left me.

"Is it not obvious?" he asked, pushing back his curls and rubbing his hand over his beard, the length slightly longer than I recalled and filled with more grey. Whatever he had been up to over the last two weeks had revealed his age in a way that I had only seen when he was at his lowest points. It made my heart hurt to look at him like this, but I brushed off the pain, keeping myself unreadable as I cocked my head the other way and silently stared at him, waiting for him to go on. But he didn't.

"How much do I owe you then? I'll pull it from

Bea's money if I really have to. You've put me in a shitty position Nat-."

He cut me off with a growl of frustration, "I don't want your fucking money. That isn't, what? What the fuck? Juniper, how do you not see what this is?"

I blinked hard, and he shook his head, pushing his hair back, his fingers resting in the dark curls as he blew out slow, steady breaths, attempting to calm his temper in a way that so rarely worked for him.

"I don't get it," I mirrored him, shaking my head and running my fingers through the ends of my ponytail. My lips pursed tightly as I stared at him and waited for an explanation.

"What do you want me to say?" He dropped his hand, taking a few steps towards me and opening them both palms up to me. His brows furrowing, his jaw tense. His hands began to shake, and I watched him curiously as he slowly forced himself into composure.

It lasted all but five seconds before he exploded, his hands flying up in the air as he advanced on me, fire in his dark eyes as he yelled at me.

"I love you, ok? There! Is that what you wanted to hear? Is that what you needed? My admission of love? Well here it is sweetheart. I fucking love you."

My jaw dropped, brows shot up, gasp filling my throat. I couldn't believe what I was hearing. Maybe it *was* a dream. I moved to pinch myself, but he was too close, too aware of my movements. His hands locked around my wrists, holding me firmly in place. He dropped to crouch before me, still gripping me as he lowered his voice and stared into my very soul.

"This is real, Juniper. My feelings, for once, I am

certain, are real. Intense as all hell, but real. *You* are the reason I'm here. Your dream is the reason I did all of this. And right now, I am fucking terrified, because there's a high chance, especially with the way that you're looking at me right now, that I fucked up even more by doing this. I thought it was the right thing to do, when you had told me I'd have to earn a way back into your life. but…" He trailed off, his voice faltering as he searched inside me and wet his lips repeatedly, his throat bobbing, unable to force any more words out.

"You really fucked up," I whispered, my voice cracking with emotion.

He bowed his head, his hair flopping onto my knees, and suddenly I was too hot.

"Nate," I panicked, thrashing out of his hold. "Nate, I'm too hot. Get off."

He released me, quickly standing and taking a step back, "Get your coat off, now," he commanded.

I did as he said, ripping it from my body and launching it onto the floor. My breathing was coming in rapid pants, unable to inhale enough to fill my lungs. "What's happening to me?"

"You're having a panic attack," Nate explained, taking my hand and dragging me to the bar. He pushed me down onto a stool, then rounded the bar and filled a tea towel with ice. He took my hand again and turned it over, placing the ice against my wrist.

"You'll be fine, Little one," he soothed, "just try to focus on those breaths."

I couldn't. I stared at him and opened my mouth to shout, to tell him he was wrong. That this felt more like a heart attack than anything else. I had seen him have panic attacks, and I had coached him through them, and this did not feel the way his had looked.

"Find something square, or rectangular and focus on it," he said, but I wasn't paying attention.

Nate pressed the ice to my other wrist, then grabbed my chin between his thumb and finger, "Focus on something."

"I ca-."

"You can."

His grip tightened, and I glared at him. Then realised that the frames of his glasses were rectangular.

"I'm focusing," I gritted out.

"Good girl," he murmured, "now start at the top left corner, inhale as you track the line along to the top right, exhale as you move down to the bottom right, inhal-."

"I get it!" I snapped, noticing his brows drop but he stayed silent.

I did as he had said, inhaling and exhaling as I traced the outline of the frame. It felt like the dumbest thing in the world, but as he released my chin and pulled away, breaking my focus, I realised that I was calm. My breaths were steady, and my body temperature was bordering on chilly.

"Better?"

"Better," I whispered. Pulling away from the icy tea-towel and wrapping my arms around my body. The thin brown jumper I had thrown on for travelling this morning doing very little to now keep me warm.

"Shit," he breathed, then disappeared down the small hall that led to my office. He opened the door and came back out a minute later holding a well-worn leather jacket, offering it to me with a shrug. "This might be better than putting that coat back on."

I looked at the jacket in his hand, and reluctantly took it, accepting that he was probably right. I needed an extra layer, but I didn't need a coat that could probably double up as a duvet.

"Why?" I finally asked once he had gone back behind the bar and made us each a strong coffee. "I still don't understand. Why *this?*"

Nate leaned against the bar in the same way that I always had done back when we were a 'we'. His eyes locked on mine as he calmly spoke, "Because you deserve this. And you ought to have someone better than me. So it just made sense in my head that if I was going to earn you back, I needed to give you what you deserve. And maybe if I pulled it off, it would make me a better man. Which I can hear it, it's selfish, but so is wanting you."

"You said you lo…" I paused, swallowing hard, unable to repeat the words. "Did you mean it?"

"I'd never have said it if I didn't. And really, how could I not, you bewitched me the moment I first laid eyes on you, Little one." His smile met his eyes and my heart melted.

But the puddle in my chest quickly curdled. Because I was no longer the same girl that he had met all those months ago. I had let this dark, twisty creature loose. *He* had helped me do it. Now, I was someone entirely different. If he saw this darkness inside of me, would he still look at me like I was the sun?

As if reading my mind – in the same way I always used to read his – he spoke again. "I may have fallen for your light side, but that darkness that you're letting run wild now was always there, I could always see it. It doesn't make you any less worthy."

He raised a brow at me as if to say, *'I should know'*, then sipped his coffee. My head was spinning, my thoughts at war with themselves. I took it all in. My new bar, created the way I wanted it, *for* me. The way Nate was looking at me with such sincerity in his dark eyes. The words, the grand fucking gesture. All of it making me want to launch myself over the wooden surface and never let him go. But then there was the other side of it all. He had left me, and hurt me. I didn't trust him. And my dreams weren't in line with this new reality anymore. I was tired and haunted, and I didn't know which way to go. Would I be a pushover if I forgave him? Would I be able to heal from all of the sadness in my past? So many questions.

"I need some time, some space," I whispered.

Nate put his mug down and nodded sadly. "I understand."

"I'll call you?"

"You will," he said, so sure of himself, even as his mouth dropped and the light in his eyes dulled just a fraction.

Exhaling heavily into my mug of coffee as I raised it to my lips, I sipped slowly, and closed my eyes, listening to the sound of Nate moving around the bar. Freezing as his hand rested for an agonisingly brief moment against my shoulder. Then listening once more for the sound of the door closing.

Once he was gone, I opened my eyes, put the mug down, and pushed it to one side, resting my forehead on the cold surface of the bar as I let my thoughts spin in frantic circles.

The sound of the door crashing into the wall behind it not five minutes later had me bolting upright and spinning on the stool. Hands slammed down on the bar on either side of me, and ice-cold lips pressed hard against mine. He pushed his tongue against the seam of my lips, and I granted him passage without hesitation, winding my arms around his neck and drawing him closer as the sweet taste of him coated my tongue.

I let Nate kiss me like I was his reason to get up each morning. And my mind turned silent as I let him in, realising that I didn't care what the destination was, I wanted to venture on whatever journey he wanted. I wanted him. And why the hell should I deny myself of that? He had done all of this to prove himself to me. If that wasn't the perfect way to build back my trust, I wasn't sure what was.

"I'm sorry," he murmured against my lips, pulling back a little. "I'm so sorry, Little one. I know what you said, but I couldn't. I, I've waited long enough. I've gone my entire life not knowing what I want, not trusting how I feel. I'm too old to wait around and not bother fighting for what I want. You're it, Juniper. And I will stand here, in this very spot, until you either tell me you feel the same, or I collapse and die."

He pulled back further, his intense stare locking on mine, telling me he meant every word.

"You're it for me too, Nate."

18

Nate

<u>2 weeks ago</u>

My chest hurt, it felt as though when she had walked out of the door that she had ripped out the beating organ caged inside and tossed it aside like it was nothing. Which, really, was exactly what I deserved.

I had realised far too late that she was the fucking one. And I was still finding it hard to believe that I was even having those types of thoughts. I had given up on the idea of love in my twenties, or maybe it had been in my teens. The point being, I had resigned myself to a life with no real direction, unreachable dreams, and stolen nights of fun long ago.

Then I met her.

I fell for a girl who tasted like sunshine, she warmed me on my coldest days. And that feeling only intensified when I realised that she had storms inside her too, ones that could battle with mine, if she would only let them.

Juniper could handle me in every way possible.

She would make me a better man. A stronger man. The man she deserved.

But how could I become that without her. She had closed the door on me, *on us.* I needed her by my side, helping me to grow. I *wanted* to earn her, but how the fuck was I going to do that? How the hell could I show her that I was right for her?

I knew I wasn't enough.

I also knew that I was too damn stubborn to give up. My sights were finally firmly set on her, and I would push myself to my very limit if only to spend one day with her as mine.

I left the bar and took up residence leaning against the wall just a few feet away, keeping my head low as I kept an eye on the place until either Juniper or Hannah came to open properly.

Hannah arrived an hour later, and I groaned as I pushed away from the wall, my muscles stiff from being frozen in place for far too long. Once she was inside, I made my way back up onto the main stretch of road. I aimlessly walked for what seemed like hours, and maybe it had been. I only stopped when I reached the edge of a cliff, the same cliff where Juniper had played out my biggest fantasy. I stood in the spot where I had held her and stared out to sea. The view was idyllic, the water so still you'd think the earth had stopped moving. A heavy sigh left me in a cloud of breath, and I fumbled around, pulling my phone from my pocket and dialling Shane's number.

"Nate, my man. How'd it go?" His booming voice instantly warmed me, even though I could barely feel my fingers.

"She didn't want to hear me out. But I was right, she's the one."

"So, where does that leave you?" he asked.

I balanced my phone to my ear with my shoulder and shoved my hands into my pockets, "I need to win her over, I need to do something to prove to her that I'm really all in."

Shane hummed loudly. I could picture him thoughtfully playing with his short beard. "You got any bright ideas?"

"It would have to be something meaningful. Something that would impress her *and* show her that I want the same things in life as she does."

Shane threw out a few suggestions, all of which I shut down. None of them felt personal enough, *meaningful* enough.

"Tell me about her," Shane finally said after I had groaned at his sixth suggestion. "What does she like, what does she want?"

"She likes breakfast, and the sea. She doesn't like being too hot. She likes having her hair played with, and her back stroked. She's a big fan of music, she says that music makes her feel alive, no matter what style it is. She wants to turn her bar into a successful music venue-."

"Yeah, that place could use some work," Shane cut in, "maybe you could write her a song?

"I've already written her a song," I explained.

"Does *she* know that?"

I doubted it, I doubted she had even heard it. I had

a badly recorded version of it on Spotify, and I highly doubted she had stalked me and found it.

"Even if she does, it doesn't feel like enough. That feels like something I'd do on an anniversary, when I forget what day it is and panic."

Shane chuckled and I grasped my phone and sat my ass down on a nearby bench.

"So you want to do something big?"

I watched a bird soar low in the sky. Juniper wouldn't make this easy for me. She never wanted me to take the easy route in life. She pushed, and she deserved someone who was willing to do the hard shit, no matter how much they didn't want to. "Yeah. Something life changing, something that shouts *I want what you want*."

"Mayb-."

"Holy shit, that's it," I cut him off, my free hand flying up into my hair as I jumped up from the bench and ran down the hill to the hotel at the bottom where I had checked in this morning.

"What's it? What the fuck are you doing?"

"Running," I panted, "hang on."

I pulled my phone away from my ear as I ran, not bothering to hang up and call him back. A few minutes later I pushed through the door to the hotel, ignoring the receptionist as I passed her. Bringing my phone back against my ear, surprised that Shane had stayed on the line. "I'll make her dream come true. I'll show her that I want the same, that together we could have whatever she wants."

"Exactly what I was about to say," Shane grumbled down the phone.

"Great minds think alike, my man." I grinned,

winding my way around the hallway and fishing out my key then glancing around the hotel room as I stepped inside.

My heart sank as the reality hit me. The room was bare, the bed uncomfortable, the carpet stained. I couldn't afford a decent place to stay. And if I couldn't do that, how the fuck was I going to pay for her bar to have all of the work it needed done?

"Oh fuck."

"What is it?"

My mood had dropped so low I was certain I'd end up falling into a spiral. But for her sake I needed to *try* to not let that happen. I couldn't be defeated at the first hurdle.

I explained it all to Shane, then told him I needed some time to think as I hung up. I slumped onto the bed, falling backwards, and staring at the ceiling with its yellowing patterns. I would have to come up with something else.

A few moments later my phone rang, and I glanced at the caller I.D, wondering why the hell Shane was calling me back after I had just asked for space. I declined the call, and then declined it again a moment later. The next thing I knew there were ten single lined texts coming through one after the other, and as I scanned over each one, I pushed myself further back upright, until I was back on my feet with wide eyes and an excited grin splitting my face.

I read the last message over and over. Shane's brilliant idea sinking in and feeling like the perfect solution.

Shane
I can guarantee your words will make a pretty penny. Enough to do it all, and then some.

I had twelve original songs written, and an incomplete one that I may never finish. Of those twelve, there was only one that I wasn't sure about selling. *Her* song. She had inspired so many little lines, but *that* song was entirely her.

Eleven songs then. Eleven songs that – if I gave everything that I had worked for these past few months up – I wouldn't need. I had blown it with Limelight anyway, and I honestly didn't give a shit. I had written so many songs that I could make a decent amount of money from, and with that money, I could make her dream a reality.

Nate
Let's talk. Let's make this happen.

With Shane and Hannah on board with my plan, things were coming together far better than I could have hoped. Juniper was going away to visit her sister for four days, which gave me just enough time to hopefully pull off everything I wanted to do for her. The biggest challenge was one I needed to deal with sooner rather than later though; getting those old bastards who so obviously hated every bone in my body to not stand in my way or spill my plans to the girl I was trying to win back.

Confronting them was not something I was

looking forward to, especially after the last time I had seen the twins. But I knew that I needed to. I'd have to put my feelings towards them to one side and hope they would be willing to do the same.

My head was spinning with everything going on, and from time to time it was becoming hard to remember *why* I was doing it all. But then I would see her, going about her day, completely unaware of my presence, and my head would suddenly clear.

I watched her as she dragged her suitcase up the slope to meet the car that had been sat waiting for the last ten minutes. Sinking my face deeper into the shadow of my hood so that she didn't spot me, I chewed on my bottom lip, praying that my plans didn't fail. I watched her climb into the car, then once it was completely out of sight, I moved. Pushing away from the wall and strolling down to Kim's.

Exhaling slowly, I opened the door, and stepped inside. Locking my gaze on Hannah and attempting to ignore the instant protests that came my way from the men sitting at the bar.

"Dude's, hear him out," she said firmly, placing a bottle of whiskey down on the bar beside four small glasses.

"Why the heck should we?" A twin snapped, standing up and cracking his knuckles.

I kept my focus on the girl who had agreed to help me, walked to the bar, and filled one of the glasses with a thumb of whiskey. I sipped, then turned to the three men, meeting each of their eyes individually. When my gaze finally landed on the angriest one, I realised that I might not be able to pull this off after all.

He stepped towards me, "You're not welcome 'ere. Get out, before I throw ya out."

"He *is* welcome," Hannah said with an irritated sigh.

"I need to talk to you all about something," I began, but the angry one stepped closer, this time cracking his neck as he snarled at me.

A hand shot out in front of him, and another of the men stood up. Carl, the one who had always seemed to hate me just a little less than the other two, placed himself between myself and – at an educated guess – Hadley. "Don't be so hasty, Had. I don't think he's dumb enough to come in here unless he has a bloody good reason."

"He *is* dumb though," Hadley sneered, taking a step back, and tossing me a filthy look. "He left our Juney, he's the biggest fuckin' idiot to ever walk the earth."

Hannah sighed loudly again and poured large measures of amber liquid into the remaining three glasses, sliding them to each of the men as they returned to their stools.

We sat in a line along the bar, and I poured myself a second measure as all eyes locked on me. Hannah's were the only ones that held any kindness. She nodded encouragingly at me, then turned her back, busying herself behind the bar, but remaining close. I'd like to think it was out of solidarity, but I could never be too sure. Trusting peoples' motives had always been a struggle.

"Well?" The silent twin piped up.

It was now or never.

"Why should we trust you?" he asked once I had

explained what I was hoping to do.

"Because I care about her, and so do you," I rested my elbow on the bar, turning my body to face the men. "You don't have to like me, that isn't what this is. *You're* not the one I'm trying to win over here."

"She's too good for you, we shouldn't let you do this." The angry one scowled at me as he spoke, his eyes narrowed into thin slits shadowed by grey brows.

"You're right," I shrugged. "But what's more important to you? Spiting me, or making her dreams come true?"

They all glanced between themselves, and I sipped my whiskey as I impatiently waited for any of them to speak. I was all out of persuasive words, so all I could do was hope that their love for this girl was enough.

And if it wasn't… Well, I'd find another way around it, because there wasn't a chance in hell that I'd be walking away again. I wasn't letting fear rule me anymore, not when it came to that girl. If I had to get myself arrested for hospitalising an OAP, so be it. I'd leave the funds in Hannah's capable hands and serve a sentence, knowing that the girl who changed my life was able to live the one she had always wanted.

"I know a few guys who could make some of the things you've suggested happen, and they owe me," Carl said, turning to me with a sparkle in his usually dull eyes as the other two gave me begrudging nods.

Oh thank fucking God.

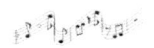

Present

"You're it for me too, Nate," she whispered, her lips puffy and voice hoarse as even more tears streamed down her face.

I crushed my lips to hers again, pushing her back against her brand-new bar and twisting her loose ponytail around my fist. I groaned into her mouth, and she playfully nipped at my lower lip before breaking our kiss and smiling up at me.

"I'm so sorry, Little one," I murmured, locking her gaze in mine, watching as the storm in her eyes intensified.

"You better be."

She pulled me closer, my lips hovering over hers. She untangled her arms from my neck, dragging her red polished nails down the outside of my arms, digging deeper as she passed the hem of my sleeves. I groaned, and she gasped, our breath mingling. Hot, tense, and desperate. Her lips parted, jaw stiffened. Her voice came in a low growl, the sound making my cock to pulse needily beneath my jeans. The girl I left behind had turned into a woman who knew her worth and wouldn't settle for anything less. Her newfound power, mixed with the darkness that she had supressed for too long, had me falling even deeper in love.

"Show me how sorry you really are, Nate."

I wet my lips, my tongue brushing against hers. "Get your sweet little ass up on the bar, Little one. And get comfy. This apology will take a while."

She did as she was told, boosting herself up on the bar and staring down at me. I swear I had never seen anything more perfect in my life. Her, in my leather jacket, with black over the knee socks that left just the tiniest slither of golden skin between them and the hem of her dark green cord skirt. She parted her thighs, exposing more of that tempting, soft skin.

I sat my ass down on the stool that she had been sitting on a few minutes ago and gazed up at her. My cool fingers dragged a hiss from between her teeth as I gently pushed her skirt higher.

"I've been so stupid," I confessed quietly.

She hummed in agreement just as my fingers reached her underwear. My apology would take time, *so much time*, but I wouldn't tease her. Instead I'd make her come over and over, until her vision blurred, and her entire body turned limp. And then I'd take care of her, soothe her and make sure she knew exactly how precious she was to me.

Her hum turned into a gasp as I hooked her panties with one finger, dragged them to the side, and plunged another into her. The gasp turned into a moan as I dragged my finger out, ensuring the angle let me graze over her clit, my still ice-cold ring no doubt the main culprit for her breathy shudder. A second finger joined the first, and I pushed deeper this time, then curled them inside her, watching her eyes flutter closed as her breaths became ragged and she moaned my name. Her walls tightened around me in no time, and I couldn't help the smug smirk that lifted the corner of my lips.

As her orgasm built her eyes flew open, and her jaw dropped as she met my gaze. "Don't look at me like that," she panted. "Cocky arsehole."

A dark laugh caught in my throat. "I have good

reason to be cocky, Little one. Look at you."

Her teeth crashed together, and she snarled at me. But a second later irritation flashed in her eyes, and she bit down on her lower lip, threw her head back, and cursed my name on a laugh while tightening around my fingers even more than before. "I'm gonna, plea-."

"No begging, this is for you baby, not me."

The noise that left her as she let go, soaking my fingers, was something I would never tire of hearing. And the look on her face as she sucked down heavy gasps of air would be imprinted in my mind until the day I died.

Juniper Bolton was a fucking goddess.

"I-," she pursed her lips and shook her head, "I'm still so angry with you."

"Yeah?" I cocked my head, slowly running my gaze from her eyes to her pussy as I pulled my fingers from her and pushed them between my lips. I met her gaze again and licked every last drop of her release from my skin while she tried her hardest to keep a scowl on her face.

She succeeded, clearing her throat before speaking. "Yes. This," she gestured around the bar. "It doesn't make everything go away. And what you just did," She sighed heavily, "Nate, you can't fuck things better."

"No, it'll take time, I know. And if you need to scream and shout at me then please, go ahead. Get it out of your system."

"Of course I want to scream and shout at you!" She threw her arms up then slammed them down on the bar.

"Go on then."

She smiled, then began to shout. But the moment she opened her mouth I dove between her thighs.

"You're a comple-*ohmyfuck,*" she moaned as I sucked her clit while attempting to rip off her panties.

Once they were off, I spread her wider, and glanced up at her, "Go on, tell me all about it. I'll just be down here, taking it."

"How am I supposed to be-."

"Mad at me while I'm doing this?" I finished for her, then flicked my tongue against her clit.

She whimpered, then pulled herself together. "Exactly."

"You can do it. You *will* do it. Because if you stop, so will I."

"Oh." Her lips parted, and a moment later she was shouting again.

My tongue lashed at her, and I sucked and nibbled her through orgasm after orgasm, refusing to stop until she was done chastising me. Until she had said everything she wanted to say. She called me every name under the sun, told me I was a selfish bastard for what I did, and I hummed my agreement against her delicious pussy.

"You know how it feels to think you're not enough," she screamed, "why did you do it?"

I pulled back, replacing my tongue with my fingers. I hadn't spoken once; I had given her the space and freedom to speak without my input or argument. But this was something I felt I needed to say.

"I was scared. It's not right, it's not an excuse, it's just… a reason. I was so scared of how I felt, and what it would do to me if you ever left me, so I left first, because doing it on my terms hurt so much less. You're right, I was selfish. But I'm trying not to be so selfish now. I know what I want, and I'd rather get hurt beyond repair than not try to show you how I feel. I want to be, no, I am *going* to be better, act better. I will be the man *you* know I can be."

Tears filled her eyes, but she blinked them back as a moan fell from her lips.

I had said what I needed to, so I put my mouth back to good use, thrusting my fingers into her too as I devoured her.

"If you ever, and I mean this, Nathaniel. If you ever pull that shit again, there will be no coming back. You're either in it for good, or not at all."

"I'm all in, Little one."

"Good," her voice wobbled, but I didn't look up. I knew she was about to cry, but she was *also* about to come. I flicked my tongue viciously against her, and as she screamed, her voice breaking and fists slamming repeatedly on the bar, I swear she said that she loved me.

"I mean…" she panted, "ignore that."

I straightened up, wiping my beard. "So I wasn't just hearing things?"

"Yes, you were." A deep red blush ran its way from her chest to her cheeks. Her eyes darted around the room, refusing to meet mine.

"Juniper," I coaxed, but she ignored me, closing her legs and pulling her arms closer to her sides, her fingers gripping the edge of the bar.

"Juniper," I repeated, and she turned her head, glancing over her shoulder and swallowing hard.

"Juniper." I finally snapped, standing, and

grasping her chin, holding her face in my hand and battling to turn her head. I was stronger, but she put up a good fight. My thumb pressed hard into her jaw, and for a moment I worried I might actually hurt her, but then she gave in.

Her face turned, but she had closed her eyes.

"Open," I commanded.

Her mouth fell open, and her tongue lolled out. I bit back the smile and swallowed down the laugh bubbling in my throat.

"You're not funny, Little one. Now open."

This time she chose to open her legs. I pressed my body closer to hers, and brushed my nose against the tip of hers, "Still not funny. Open."

This time she did what I wanted. Her eyes hesitantly opening and locking on mine. The storm I had seen in them when I had started to apologise had calmed, replaced with the sparkling ocean I knew so well.

"You know how I feel. I would never have done all of this if I hadn't meant what I said last week. I already told you that I love you, and you are it for me. Please don't shut me out over three words that you might not feel entirely ready to say."

"You really meant it?"

"I get it, you don't trust me. I wouldn't if the roles were reversed. But I do, I mean it. Your dreams are my dreams now, your future, mine. I want to be beside you through it all."

"What if *this* isn't my dream anymore?" She pulled her lip between her teeth, dropping her gaze.

"What do you mean?" I asked, tightening my hold on her chin, prompting her to look at me.

Her eyes remained locked on my chest, "What if I was giving up on this place? What if I was done?"

I dropped my hand, resting it on her knee, my thumb rubbing circles over the top of her sock. "Why?"

She hesitated, her grip on the edge of the bar tightening. "Because I don't have what it takes to make it. Because I'm haunted by ghosts in this place. Because this place isn't ready for the dream I've been clinging to." She glanced up through her lashes. "Come on, Nate. This was never realistic, was it?"

I tried to consider her reasoning for a moment, but my arguments were coming too fast. "You are incredible, you made it. You already did it. All I did here was make what you already had sparkle. This is all your idea's. So don't give me that shit. And this town is ready, if they weren't they'd have shut you down years ago. You've given the people a place they didn't know they needed. And as for being haunted, we all have ghosts, Juniper. They will follow you anywhere you go. You just learn to live with them."

I turned my hand over, offering her my palm. I helped her down from the bar and tossed her torn panties in the direction of a bin. I missed and she giggled awkwardly.

"What do you need right now? Shall I talk, or distract?" I asked.

She looked thoughtful as she shuffled from foot to foot, but when she finally looked up at me, her eyes said it all. "Fuck me, Nate. Fuck all of this confusion away. We can talk after."

"As you wish."

She smiled wickedly at me, and before I knew it, I

had taken her on two tables, and she was finally spread out on top of the stage. I slammed my way inside her, driving my cock home, where it fucking belonged. Like before, I didn't let her beg, even though she attempted to. I knew that she enjoyed doing it, but I wasn't going to take that control away until I was sure that she believed I was ready for the real deal.

Which I was.

Hell, I had even managed to use some of the money I had made from my songs to pay for sessions with a private therapist, who not only specialised in personality disorders, but had one. If anyone was going to understand me, it was her.

Juniper thrashed around on the stage, the perfect platform that I had made sure was ready for her today. I had no idea that the first performance it would see would be this private show, but it felt fitting.

I flipped her over, repositioning us so that she was on her knees, looking out over the bar.

"This is all yours." I declared, twisting her ponytail around my fist as I fucked her hard until she was shrieking and shaking, and I was filling her tight pussy. "And so am I."

"Mine," she breathed, and I fell back onto my ass, pulling her with me. I held her body close to mine, stroking her hair as she snuggled in and gazed blissfully around the room. "What time is it?"

I glanced at the clock on the far wall, "3pm."

"Holy shit," she laughed. "We've been making up for hours. I'm surprised we've been left alone for this long."

"You can thank Hannah for that," I explained,

fidgeting until I was a little more comfortable. "She's been incredible."

"I bet," Juniper hummed. "I suppose we had better clean up and set up for the day."

"Nuh uh," I shook my head. "We're going to clean up, lock up, and spend the rest of the day in a bubble."

"We can't," she protested, but the way her body slumped heavily against mine was enough indication that she wouldn't fight me if I insisted. "Ok, maybe we can. But not the bubble part. We need to do some serious talking."

"After food?"

She nodded and wriggled out of my hold. "Chips and ice-cream?"

I stood up, offering her my hand, "Chips and ice-cream."

19

Juno

A shriek tore through my throat as I bolted upright in bed, my chest was tight, my skin coated in cold sweat while I blinked tears from my eyes.

"What is it?" Nate mumbled, his hand swiping through the air as he sleepily searched for me. He finally grasped my arm, the contact grounding me faster than my awful attempt at breathing myself back down would have.

"Nightmare," I whispered, my voice wobbling. I attempted to lay back down, but the moment my head hit the pillow a wave of fear slammed into me. I bolted back up, clutching the duvet as though it might save me from the ghosts.

Nate's thumb swept up and down my arm, "What do you need?"

"I don't know," I confessed weakly.

He released me, switched on the lamp on his side

of the bed, and fumbled for his glasses. He slid them on, sat up, plumped his pillow, and leaned against the headboard, dragging me closer and tucking me under his arm. His fingers painted swirling patterns across my skin as he reminded me of the square breathing technique that he had taught me that day that I'd had my first real panic attack.

"What was the nightmare about?" he asked.

"That morning."

I snuggled closer to him, feeling safe in his hold.

"Oh, Little one," he murmured against my hair, kissing the top of my head. "I wish I could make it go away for you. Do you think it was a one off because you're stressed about tomorrow? Or do you think it's happening because of something else?"

Tomorrow marked the big opening of Kim's to the public. I had reluctantly agreed to keep the bar closed for two weeks to allow for the final touches to be added, a big opening night to be planned, and for me and Nate to work out where we stood with each other. It had been good for everyone. Hannah had taken the time to go away for a while with Shane, and when she came back, she announced that they were an official item and that he would be moving down here and taking a step back from his duties at Limelight. He was still a partner, just a far less active one, which apparently the woman he worked beside was thrilled about. From what Nate had told me, she seemed like a bit of a control freak.

It had also been good for my old dudes, who were *slightly* warming to Nate. Seeing them together had shocked me so much that I had genuinely thought I had died. But apparently it was my weekend away that had brought them close enough to not hate each other, which in my eyes was wonderful. I would never expect him to be included in their group, even though he was close to qualifying for old dude status, but the way they interacted now was better than I could have ever hoped.

Nate and I were finding our feet. It was messy, and at times I wondered if he felt as though he was walking on eggshells, but he assured me that wasn't the case at all. He was just adjusting. His therapist – who he would be seeing twice a week – was amazing, and together they had quickly made a plan for his treatment. After his first session she had realised that he needed to know what was coming in advance in as many parts of his life as he could. So knowing what they'd be working on each session before it happened was great for him. And I was learning too, I was making sure to be open about what I was doing, and how I was feeling. It was strangely freeing, being able to just say what was in my head without worrying. Nate appreciated my efforts and told me so daily. He spent each day making sure that I never doubted him, and even though it was still early days of our fresh start, my trust in him was growing faster than I ever thought it could.

"I think it could be stress, but I dunno." My breathing had returned to normal. The nightmare fading from my mind. I hadn't had one since before I had visited my sister. I thought that it was my home that caused them, but I had been sleeping here every night since I got back. So maybe it was something else that was bringing them to the surface. "Maybe I need to talk to a professional."

"I could ask Pen if she would mind seeing you for

a couple of sessions?"

"No, that wouldn't feel right, she's *your* therapist."

"Ok, how about I ask her if she knows anyone? Would you take a recommendation from her?" he asked, rubbing his jaw along the top of my head, his stubble catching on my hair. Come morning I'd probably have a frizzy nest on top of my head thanks to him.

"That I'll do." I nodded, laughing to myself as I realised, I was making the frizz worse.

Nate's body relaxed, and I melted into him. "Do you want to talk, or sleep?"

"I don't think I can do either."

"Do you want me to play?" he offered, and I nodded again.

"Play me somethin' pretty, old man."

He groaned as he leaned over and grabbed his guitar from its place hanging just beyond the bedside table. "I think I preferred it when you called me baby."

"Fine, *baby.*" I snuggled closer, and he trapped me with the neck of the guitar. I rested my head against his collarbone, and closed my eyes, letting the warm earthy scent of him, his gentle plucking, and soft words soothe me until I was on the edge of a dream, about to be pulled in.

I gave in, and when I woke again, it was to Nate cursing as he stubbed his toe on the dresser and hopped around in just a pair of tight black boxershorts. I giggled as I watched him, then ducked my head under the duvet as he spun and glared at me.

"It's not funny, it really fucking hurts," he complained, "after this weekend we're going house hunting, this place is too fucking small."

I yanked the duvet down, staring at him in wide eyed shock. When we had agreed to work on things, I had suggested that he stay at my place until we had a clearer idea of our lives moving forward. I didn't want him staying in some crappy hotel. But we hadn't discussed our living arrangement since. I had presumed that he might want his own space at some point and might rent somewhere, or he'd disappear up to London occasionally, keeping his flat up there for time away from me, but apparently, he had different ideas.

"You mean for you right?" I asked.

"No, I mean for us." His brows dropped, and his expression slipped from pained to sad. "Unless you don't want that?"

I mulled over the idea for a moment, and he slumped down onto the foot of the bed, muttering under his breath about being a complete idiot.

I shuffled down the bed, dragging the duvet with me to stay warm, and wrapped my arms around him from behind, snuggling into his back. "I'm all in, baby. But how the heck are we gonna afford a house?"

"I have news, but I wanted to wait for the weekend to be over before I told you. This is your time in the spotlight, Little one."

"Tell me," I pushed, squeezing him tighter. "Tell me, tell me, tell me."

He groaned and shivered as I placed kisses along his shoulder blades between each word. "Shane wants to help me start up song writing. As a career. And this time I wouldn't be outright selling them, I'd keep my name on everything. With his contacts, the money I have leftover, and the income from Kim's, we can afford to move. Nothing fancy, just something big enough to move around in. Something that is ours, something new."

I trailed more kisses up his neck as he spoke, then nibbled his earlobe. "This is fantastic news, I'm so proud of you."

He tensed and I exhaled slowly, needing to get this through to him.

"I mean it," I promised. "And you are worthy of that, you've earned it. And I think moving would be a great idea."

"You don't think it's crazy?" he asked.

I shook my head, nuzzling my nose into his neck, "Nope, a little bit scary maybe, but not crazy."

"I like doing the scary things with you though," he whispered, and I grinned, holding him even tighter as I pushed forward and kissed his cheek.

"Me too."

"So it's settled then? Monday morning we can start looking?"

"Of course. And we'll have a little extra too. I'll put that money that I have saved towards somewhere new." I said, shocking myself as the words left my mouth without conscious thought.

Nate stiffened again, then twisted slightly to look at me. "The money you refused to…"

"Yeah. That money." I considered what I was doing, what I was *saying*, wrapping my arms tighter around him. "You won't take it for what you did to the bar, and she won't take it for her future, so this, this is where it should go. And if she's ever in trouble, she can come live with us and we'll look after her, wont we?" I narrowed my gaze at him, knowing he knew that there was only one right answer.

"You're finally listening to *everyone* then," he teased, "I'm glad you've accepted it at last."

"It feels weird." I admitted, still shocked by my decision. Up until a fortnight ago I was completely concrete on my decision to keep it safe for her. No one had managed to sway me. But when I had sat on that stage, feeling like I was about to lose something too soon, and fear had struck me so sharply, I had offered it up, begrudgingly. This, making a choice that I *wanted,* felt so much better. I didn't feel guilt like I presumed I would. I felt… fine. "But yes. At last."

"I'm proud of *you,* It's about time you put yourself first."

"It is, isn't it. Now how about you put me first too and get your ass back in this bed. I need some help releasing some of this stress and anxiety."

He turned, pushed me onto my back, and crawled up my body, peeling the duvet down as he moved, his eyes locked on mine as a predatory growl rumbled in his chest. I squeaked like a mouse, and he pounced, his lips on mine, hands tangling in my hair, hard cock pressing against me through the layers of fabric between us.

"We had better be quick, your sister will be here soon."

I groaned, pulling away, "Maybe I can come up with an excuse to delay her?"

"Absolutely not. Come on, Little one, you know that I can easily make you come in less than five minutes," He grinned, then dropped his head, his lips grazing my ear. "And once everyone leaves Kim's tonight, I plan to fuck you on every surface."

"But we alrea-." I began, attempting to point out that we had kinda already done that a couple of weeks ago.

"*Every* surface." He pushed his cock hard against me, and ran his fingers down my body, slipping my sleep shorts down to my knees. I wiggled them the rest of the way off as he pushed his boxers down and dragged the tip of his cock through my arousal. "I'll start at the door, pinning you to it by your throat. Then we'll make our way over every single table, maybe I'll pull up a chair and feast on you, maybe I'll bend you over and…"

He thrust into me, causing me to cry out. "You get the picture."

I nodded eagerly as he slowly fucked me. "It'll be the perfect opening night."

"All thanks to you," I panted.

He picked up his pace, throwing my leg up over his shoulder, hitting me deeper. "*Our* hard work will pay off, just you wait."

The way he spoke about us as a team was sending me over the edge. With the combination of his cock, his words, and his fingers sliding between us to tease my clit, I was detonating in less than five minutes, just like he said I would.

He grinned, then pulled out. I frowned at his cock, then reached out for it, not wanting to leave him this way, but he got up off of the bed with a dark smirk. "I can wait. Especially as tonight, I'm going to make you beg."

He stroked himself a couple of times, and I scowled at him, wanting to take over and fill my mouth with his cum, but he wasn't going to let me. I would have to get up and find myself another breakfast.

He tucked his cock away and pulled on some joggers and a tight fitted t-shirt. I wrinkled my nose in disappointment and sighed, "I better go shower."

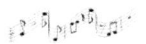

I scrunched my damp hair, running a handful of serum through it to avoid any frizz, then twisted it up, securing it with a chunky claw clip. I had chucked on a sage green jumpsuit that Nate had told me made me look like a sexy plumber, and had paired it with some fluffy socks. I really needed a new pair of slippers, but with Christmas only a couple of weeks away I was hoping I would be gifted a pair by somebody. I had been dropping enough hints.

The doorbell rang, and I flew from my bedroom into the hallway, almost tripping over a pair of black boots before yanking the front door open. My sister came dancing over the threshold, accompanied by another girl.

"Bug! I hope you don't mind me bringing Cece with, but the boys are stressing, and I thought she could do with a break," Bea said as she pulled me into a tight hug.

"Of course I don't mind." I smiled over my sister's shoulder at the blonde girl I had met on the karaoke night out.

"Thank you so much, Juniper." She gave me an exhausted looking smile and I laughed lightly.

"Please, call me Juno. And my door is always open, if you're ever around and need a break."

"I'll keep that in mind when we're next this way, no doubt we'll be showing our faces quite a bit. Are you excited about tonight?" she asked, slipping her shoes off.

I led the way through to the kitchen, "I'm so excited, and really *really* nerv-." I stopped dead in my tracks, the sight and smell rendering me momentarily speechless. "You're cooking?"

Nate turned around, forcing a scowl off of his face as he glanced between me and our guests. "Badly."

"It doesn't smell bad at all," Bea said, stepping forward with her arms wide. "It's nice to meet you, Old man."

He froze, the scowl returning as she wrapped her arms around his waist. He pulled himself together, and reluctantly hugged her back with one arm, the other held in the air with a greasy spatula in his hand.

"Less of the old," he grumbled, "but it's nice to meet you too."

"This is my friend, Cece," Bea explained, releasing my man and waving at hand at the woman by my side who was struggling to hold back a laugh.

Nate gave her a nod, then turned back to the oven, flipping eggs and bacon around in the pan.

Cece snorted a laugh, and Bea flopped down into a chair with a big smile on her face.

"He's not much of a people person, is he?" Cece asked.

"Nope," Nate said, his back still to us.

"You'd get on so well with E," she said, dropping down into the chair beside Bea.

My sister nodded in agreement and went on to explain all about the band who had agreed to join them tonight. E was their frontman, and although he came across to the fans like a charming gentleman, he was, in fact, possibly an even moodier bastard than Nate.

"Sounds like my kinda guy," Nate said, plating up the eggs and bacon. He placed plates on the table, along with toast and butter in a little rack that I wasn't even aware I owned.

It was a tight squeeze for him to move around us all in the kitchen, and once he had made us all coffees, no doubt trying to get on my sister's good side – a smart choice – he stood behind me, leaned down, pressed a kiss to my cheek, and whispered in my ear. "See, we definitely need more space."

I swatted playfully at him then dragged him into the seat beside me, and for the first time since meeting, we ate breakfast together.

"I didn't know you could cook?" I declared once we had eaten, and Bea and Cece had vacated to the lounge to go and make some calls. They were dealing with some new drama that I was luckily not getting dragged into. I wouldn't be able to handle that today anyway.

"I can't, that was a complete fluke," Nate said, clearing the table. "Maybe, when we have a decent sized kitchen, you could teach me some recipes?"

"I'd love to." I wasn't a pro by any means, but I could do all of the basics and follow most recipes. "And maybe you could teach me somethin' too?"

"There isn't a lot that I know that you don't."

"Guitar," I said quietly, "I've always wanted to learn to play an instrument."

His eyes lit up, and the excitement radiating from

him warmed me all over. "I can definitely teach you that."

I mirrored his smile, jumping up to kiss him before snatching the cloth out of his hand and shoving him towards the door. "You cooked; I'll wash up."

"You just want me to go and bond with your sister," he groaned, and I grinned again.

His phone started ringing loudly, and he pulled it from his pocket. His brows pulled together as he answered, turned away from me, and headed to the bedroom. The last thing I heard before he closed the door was him asking whoever was on the other end if it was done.

In an attempt to trust him, I remained in the kitchen, but I couldn't help but wonder what was going on in my bedroom. Was what done? I hoped he might tell me when he had finished speaking to whoever had been on the phone, but the longer the door stayed closed, the more I worried that he might avoid me.

Nate didn't need to tell me everything, but the look on his face before he walked away was concerning to say the least. Whatever was going on was important.

I began scrubbing at the pan in the sink, repeatedly blowing stray hairs out of my face as I vigorously cleaned. Bea came wondering in as I pulled the far too big yellow marigolds from my hands and tossed them over the top of the tap, soapy suds dripping from them in annoyingly loud splatters.

"You seem tense," she said, rubbing wide circles on my back. "Wanna talk?"

I shook my head, then sighed, lowering my voice. "I'm worried, Nate took a call over twenty minutes ago, and he's not come out of the bedroom since."

"Maybe he's still on the phone?" Bea suggested, glancing where I was staring through the doorway towards my bedroom. "You've got to try to trust him, Bug."

"I am," I snapped, then blew my hair away from my face again. "Sorry, I didn't mean to, I, I'm trying, and so is he." I nodded to myself. "We're good. We're learnin', and we're happy, he'll tell me if it's important."

"He will," Bea agreed, "and I am so glad you're happy. You seem more like yourself now."

"Look at us." I smiled at her and wiped my thumb under her eye where her perfectly painted on eyeliner had smudged. She batted me away but smiled back down at me. "All happy."

"And successful," she added.

I tutted and shook my head, "Don't jinx it."

She laughed, and dragged me into the lounge, pulling me down onto the sofa with her. We sat and chatted just us three girls for a while and I ended up so wrapped up in the excitement from bonding with Cece, who was enthusiastically planning a load of marketing strategies for me, that I didn't even notice Nate enter the room. It was only when he stood by the window and cleared his throat that I even looked up from her tablet.

"Can I speak to you, alone?" he asked, his gaze locked on me. His eyes were dark and twinkly, like he was happy and mad all at once. The intensity of his stare had me nodding and getting to my feet straight away, apologising to Cece for the interruption and promising to get back to it when I was done talking to Nate.

He took my hand and pulled me into the hallway.

"I was going to wait until we were properly alone, but I can't."

"What is it?" I asked, chewing on the inside of my cheek and gripping his hand tightly.

His thumb stroked the back of my hand as he leaned against the wall and blinked a couple of times. "I didn't want to say it in there, since I don't know who knows." He glanced over my head towards the lounge, then lowered his voice to a whisper. "But it's gone away, for good."

"What has?" I squinted at him.

What the heck was he talking about?

"Your ghost." He widened his eyes, and my jaw dropped.

"You mean… how?" I breathed.

Nate pulled me closer, cupping my face, his thumb caressing my cheek. "I called in a few favours, spoke to the right people, and it's gone. No one will be able to hold it over you again. Not that they should anyway, but we both know how these things can get twisted."

Tears stung the backs of my eyes. "Nate," I praised, pushing up on my tiptoes to kiss him. "You're my hero, you know that?"

"I'm not, Little one. You never needed saving. You just needed someone by your side, cheering you on. Someone in your corner when you needed a break. You are so much stronger than I think you realise. Making this go away was just a small way of me showing you that I care. I hope that maybe this, therapy, and moving might help to banish your nightmares, but really, Juniper, you are your own hero."

I laughed, thanking him and kissing him again. "I love the way you see me."

"I love the way you look."

Scanning the room, I couldn't fight the smile creeping over my face. The doors were open, the music was blasting, and faces new and old surrounded me. I had Hannah on one side, pouring a messy pint, and my old bar manager, Clem, on the other, lining up a row of shots. My best friends were sitting up at the bar with red faces, and glazed eyes from an entire afternoon of celebrating. My sister was sitting at a huge table, her band and her friends all around her. Cece's guys were up on the stage setting up. And walking down the corridor and through the archway was a man, a man who wore an expression that said he hated everyone and everything. Until his eyes met mine, and everything in them softened.

Nate stepped behind the bar, wrapped his arms around my waist, and nuzzled into my hair. "Everything is perfect."

"It is," I agreed, spinning in his arms to face him.

"Want me to take over for a while? Give you a break to enjoy this?" he asked.

"Not yet." But I almost changed my mind as the sound of a symbol crashing snared my attention, and the music blasting through the speakers faded away, making way for One Last Time to start their set.

Elijah Knox, their frontman, smoothed back his bleached blonde hair, grabbed the mic from its stand, and began to pace the stage, addressing the crowd in his signature charming way. I could see why Cece had thought he would get on with Nate. They were both capable of switching on the charm, when it suited them.

I recognised a few of their songs, and found myself getting more and more distracted as they played. Wanting so badly to step away from the bar and join in with the crowd of fans jumping around in front of the stage.

Bea appeared in front of me, and I passed her a pint glass filled with water. My sister would limit herself to one alcoholic drink before a show, something the bands performing tonight all had in common. After the one drink it was strictly water until she had performed.

The rest of her band joined her, then they all disappeared down the corridor and through the door that used to be a giant storage room. Nate had fitted another door to the other end of the room, which exited to the side of the stage. It had taken far too long to clear the room out and set it up as a backstage area for the performers, but our hard work had paid off. The whole place felt as though it was a real venue. And now, with epic vocals bouncing off of the walls, and sweaty bodies throwing themselves around to the rhythm of the music, I could finally see that my dream had come true. It was real, and I was so glad I hadn't walked away.

One Last Time finished their set and announced that Deity would be on shortly. A moment later the bar was crowded with people, all wanting to quickly get a drink down them before the headline act made their way onto the stage.

Cece shoved her way to the front, grabbing my

hand over the bar. "You coming?" she panted, her voice hoarse, no doubt from screaming along to One Last Time's set.

"Go," Nate pushed, nudging me towards the end of the bar and stepping up to take care of a group of guys. I hesitated, not sure that Nate knew what he was doing, but as he forced a smile and poured the perfect pint, that worry disappeared. I stepped around the bar, and hand in hand, Cece and I made our way 'backstage' to wish my sister good luck and praise the guys who had just rocked my venue.

My *venue*.

"I did not expect to find a place like this in Lyme Regis," One Last Time's bassist said as I slumped down onto the sofa beside him and one of the guitarists. "How the hell did you manage to pull this off?"

I laughed, "With a hell of a lot of help."

"My little June-bug is being way too modest, she's always had the drive to make this happen, and the balls to make things fit where other's think they shouldn't," Bea said, glancing over her shoulder at me from the doorway as she leaned against the open door, waiting for her band to get themselves sorted out on the stage.

"I do have pretty big balls," I said smugly.

"I bet mine are bigger," the guitarist sitting next to Cece declared, "Right Sweetheart?"

The drummer nodded, his grin wide as he jabbed the guitarist with one of his drumsticks, "Massive, the biggest I've ever seen."

The band started to joke around, until Bea spoke over everyone, declaring that they'd better shut the fuck up, and pay attention. And that maybe if they watched carefully, they could learn a thing or two. She gave them each a cocky salute, which all but one of them rolled their eyes at.

Elijah snatched the drummer's sticks and launched them at Bea, narrowly missing her as she bounded through the doorway and up onto the stage. "Fuck you, Beatrix. You learned everything you know from me!" he yelled, but there wasn't a chance in hell of her hearing him over the roar coming from the other side of the wall.

The band all got up and crowded around the side door, but I left them, making my way back out to the bar, quickly checking on my staff, then losing myself in the crowd. When I finally battled my way to the front, my sister was starting her first song, the one she had written the day I had told her I was going to turn our parents' restaurant into a bar.

"This one's for you, Bug."

Her gaze locked on mine, and as she sang, the warmth of her voice wrapped around me. I sang the words back to her with tears in my eyes. We were all grown up now, living our lives in ways that I knew would make our parents proud. Even with all of the ups and downs, the mistakes and the losses, we had become everything they had always wanted.

As their set finished, thick arms banded around my body. I twisted my fingers between his. "How you feeling, Little one?" Nate whispered in my ear, his warm breath sending a rush of heat between my thighs.

"Like I never want to let go of this feeling."

He hummed happily against my hair, whispering

promises as I stared up at my sister, watching as joyful tears ran down her perfectly made-up face. "Everyone give it up for the woman who had an epic dream. She gave us a place to enjoy music. Well done little sis. I love you."

The venue erupted with cheers, the excitement vibrating off of the walls and through my body, It felt exactly how I had always imagined it would. And I knew I had been a complete idiot to have ever considered walking away. I would never doubt myself like that again. And if I ever tried to, I knew there would be an army of people ready to stop me.

My friends, my family, him.

20

Nate

Epilogue

2 years later

Tears filled my eyes as the music started up and I turned, finding her gliding slowly towards me. I pressed my tongue to the roof of my mouth and pinched the skin between my thumb and forefinger, but it did nothing to stop that single tear from sliding down my cheek.

    I ground my teeth together in a further attempt to stop myself from crying, but another tear fell as her ocean eyes locked on mine and she tucked her soft pink lips between her teeth, biting back a smile and failing a moment later as it split her face, her cheeks rising high as she laughed, bowed her head, and started to sway her way towards me. Earning herself an echo of laughter from the rows of guests that she passed.

    She twirled in her floaty, white dress, then

bounded down the aisle, my girl far too impatient and excitable to stick to a traditional march for long. She threw herself at me and I held her tight, breathing in her sea salt scent and twisting my fingers through the ends of the lose, long curls that fell down her back.

"You look beautiful," I growled, tightening my hold on her until I had pushed back my tears and felt composed enough to get through the rest of the ceremony.

She took a step back, taking my hands in hers and raking her gaze over me with a dark flash in her eyes, "And you look damn near edible."

I noticed Shane's expression out of the corner of my eye, a smug grin on his face as he pulled Hannah closer. He had picked my suit.

Standing up in front of anyone and declaring my undying love and devotion to a woman had seemed like a joke before I met Juniper. I had never thought about whether I would wear black or blue, or if I would want oxford or brogue. Apparently, there were choices to be made, and after shrugging my way through my entire fitting, Shane had stepped in and taken lead. Without him, I wouldn't be standing up at the altar, gazing into the eyes of my wife-to-be, wearing a perfectly fitted black and silver pinstriped suit – which according to Hannah made me look like a 'Hot Business Daddy', whatever the fuck that meant, it was apparently a compliment though.

The vicar cleared his throat, drawing our attention to him as he raised his hands and dove straight in, welcoming everyone and rambling on about our love. I barely heard a single word he said, all I could think about was how bewitching my girl looked, and how fucking lucky I was to be standing here, taking this massive step in our lives together.

I had it all. Work that I loved, writing music for incredible artists by day, helping my girl at Kim's by night. A *house* by the sea where Juniper could run from our door, over the stones, and straight out into the water. A great friend in Shane. Acceptance into the local community. Brand new skills to handle my mental health, along with a therapist who after two years had finally decided that I was ready to leave her behind – not cured, but able to move on with my life knowing that I am more than my diagnosis. And *her*, my Little Juniper. My…

"Nathaniel?" the priest leaned forward, "Are you with us?"

"Sorry, yes," I muttered, blinking hard and attempting to work out what part we had got to.

Did I need to say anything? Or had I just zoned out and made it too obvious or something?

"Vows," Juniper mouthed at me with a raised brow.

Of course.

The vicar guided us through the words we had selected, and within no time at all Juniper was sliding a platinum ring onto my finger. I had removed all of my usual rings for today, not wanting anything except this token of our love to be decorating my fingers.

Juniper held her hand out to me, and I pushed the matching band up to meet the teardrop diamond that I had placed on her finger ten months ago.

"I now pronounce you husband and wife," the vicar announced joyfully.

She knocked me back a step as she threw her arms around my neck and kissed me as though her life depended on it. A roar of laughter at her continued impatience rang around the church, followed by clapping and cheering. I twisted, dipping Juniper as I lost myself to her lips, and the cheers got louder.

"My husband," she gasped, tears rolling down her cheeks.

My thumbs brushed them away, careful not to smudge her makeup, "My wife."

Making our way down the aisle hand in hand was the best feeling I could imagine, each step had me feeling like I was floating. We followed Bea, who was practically bouncing up ahead of us in her burgundy bridesmaid dress. Juniper thanked each person who congratulated us, and I couldn't wipe the smile from my face. It didn't matter to me that these people – though they had accepted me – were mainly speaking to her. Nothing at all could dampen my mood. We had come so far. My wife was happy, successful, and free from so much of her past. Our pasts didn't haunt either of us anymore, and we both looked forward to the future.

"Welcome to the family, General Grump."

I shook my head at my new sister-in-law, still hating her nickname for me, but after almost two years I was certain it was one I would forever be stuck with. Even her guys called me General Grump, or Gen for short.

I wrapped an arm around her shoulder, pulling her close as we all stepped outside the small church. Bea was a fantastic woman, a far better sister than my own had ever been. I wasn't sad or bitter about my family not being at my wedding, because I had everyone I needed right here.

It was the middle of January. It may have been bloody freezing still, but we had luck on our side as the sun shone high in the sky. I released Bea, and pulled Juniper along a path, separating us from the crowd leaving the church and attempting to hurry her along to the car that was waiting for us. But she was content taking her time, telling me how happy she was. I listened as we walked, drinking in every movement, the way her brows jumped up when she reached an inflection in a sentence, and how her eyes crinkled at the edges when her lips tipped up. She bounced slightly as she walked, her arms forever moving, covered in tiny goosebumps. She batted my arm when she caught me staring at her chest, calling me insatiable as I refused to tear my gaze away from the deep 'v' of her dress. My thoughts turned filthy, and I acted on impulse, bending, wrapping my arms around her thighs, and tossing her over my shoulder.

Juniper shrieked and smacked my ass with her small bouquet, "Put me down before you throw your back out!"

I picked up my pace, outrage spurring me on. I dropped her ass on the hood of the car, tearing one of the ribbons that someone had tied to it and causing Juniper to narrow her eyes at me.

"You broke the rib-."

I cut her off with a kiss, pushing my tongue between her lips. She kissed me back, then bit my lip as she pulled away. Her expression had turned dark, her pupils blown, breath coming in needy pants.

"Get in the car," I growled.

I stepped back to allow her to do as she was told, and once she was safely in the back of the car I hopped in the drivers' seat, sped away from the church, and pulled up on the side of a quiet road where no one would find us.

"Everyone will wonder where we are," Juniper said as I unclipped my seatbelt.

I climbed out of the black Mercedes and opened the back door. Juniper slid along to the other side, but I wasn't planning on joining her in the car. I snared her ankle as she crossed her legs, and I dragged her back towards the open door. Once her feet were out of the car I dropped to my knees, not caring about the dusty mud that would be clinging to the dark fabric. "You better hurry then."

She excitedly gathered up the skirt of her dress, and I ducked under, realising I was the luckiest man alive when I found her completely bare and already soaked for me.

"No panties?" I asked, "Did you stand up in that church and commit your life to me with no fucking panties on?"

She laughed and wriggled herself to the very edge of the seat, spreading her legs as wide as she could in the doorway. "Of course I did. Start as you mean to go on an' all that."

Jesus, fuck.

Speechless and hungry I leaned forward and began lapping and sucking at my wife's perfectly delicious pussy. She moaned and began to grind, her hips bucking and fingers grasping the back of my head through her dress.

I fucked her with my tongue before slipping my ring and middle fingers into her dripping cunt, pushing all the way in so that her juices coated the band that she had placed on my finger. I twisted inside her and flicked my tongue over her clit until she was begging me to let her come.

"Please, I need to come. Let me come, Baby."

"More."

"Please, I can't hold on, it feels too good."

"Who makes you feel good?"

"You do, you do, *you do*," she cried, thrashing and gripping my fingers. I pushed her further, replacing my tongue with my thumb as I hummed thoughtfully, wondering if I could push her for another minute.

The needy pleas that continued to fall from her lips we enough to convince me to give in though, and seconds later I was giving her what she needed.

"Come for me then, Little one. Show me how good I make you feel."

Her body convulsed as she flooded my fingers, and I pushed my tongue back between her thighs, licking up every last drop of her until she collapsed back across the seats and shuddered with a breezy laugh.

"Right, let's get going then," I decided, straightening up and adjusting her dress.

She stared up at me with her brows pinched, two adorable little lines sitting between them that I leaned down and smoothed my thumb over.

"When I fill you for the first time as your husband, Little wife, I will not do it by the side of the road."

"But you'll do *that* to me by the side of the road?" She cocked her head, her lips pursed with a smile attempting to tug at them.

"Of course, you can't expect me to wait for that. I'm addicted to the taste of you and the way you squirm."

"And here I was thinking that you just loved making me happy," she said with a click of her tongue.

"That too." I winked, lifted her legs back into the car, and closed the door to the sound of her laughing.

Loud cheering met us as we pulled up beside the hired car that Bea was leaning against, her heavily tattooed arms folded over her chest, and a stern look on her face. Our guests were all crowded in the carpark at the top of the hill and were looking slightly on the chilly side. For a split second I felt a pang of guilt for keeping them waiting out in the cold for us, but then I glanced in the mirror at my bride, and the stab went away. I'd have made them wait hours if she had asked me to. If anything, they should all count themselves lucky that I had enough self-control to wait until later before I claimed her completely.

Bea opened my door, glaring down at me. But her glare quickly morphed into a smirk as she glanced between my face and the back seat. "Thanks for joining us. So glad you could fit this into your busy schedule," she sassed.

"You are *very* welcome," I said with a straight face as I nudged her out of my way and stepped out of the car. She huffed dramatically before slinking off to join the other guests and allowing me to assist Juniper out of the car.

Everyone cheered again as we led the way down

to the hill towards the beach where one of the photographers was waiting for us to take photos outside the venue.

Once we had posed for a million snaps, and our guests had complained at least fifty times about being cold, we made our way inside Kim's. The transformation the place had gone under just for our day was incredible. Floral arrangements sat on each table, and each chair was covered in white fabric tied with black, red and silver bows. The place still had its usual edge to it, but it was elegant in all of the right places. A buffet had been set up along one wall, our cake sat on a table beside the stage, which was maybe not the safest place for it, but it looked perfect, tall tiers of white fondant with red sugar roses cascading down one side. The stage was set up, ready for the speeches that would be made after we had eaten, and the bands that would be playing after that.

We had roped Bea into playing, but tonight she wouldn't be accompanied by the entire band. Another band who had played a recent tour with our friends in One Last Time were also going to play tonight. I loved their sound, and they were a good alternative for One Last Time, since our friends wouldn't be joining us following the events of the last week. Elijah had called this morning to wish me luck and give me a hell of a lot of unsolicited advice, and Asher had sent a huge gift that I was quite frankly dreading opening. The man didn't know where the line was when it came to gifts, although his girl had said that he was getting a bit better at controlling himself.

"Holy shit," Juniper breathed as she spun in a circle, holding her flowers to her chest as her eyes lit up.

"Shit," Carrie repeated, and I clamped my hand over my mouth as Junipers eyes widened with shock. "Shit, shit, shit," the toddler sang as she ran past us towards her dad.

I held back my laughter for as long as I could, but it exploded out from behind my hand. Juniper gave me a worried look, then searched the room for the little girl's mum who was luckily nowhere to be seen.

"If she finds out that was me, she's going to kill me," Juniper whispered, still searching.

"Just blame me," I offered, taking her hand and holding back more laughter as the little girl screamed 'shit' at the top of her lungs. "She can't even say your name anyway, no one will know."

Juniper nuzzled into my neck, laughter spilling from her lips against my skin. I watched the little girl grin up at her dad and wondered if I had been too selfish when I told Juniper that I didn't want to be a father. I had bought it up last year, and she had said that she didn't mind, that kids were never something she had even considered. But I wondered if she was just being agreeable. My girl was so much more sure of her mind now than she was when we had first met, so I should have believed her when she said it, but a tiny part of me didn't.

"You sure you don't want one?" I asked, dropping my mouth to her ear.

"One?"

"A kid."

She pulled back and pursed her lips, "I love kids, but I love our life more. I don't feel like I'm missin' out. You're not being selfish; I don't care about that stuff."

My brows pinched and she laughed. "I can read you, remember."

"Not always," I pushed, "Sometimes you get me completely wrong."

"That was one time," she protested, releasing me and placing her hands on her hips. "Unless you count that time I thought you wanted me to push you off of the edge of that pool, you looked like that was what you wanted."

I snorted at the memory of her flying at me as I stood sipping my coffee on the last morning of our break away a couple of months ago. She grinned at me, all teeth, my sunshine girl always able to make things light. We didn't argue about much, and she still let her darkness creep out, but she had found her light again so much more in this past year. Light or dark though, she was always kind. And that was what had pushed me off the deep end. Her very essence. It didn't matter if she was laughing and teasing, or screaming and crying, it was always there. She was the type of girl who made the world a better place without even trying. And she made me a better person. Not a perfect person, but better.

The best version of me.

"Ladies and gents, please find your seats, then help yourselves to food," Hadley announced over the mic in the middle of the stage.

Everyone did as they were told, and in no time, we were all completely stuffed and laughing our asses off at Shane's speech. Bea got up next, keeping her words short and sweet as she blinked back tears, and the old dudes followed, hugging her as she went back to her place beside Juniper.

"Give it up for Juney, we are so proud of you."

Jeremy finished, and Hadley snatched the mic.

"And Nate, you're not the worst."

Carl nodded in agreement, and the three of them started to laugh loudly until one of the twins started choking, turning red as a beetroot, and Juniper jumped up onto the stage to help calm him down. They all hugged her with tears in their eyes, and once they were back in their seats, I stepped up onto the stage beside her.

"Can someone grab us a couple of chairs?" I asked, and a couple of guys brought them up, placing them on the stage for me. I positioned the chairs where I wanted them and took a steadying breath. Performing came naturally to me, but performing something like this, for her, was entirely new. But what better time and place than at our wedding.

I guided Juniper into her chair and took her hand as I sat in the one beside her. "My love, today you have made me the happiest man alive. And there aren't enough words to describe how wonderful you are. Trust me, I've tried to find more."

She smiled at me, that sweet one that crinkled her eyes.

"Some of you may know," I turned my attention to our guests. "That Juniper and I didn't have the smoothest start. But what none of you know," I paused, and glanced at Shane, "Ok, maybe one of you knows. When we were apart, I wrote a song that was never sold or released. It was deep, and painful, and full of so much fear. So I won't be singing that for anyone. But when I came back to her, and she allowed me a chance to become a man who deserves her, I wrote this…"

I stood up, moving to the back of the stage to pick

up my old acoustic, Lola. I kept my focus on Juniper as I sat and strummed the first chord.

"I love you, Little one," I whispered away from the mic, just loud enough for her to hear before I dove into the song that I had spent many sleepless nights working on.

"...and after all is said and done,
I know, my sweet starburst,
you are the one."

I plucked the strings, as I closed my eyes, forcing back tears and pressing my forehead against the mic. Concentrating hard on my fingers. Ignoring the people in the room who weren't her. I stole a glance at her, finding her sitting with her hands pressed to her chest and her lip drawn between her teeth. Her expression was so full of excitement and love. Enough to push me through the final line of this song.

"You bring me hope,
and joy and sun.
sweetest starburst,
my only one."

I watched my girl as she released her lip, her smile wide and contagious. "You soppy bastard," she cooed, getting to her feet, and taking my hand.

I handed my guitar to Bea, who was hovering at the edge of the stage, and took Juniper in my arms, kissing her before sweeping her off her feet and making our way down to the floor in front of the stage. Bea replaced me on the stage, and a moment later she was singing a beautifully haunting version of A Twist in My Story by Secondhand Serenade. I carefully placed Juniper on her feet, then slowly twirled her under my arm. She giggled and wrapped her arms around my neck as I held her close and dipped her low, kissing her quickly, then spinning her again until her giggles were louder than her sister's voice. Halfway through the song she turned to Hannah and beckoned her onto the 'dancefloor'. Hannah grabbed Shane, and other couples followed. Before we knew it, we were surrounded by a sea of people. Bea finished her song, made a gushy comment about my serenade, then jumped to her feet and dove straight into some of Deity's most popular tracks. She was joined on the stage by a couple of the guys and a few songs later she was telling us she couldn't be bothered to do anymore and was dragging the other band up to play out the rest of the reception.

    We danced and sang and drank until our feet were burning, our throats were scratchy, and I had a swell in my trousers that just wouldn't fucking quit.

    "I don't want to wait another minute to have you, Little Wife," I rasped in Juniper's ear after another group of guests had congratulated us and said their goodbyes.

    "Neither do I," she whispered, twisting in my arms, and placing her hands on my shoulders. "Shall we sneak off now?"

    "Absolutely not, I've been envisioning taking you in this pretty dress on top of the sticky bar all day. We're kicking everyone out. Now."

    "I don't think…" I cut her off with a needy kiss, biting her lip as I pulled away.

    "Ok, ok." She turned and flew across the room, grabbing her sister and whispering in her ear. Bea rolled her eyes, glared at me playfully, then started to usher people out of the bar.

Within fifteen minutes my brilliant bossy sister-in-law had cleared our bar. She shoved the members of the bands out of the front door, hugged her sister, and slipped a baggie containing a little blue pill in my pocket. "Just in case, I know you old guys sometimes struggle to, you know, get full mast," she said with a mischievous grin.

I shook my head at her and nudged her away from me. She blew me a kiss, then ran out the door, leaving me and Juniper alone.

Juniper stepped around the bar, grabbed a bottle of whiskey from the top shelf, and poured us each a large measure.

"To us," she announced, and I clinked my glass against hers.

"To us."

I sipped slowly, keeping my eyes locked on hers. "You look beautiful, I can't wait to ruin you."

Her eyes darkened, and her lips twitched. "Where do you want me first?"

"Your choice, Little one. I'll take you wherever you'll have me."

Her lips curled up, an excited glint in her eye as she licked her lips, placed her glass down, and nodded at mine.

"Well, in that case, get that down you, and get your ass up on my stage, Baby. It's your time to shine."

The End.

Acknowledgements

K. I would not have made it through this book without you. You pushed me, cheered me on, and talked me down so many times. I appreciate you so bloody much. Thank you for listening to my countless voice notes that literally make no sense, and are so often just the sounds of me making tea. You're the best, but you already knew that. I love you.

My street team. For being the best little cheerleaders. For always being so excited about my work and forever sending the nicest messages. You all spur me on.

Aly. Firstly, Happy birthday, and secondly, thank you for loving Nate. Sorry for hurting you in this, but hey, you were his second favourite guitar. Not everyone can say that. You're awesome.

As always, Costa man. I *still* don't know your name, and I'm *still* to social awkward to ask. But thank you again, for always giving me extra snacks when I look stressed. You fuel my little brain with your kindness and coffee. One day, I'll learn your name. One day.

And to you. Darling reader. Without you I would just be scribbling in notebooks and dreaming about this life. Thank you for being here. And I hope I'll see you again soon.

Support

Mental health support
htttps://www.mentalhealth.org.uk/
https://www.mind.org/
https://mhnational.org/
https://mhfa.org.au/

Special shout out to @Bianca.mc.intyre (Instagram) for being the most incredible source for anyone who may struggle with an array of mental health challenges. And for helping me to realise that I'm not alone during my own mental health battles.

Stalk Addy

Facebook readers group
https://www.facebook.com/groups/862089804490371

Instagram
https://www.instagram.com/addisoncarterauthor/

Newsletter
https://mailchi.mp/70330c606ac8/landing-page

More books by Addison Carter

The Muse Series

Inter-connecting stand-alones.

Enchanted Lyrics

Bitter Riff

Book 3

Book 4

The Mini Muse Series

Novella's connecting to the muse series.

Enchanted Lyrics Christmas

Book 1

Book 2

Book 3

Book 4

The Love and Lies duet

Gang themed MFM

The Truth

The Promise

Printed in Great Britain
by Amazon